MW00644167

bonded by death

MAGIC WARS: HER IMMORTAL MONSTERS
BOOK 2

KEL CARPENTER
AURELIA JANE

RAGING HIPPO

Bonded by Death

Kel Carpenter and Aurelia Jane

Published by Raging Hippo LLC

Copyright © 2023, Raging Hippo LLC

Edited by Theresa Schultz

Proofread by Dominique Laura

Cover Art by Jay

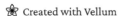 Created with Vellum

about the authors

Kel Carpenter and Aurelia Jane are the hilarious team behind the international bestselling series, A Demon's Guide to the Afterlife.

They pride themselves in being absolute weirdos, spending hours on the phone coming up with detailed worlds, and laughing about crazy ideas for torturing characters. While they believe they each have the personality of a rabid badger, people still seem to like them okay.

They share a love of coffee, travel, and tacos, and they've made some adorable tiny people with their equally weird husbands. Best friends and work wives, Kel has the audacity to live in Maryland while Aurelia lives in Texas, but they try to see each other as much as possible.

"In French, there's a phrase for the random urge to jump from high places, the irrational desire to swerve into traffic despite imminent destruction: l'appel du vide, the call of the void. Those sudden feral impulses tend to be shoved away immediately, but humans still experience them. What if you jumped? What if you touched the fire? What if? What if? When I looked at him, staring at me, the void called. What if?"

HER SOUL TO TAKE, HARLEY LAROUX

To all the women that are too damn tired from taking care of everyone else. Don't forget to take care of you.

three years ago . . .

Sweat beaded at the base of my neck as I walked down the hallway and headed to a sitting room. My mother had "requested my presence" downstairs, but for what purpose, I didn't know. I never did. This entire family was so unpredictable. For all I knew, I was walking into an ambush. My older sister would torment me. My mother would smile while I struggled against Carissa to find my magic for self-defense. Or maybe my mother wanted me to show her how much I'd "improved" so it would provide her with the opportunity to tell me again that I was her greatest disappointment.

I couldn't wait to marry Marcel and just leave. I didn't care where we went, just as long as it wasn't here.

It wasn't a big surprise that my family thought I was useless. I let them think that. My chaos magic may not have been strong, but I was smart. Everyone is dealt certain cards in life, and what matters is how you play your hand. For years, I'd been slowly and quietly preparing for the day I could leave. I had money in place. Small jobs I had managed to do in secret.

I was good at that. Keeping secrets.

Slowing down as I came to the entryway into the parlor, I took a deep breath to mentally prepare myself for whatever she had to say. As I walked in, there was an internal sigh of relief that flitted through my chest. Marcel was there, and that gave me comfort. My twin was, and though she and I weren't on good terms anymore, at least she wasn't Carissa. My mother was my mother, and may as well have been the devil's spawn for all I knew.

My momentary respite was shaken as soon as I looked into Marcel's eyes. Something was wrong. Forgetting all pretenses about the proper behavior my mother expected of me, I moved swiftly toward him, reaching out.

"Marcel, what's wro—?" A slender arm blocked me from moving further, and I turned to look at my mother. She stood at his side, then moved forward to block me. I looked at her, my brows knitting together. A smug smile graced her cold features.

"Nat," Marcel started, "I have to tell you something, but I want—"

"You are no longer engaged to Marcel, Nathalie," my mother said callously.

"Dammit, Dolores," he growled.

"What the hell are you talking about?" Looking back and forth between them, I couldn't make sense of what was happening. "We've been betrothed for three years."

"And you are no longer."

Marcel turned to her. "This is not what we discussed."

She glared at him, cocking a thin eyebrow while she stared him down with an intensity I'd never seen before. "I don't care. The girl needs to know her place, *just as you have learned yours.*"

His features darkened, but he pressed his lips together.

"Marcel?" My voice wasn't as strong as I wanted it to be. What did that even mean? That he had learned his place . . .

"Yes, go on, Marcel." I cringed as soon as I heard her. Morgan Le Fay had entered the room and began walking a slow, dangerous circle around us, speaking. Her authoritative tone carried, but the cruel, mocking manner came through clearly. "Tell the girl she's a disappointment to the Le Fays. To the entire coven. Tell her it's been decided she's no longer worthy to breed with an Abernathy."

My stomach twisted. Marcel stood there shaking with rage, but still he remained quiet. Why was he saying nothing? Why was he just standing there?

"Tell her she's been *replaced*," The Morrigan whispered as she walked past me, hovering near me. The evil she'd been consumed with radiated from her, and it terrified me.

"Replaced?" I repeated, the word shaking as my voice strained.

"By your sister," my mother said.

"If the fates chose to burden you with twins, we should be thankful at least one of them isn't useless," The Morrigan sneered, digging the knife in deeper.

My heart dropped into my stomach as my breath left my lungs violently. My throat tightened, and tears stung the corner of my eyes. Kat stood there, completely expressionless, not even meeting my gaze. She wasn't smug. She wasn't happy to hurt me at this moment. She looked . . . dead inside.

I wanted to argue. To tell them that Marcel and I were in love with each other. That we had chosen each other. That he didn't love Kat, and that Kat didn't love him . . . but it wouldn't matter. They didn't care about any of it.

They cared about Kat's magic being stronger than mine. They despised my existence, and that wasn't news to me.

And Marcel said nothing to defend us.

I realized nothing was keeping me here anymore. All the preparations I'd made for the life I'd build with Marcel had been preparing for my own life. One I would make for myself.

My jaw hurt from how hard I'd clenched my teeth together. I couldn't speak, and I refused to let them see me cry over it. So I turned on my heel and headed for the door, hearing Marcel call for me as I stormed out.

It was time. It was time to take care of myself. To become the woman I wanted to be. It was time to walk away from the toxicity this entire family exuded. I wouldn't be their punching bag anymore. I wouldn't let them dictate my life and determine my future. No more.

"Nat, wait!" Marcel grabbed my wrist as I walked down the driveway, heading to my car.

Spinning around, I used all the momentum I had to slap him in the face. His head jerked to the side with the impact, and the instant stinging on my palm throbbed.

"Let me go," I spat, yanking my arm away from him.

"Nat, please, let me explain—"

"Explain?" I repeated with a laugh, taking a step back. "Explain what, Marcel? How you just stood there and let my mother and The Morrigan tell me I'm not worthy of you? Or how you didn't speak up when they said you were marrying my sister because you already knew that's what they were going to say? Or how you began that conversation before my mother cut you off, so you were going to be the one to tell me—right then and there—that you agreed to *MARRY MY TWIN SISTER*? Tell me what *exactly* it is you want to explain."

"I don't want this," he argued, running his hands

4

through his hair. "I don't want to marry Kat. I want to marry you!"

"Then why the fuck are you going along with it?"

"Because I have to. Because I—" Marcel stopped, scrubbing his hands down his face. "I just . . . can't tell you why."

"You can't tell me? You've never kept a secret from me. You tell me everything, but suddenly you can't?" While I saw pain in his eyes with every word I spoke, there was something else in the way the corner of his eye twitched. The way his eyebrows formed a slight frown as soon as I'd said the word "secret." It was guilt.

"But you have . . . You have been keeping secrets from me . . ." How could I have been so stupid? So naïve and blinded by love, that's how.

Closing his eyes, he sighed. "It's not what you think."

"Then what is it, Marcel?" The silence between us expanded until I understood he wasn't going to answer me. "Why won't you trust me with this? Just give me this answer. That's all I'm asking for."

"I'd give you anything, Nat. Trust isn't the issue," he said, reaching for my hands. He held them in his, pleading with me. "I just need you to trust me. Trust that I love you and I am doing what's best for us."

"What's *best for us*?" Anger and hurt and pain tore through me. Jerking my hands from his embrace, I took a step back. And another. And another, until my ass bumped into the side of my car.

Disgust filled me. My stomach roiled. I felt used. Cheap. Disposable. As those words settled over me, a voice in my head reminded me that I was better than that. Better than what they believed me to be.

"I'll fix this, sunbeam," he said, stepping toward me. I

held a hand up and he stopped. "I'll find a way to make you understand. Prove to you that we're meant to be together."

"You've already proven yourself just fine," I whispered, shaking my head. Reaching back, I slipped my fingers under the handle and opened the door. "Stay away from me."

"I won't stop until I make you understand. I'll make you understand, and I will win you back, Nathalie. I swear it."

"Goodbye, Marcel. Go back to your fiancé." Without so much as a glance in his direction, I closed the door and pulled a hidden key from under the seat to start the car.

As I drove down the driveway, I saw Marcel in my rearview mirror. Standing in the same spot, he looked like nothing more than a statue framed by the Le Fay mansion in the background.

One day I'd return, no doubt.

One day, I'd burn this miserable place to the ground.

NATHALIE

My heart was battered. Bruised.

Not broken, thankfully. In some ways, Lucifer saved me from that. While he was a jealous and possessive stalker, him waking me that day at August's apartment so I could hear Sasha say they were mates . . . it was a cruel kindness.

One I was pissed at him for, because I didn't know how to be grateful yet.

In time, I would.

Probably.

"Get some sleep, Nathalie," Señora Rosara said quietly. She wasn't exactly a kind woman, but she had a soft spot for certain people. I was one of those people, and she knew what this would cost me. Something I hadn't even let myself consider. It was different when the choice was taken away, though. I may be pissed at August and not have wanted to hurt Sasha—but there was still a choice involved for everyone. I was choosing not to finish the bond, rather than watching him move on with the woman he swore to hate.

Fuck. The idea of him going through with it made me

angry, but the idea of him not . . .

I didn't usually feel guilt. It wasn't a useless emotion, contrary to what Lucifer thought. I just made the right decisions. I didn't have a reason to feel guilt most of the time, but if August refused to help us find Sasha simply because I was in the picture . . .

Looking down at the glass bottle Señora had given me, my fingers gripped it tight enough my knuckles turned white.

"I'm not sure if I can." The words slipped out without meaning to. I grimaced. Señora cast me a sympathetic smile.

"There's nothing more you can do for your friend. That's my job now. Take the *pendejo* with you."

She motioned to Marcel, who glowered at being referred to as a dumbass.

I mean, if it quacks like a duck . . .

"Let me know if you need anything." There was no point arguing with her. Not when she was right. I may be stubborn, but it wasn't for the sake of being difficult. I recognized defeat when I saw it.

She gave me a tight nod before motioning with a thrust of her chin that it was time for me to go. I walked out of her back room and into the shop with Marcel on my heels without needing to be told.

The trek to the elevator was a blur. I was so stuck in my head and the decision I'd made that I didn't realize the predicament I was in until the elevator doors opened on my floor and Marcel stepped out with me.

"Shit," I cursed under my breath.

I never, ever brought anyone home.

Did I say *never*? Because I meant it.

Really. It was true. I could count on two hands the

number of people I'd let enter this apartment. Over half of them were life-and-death circumstances.

My *pendejo* ex certainly didn't count as that.

I scratched the back of my head, stalling, when he spoke up. "Please don't tell me you're considering making me sleep in the hall."

I wasn't, but now that he'd said it, the option was appealing. I wanted to be alone.

"It's not just me I need to consider. I have a teenage girl who lives with me now."

"What the fuck, Nat?" Marcel squinted at me. "First, I'm not a pedophile. I take offense that you think I'd try to seduce a child."

I groaned. "That's not what I meant."

"Second," he continued. "I'm only interested in you. If you truly don't trust me, we can share your bed. That way you can keep an eye on me—"

I laughed. It was a little forced, but his bullshit made for a good distraction. "Hilarious, and also no. That's never going to happen."

Marcel shrugged. "Just proposing options."

I rolled my eyes, letting myself stuff down the negative things I didn't want to feel. "It's not you hitting on Mist that I'm worried about. She freaks out around men. She's been through . . . a lot. She's an abuse survivor."

Understanding flashed through his eyes. "Oh. I, uh . . . I see."

Tempted as I was to put him in the side room or on the couch, if she woke up in the middle of the night for any reason and found him, things would end badly. While damaged, she wasn't helpless; Piper had saved her life by turning her into a siren, a legendary creature with the power to compel people to do anything they want.

In the interest of being able to safely house and take care of her, I was immune to her magic, along with a select few who Piper had protected from that ability of hers.

Marcel was neither a caretaker nor under protection. I also wouldn't ask for it to be extended to him.

The girl was still wary of Anders and Ronan, and they'd both been there since the day she was rescued. Ronan was mindful where Mist was concerned, but his sole focus was always on Piper and their children. She never said it, but the way he ignored her seemed to put her at ease more than anything. She didn't want to be seen. Anders was harder for her to accept because he actively made an effort to be quiet and respectful, but also comforting. Friendly. He didn't ignore her existence, even if he always gave her space. She was only now coming around to speaking to him with something resembling ease. Marcel would amount to little more than a threat to be eliminated in her space.

I bit the inside of my lip. The weight of the day was bearing down on me, a burden I didn't want to shoulder.

"You'll sleep in my room *on the floor.*"

Marcel smirked, like he'd somehow won the debate.

"This is temporary," I insisted as we approached my apartment. "Tomorrow you'll need to go somewhere else." I defused the bomb strapped to my door that Piper had put in back when we lived together. It flashed red as the knob read my magical signature and let me through. Marcel watched me with interest.

"Is that what I think it is?"

"Probably," I replied, opening the door and waving him through. "I'd advise against trying to break in if you like living."

He chuckled, stepping through the door with an odd sort of respect. He took his shoes off next to it, before silently walking around my small living room and spotting the side room that held a cot. He quirked an eyebrow at me.

"Mist can't even see you," I explained. A flush crept up my neck even though I was telling the truth. "It won't end well."

He snorted like it was funny, but I didn't miss the way his shoulders tightened. "Sneaking me in like a dirty little secret," he mused. "I suppose I don't deserve anything more." He tried to be unemotional about it, but I saw the tension beneath the surface.

When we were two young, *dumb* kids, he was touchy and possessive when it came to me. He wanted to make it known that we weren't just betrothed, we were *together*. I hadn't been keen on that since he'd taught several classes I was in. I'd already been picked on enough. I didn't need the added insults about whoring myself out to him for extra "help."

That still didn't stop him from making an example of anyone that got too close back then. The other witches and warlocks just assumed he was weird about it because we were betrothed. Half the kids in our coven were the same way. It wasn't uncommon for our kind, so it didn't mean much.

Marcel and I were one of the rare few that had fallen in love with their chosen match, and like all fairy tales—the real ones, not the cartoon movie versions—we ended in tragedy.

"Hardly," I scoffed. "I just value her sense of safety and won't sacrifice that to feel more at ease for the next six hours. Unlike her, I'm an adult who can handle being uncomfortable without spiraling."

His dark eyebrows lifted. "There was a time when I *was* what made you feel secure."

My skin prickled. "Shower is at the end of the hall. I don't want blood on my things, so unless you've changed your mind and would like to sleep outside, you need to use it. Quickly. There are soundproofing enchantments, but I don't want her seeing you."

I turned on my heel and didn't look back, not even when I reached my room, but left my door open. I quickly readied myself for bed, knowing I needed to be able to keep an ear out in case Mist opened her door for any reason.

I'd have showered under different circumstances, but I wasn't willing to leave Marcel alone in my room for any length of time. Wet wipes it was.

I changed quickly into sweats and a tank top, cleaning my bits and washing the dried blood from my knees with methodical movements.

The water turned off right as I tossed a pillow and blanket on the floor, then climbed into bed.

I turned toward the window, giving him my back as he entered my room. The lock clicked shut. Despite the logical part of my brain, my heart started to hammer. Not out of fear . . . out of excitement.

When I was younger, Marcel and I had been hormonal teenagers. He came to me in the middle of the night more times than I could count, and there were times I went to him. I'd given him permission to wake me up when he needed me. Sometimes he needed comfort from the nightmares that plagued his youth, and sometimes it was for . . . other things.

It was the latter that replayed in my mind now.

He'd liked to finger me to the edge of an orgasm and then shove himself in me so that I climaxed right as he entered me. It was one hell of a way to wake up.

It had been years since he'd snuck into my room in the

middle of the night, but the similarities pulled at me, creating an ache that begged to be filled.

He was right earlier. He had been my haven once upon a time. A part of me still saw him as that and longed to feel our connection once more, even though he'd done everything in his power to ruin that . . . to ruin *me*.

Marcel chuckled at the sparse accommodations I'd given him. All things considered, he was lucky I wasn't insisting on the hallway. If not for the altercation between him and the señora, I might have. But she lived across the hall from me, and I wouldn't put it past her to turn him into a cat if he couldn't control his stupid mouth. So here I was. Twisted up inside for too many reasons, him being one of them.

Quiet footsteps and deep breaths were the only sounds in the room as he took a moment to get settled. Inexplicable sadness filled me, curtailed by annoyance at my own feelings. Several minutes passed in tense silence.

"Goodnight, sunbeam."

There was a time that nickname filled me with peace.

Alone in my bed with only my thoughts for comfort, all I felt now . . . was lost.

If Sasha could see me, maybe she'd be comforted by that.

Dead or alive, we were both wandering, searching for something we might never find.

HOURS PASSED.

I tossed and turned, but despite the exhaustion weighing me down, sleep never came. Not three feet from my bed, Marcel's deep, even breaths infuriated me. Of course he had no trouble sleeping. Potentially killing a woman wasn't strange for a black warlock, let alone something worth developing insomnia over.

I envied his ability to be at peace with his decisions.

Because the truth was, I was anything but.

Black witch or not, we'd been raised the same way. Where I'd cracked under the pressure my parents had put on us, he'd thrived. The darkness was as much home to him as it was to Lucifer.

But not for me.

My childhood home was one of all things macabre. Stone gargoyles with glowing red eyes arched over the roof's edge—observing not just all who entered, but those who left. Skulls adorned doorways, just another measure for my mother—and hers before her—to control everyone under that roof. The skulls reported our every movement, phantom whispers in her ear. The only blessing was that Carissa wouldn't ever be able to hear them.

Our mother didn't die a conventional death. There were no remains. My eldest sister was left without our mother's skull, and that was the offering required to pass on that awful magic to the next female heir. Carissa couldn't pay the price, so that awful incantation died when Dolores Le Fay did.

I used to have nightmares that I was being followed by skeletons. Never given a moment of peace. That began to bleed into my reality.

I dreamed of gargoyles that held me down so Katherine could cut out my heart. My blood drowned me as often as Katherine did, stuffing the organ in my mouth. Either way, I died of suffocation every night.

Leaving that place hadn't taken those fears away, even

if they weren't exactly the most rational. It just showed me that despite how cruel the world could be, the house of horrors I was raised in was its own kind of punishment.

It showed me that despite my privilege, I'd lived through evils that few could survive without either becoming them, or breaking entirely.

Marcel became them.

Death suited him in a way it never would me.

I had escaped and never looked back.

We were both shaped by the world we lived in, he and I. The difference was that I didn't like what that meant, so I reshaped it.

But all the good deeds and reassuring excuses couldn't help me sleep.

I might not be that scared little girl who was thrown into the ocean and told to swim, but I was still nothing in the presence of real power. I rarely begrudged my fucked-up magic, but on days like this, it was hard not to.

If I'd been a death witch, I could have done the ritual myself.

If I'd been stronger, maybe Marcel would have let me go into the veil instead.

If I hadn't been such a fucking coward, we may not have needed to do it at all.

That last one tormented me the most. Shame wasn't something in which I often indulged, but it was hard to ignore when Sasha could die because of my choice.

"You need sleep, little witch."

I stiffened beneath my duvet. I knew the saying was "speak of the devil," but all I needed to do was think of him and it was like he could read my mind. If not for our game, I'd have wondered if he could hear my thoughts somehow.

When I didn't respond, he appeared next to me on the

15

mattress, sitting back against the wall my bed was pushed up against. His long legs pressed against my arms through the heavy comforter. I stiffened at his proximity.

If Marcel weren't here, I'd have told Lucifer to leave.

I wished I actually made good on my threat of carrying around salt instead of just saying it. For once, I would have used it. I didn't even know if it would work, but I liked the idea that it could.

"Don't give me that look," he sighed. "It's almost morning and you haven't slept a wink. Denying yourself sleep won't help Sasha, if that's what this is about."

"Go away," I whispered, not daring to speak even a single decibel louder for fear it would wake Marcel.

"No."

We glared at one another.

Or rather, I glared, and he had an absurdly expectant look on his face, like *I* was the infuriating one. His audacity would never cease to amaze me.

I rolled over, facing the other way even though it wasn't the side I usually slept on. Lucifer chuckled, stirring a fire in my gut.

Angry, hateful words like the ones I'd spewed earlier came to mind.

"You're mad at me." If he was this observant, no wonder my family could trap him. Sheesh. "What I don't understand is why."

Against my better judgment, I turned my cheek to glare at him over my shoulder. Lucifer stared patiently, waiting for me to explain.

A growl built in the back of my throat as I rolled onto my back and motioned to Marcel. The devil rolled his eyes and my phone floated over from my nightstand, then dropped to my stomach unceremoniously.

"Type it out."

I dialed down the brightness with a cautious glance at the sleeping man on my floor. Even if he did wake, he'd only see me typing on my phone. While he'd ask questions, I didn't exactly have to answer them.

I double tapped the home button and opened my notes app.

You seriously don't understand?

"I can tell you blame me for Sasha somehow, but I fail to see what I did. Distracting you was hardly the cause of her being lost in the veil."

You refused to help look for her. You refused to do anything.

He cocked his head. "She was already lost. There was nothing I could do."

I grit my teeth. *You really are a bastard. She was in love with you not long ago, and you can't even be assed to help her because you're too busy manipulating me for your own selfish ends.*

The first hint of ire lit his golden irises. He dropped his hands to the bed and scooted down. I could have sworn the mattress dipped as he laid beside me, his body pressing into mine as he placed his knee between my own, bracing himself with a forearm above my head.

"Let's be clear about this, little witch. I am a bastard where many things are concerned, but the choice to push Sasha into the veil lies with her and her alone. I did nothing because there was nothing I *could* do." He leaned close, our faces only inches apart. I breathed harder, the blanket suddenly too warm. "There were no ghosts to ask. No people I could speak with. The number of individuals who can even see me is limited to one hand—and none of them would have any greater idea why that ritual went wrong than you or I."

"You didn't even try," I exhaled.

"What part of *nothing I could do* did you not understand?"

Tears filled my eyes, as they sometimes did with strong emotion. I turned my cheek, not wanting to cry, especially not in front of him.

Lucifer wasn't going to allow that.

He grabbed my jaw with his free hand and wrenched it back, forcing me to look at him.

"You may curse me all you want. You can call me a monster. But you won't deny me your eyes. *Ever.*" His possessive tone sent a shiver down my spine despite the way I was sweating beneath the duvet. "We're going to talk about this because whatever is going on in that fascinating mind of yours is keeping you up when you should be dreaming."

I glared, because with his grip on my jaw, that was the best "fuck you" I could manage.

"Tell me what is bothering you."

"No." I mouthed the word and anger flashed in his eyes again.

He leaned closer. "I'm only going to ask one more time before I claim that kiss, and if you don't answer, the next one won't be on these lips." He ran his thumb over my bottom lip, too hard to be a caress.

I gasped. "I only owe you one."

"Two," he said firmly.

I wanted to correct him and ask what the second was for.

I wanted to be wrong.

He asked me if I'd ever choose him. I said no. I told him he was a monster.

I'd lied.

"If you don't answer, it'll be three."

"We're not playing the game anymore, asshole," I hissed between my teeth.

Lucifer laughed, his cool breath making my skin feel achy. Needy. He touched my ear with his lips.

"We made a bargain, little witch. I promised honesty, and you agreed to the same, or you'd forfeit a kiss." He pulled back, a knowing smirk gracing his stupidly attractive face. Why couldn't the devil have a unibrow and bad breath? It would be so much easier to not get distracted if he did.

"For the game," I replied.

"I swear to tell you the truth in return for your own truth, but for every lie or non-answer, I will claim a kiss," he repeated his vow. "Nowhere in there did we state a game."

My lips parted. *Goddamnit.*

This was exactly what Sienna had warned me about, and I fell right for it.

"Why can't you sleep?" Lucifer said, not giving me any time to process his trickery with words and my own foolish arrogance in thinking I'd somehow gotten around not giving more than I was willing to offer.

That didn't mean I wanted to give him this truth.

I closed the gap between us, pressing my lips to his.

Might as well pay up while not answering. Lucifer growled like a feral beast, and true to the freak I was, the sound excited me.

I parted my lips to lick the seam of his mouth and he sucked my tongue between them. A groan reminiscent of a dam breaking from the pressure ran through him.

I hated how much I liked it, but armed with the knowledge that no one would know about my moment of weakness, I fell off my high horse and into the devil's arms.

LUCIFER

She thought she was taking control back.

It wasn't hard to guess at her reasoning for kissing me first, but fuck if it didn't make me hard. Samhain was right around the corner, and I needed my little witch in tip-top shape for what I had planned.

That's what this was supposed to be about. Me forcing her to address whatever issues were eating at her so she could get some rest. Her magic never played nice when she didn't take care of herself. Even though I'd never had a caring bone in my body, I'd be more than happy to find some sap who did and yank it right out of them, use it and claim it for my own so I could do the job that none of these useless underlings were capable of. I could pretend.

That was before she touched me.

Before she kissed me like I was the air she needed to survive.

Unable to deny my own hedonistic nature, I shifted my knee, pressing it into the apex of her thighs. She jerked, and delicious heat bloomed across her cheeks.

I twisted my tongue around hers, rocking against her

just enough to stimulate her clit. The smallest whimper escaped her throat, tugging at my admittedly very minimal self-control.

Nathalie stilled, her eyes wide with blown pupils. She glanced over to the boy who was still pretending to sleep. Her expression smoothed once more when she saw the steady rise and fall of his chest. He was a good little liar. Not unlike my witch.

Where something was weighing on her, I had a feeling that what kept him awake had a lot more to do with the girl he'd obsessed over for years lying within reach, alone and asleep, as far as he knew.

At least until that delicious little whimper.

She missed the way his body stiffened, too focused on me.

As she should be.

I applied a touch more pressure as I rocked my knee against her slick heat. Nathalie bit her lip to keep from crying out, hard enough she broke the skin.

I ducked down, soothing the wound by licking the droplets of blood from her mouth. She didn't know that every drop made me stronger, just as her own desire did. She didn't realize that in partaking in pleasure, by giving into desire, I was so much closer to the living realm. I could smell it. Taste it.

Nathalie gasped as I cleaned her mouth of all traces of blood.

I was supposed to help her sleep. Her body needed it.

If she was so insistent on being stubborn, I supposed there was more than one way to achieve my goal.

I wanted to understand what went on in her pretty little head more than anything, but tasting her skin was a very close second. Besides, beggars can't be choosers.

If I couldn't have her truth, then I'd gladly take her kiss. And then some.

"We can't," she groaned, a bit louder than I think she meant to be. I kept the smirk off my face at the idea of that little prick hearing her like this for *me*. He didn't know it was for me, but he knew it wasn't for him.

Satisfaction wasn't a strong enough word for that feeling.

"We can," I disagreed, rocking into her. A slight sheen was forming on her forehead and sweat already dotted her chest between her breasts where the low-cut tank top hid little.

Her body shuddered again, as if struck by lightning.

"Not with him right there," she muttered. That her objection was his presence and not some bullshit excuse about not wanting me made the tangled feelings in my chest latch on to her—tightly, like thorns in skin, vines of obsession clinging to everything that was Nathalie. They were dangerous, these feelings. They would hurt her at some point. I knew the way I wanted her wasn't what one would call healthy.

I also didn't care.

They may hurt her, but she'd come to like the pain.

Telekinetically, I pulled the duvet off her.

"Luci . . ." It was meant to be a warning, but she dropped the second half of my name with a cautious glance at the boy again.

In the past, I'd hated that nickname. Not in the least because my insufferable prick of a brother liked to call me it.

On her lips, I could get used to the sound of it.

"Not the most creative pet name, but for you, I'll answer

to it with minimal complaints." She narrowed her beautiful brown eyes at me as I grabbed her knees and parted them.

"Stop," she hissed despite the lack of resistance. Her body screamed yes, but her delicate sensibilities about me eating her out in front of her ex needed assuaging. How she could go to a sex dungeon and fuck in front of strangers but take issue with him potentially watching was beyond me, but there it was.

"You know how to make me," I said, running my jaw along the low waistband of her sweatpants. Her arousal perfumed the air, goading me to do more.

Nathalie fisted my hair in one hand, pulling it enough to bite.

I chuckled, not minding in the slightest.

"I could have prevented it."

The quiet admission was a victory that felt strangely like a loss.

"You had no way of knowing what would happen."

I moved from between her legs to sit beside her. Nat threw an arm over her face, then sighed in frustration and reached for her phone. Her fingers tapped faster than I could keep up with.

If I'd bargained with you to find the ghosts and get the answers we needed, Sasha never would have needed to go into the veil. She wouldn't be lost.

All at once, I understood her anger.

It wasn't aimed at me, not truly. It was aimed at herself.

"Nathalie." I said her name quietly, wanting her to look without me forcing her to. She rewarded my patience with an irritated, angry stare. I'd take it.

"I'm a coward," she whispered. "I didn't want to pay the price you'd ask. She may die because of it. And if she doesn't . . ." Her unspoken words were louder than a scream.

If she doesn't die, then she'll be completely bonded to the incubus you're trying to convince yourself you don't have feelings for.

Except she was too selfless to admit that.

I wasn't capable of true remorse. The long years of existing had stripped that from me. Hindsight was probably the closest I'd inch toward regret of any form.

I didn't like hearing her talk about herself that way. Not over something, that in hindsight, I should have made crystal clear for her. Particularly when her selflessness bordered on masochism.

"I wouldn't have been able to do that even if you had asked, little witch." I waited for the words to sink in. She blinked slowly. Confusion clouded her expression. I sighed. "I can't see other ghosts. I haven't been able to for weeks. If the lack of reaction I get from necromancers is any indication, they can't see or hear me either. That's why I could not help you with Sasha then, any more than I can now."

She opened and closed her mouth. Traces of desire still plagued her, but her muscles had relaxed instantly thanks to the immediate relief she must have felt. It said a lot about how much this had been bothering her.

Her fingers tapped away again. She lowered the phone to show me her question.

Do you know why you can't see other ghosts anymore?

I tilted my head. Her expression was open instead of suspicious. "I never truly entered the veil. Not all of me, at least. I suspect that my current existence is some kind of in-between. A purgatory of sorts."

She nodded, her eyes going faraway. To that place in her

mind she refused to tell me about. I'd get those secrets out of her soon enough as well.

"Sleep, Nathalie. You're not to blame for her situation or anything that comes from it, but you can't help anyone in this state. If you keep fighting me, I will finish what you started."

Pink stained her cheeks, but she rotated onto her side into the fetal position, grabbing a pillow to hold to her chest with her legs tucked around it.

It didn't take long for her to surrender to sleep with her conscience now clear.

And in her dreams, the smallest of sighs left her lips.

"*Luci . . .*"

three

NATHALIE

I buried my face deeper into my pillow.

It smelled like books and my shampoo. Parchment and ink. Lilac and raspberries. I snuggled closer, groaning in delight at the warmth.

An insistent banging disturbed my fuzzy feelings. My tired limbs struggled to process that we needed to get up and see who was at the door.

Until my pillow moved.

Callused fingers ran over my bare arm, leaving a trail of goosebumps in their wake.

I let out a yelp, pushing away, but an arm that was coiled around my waist already without me knowing pulled back to prevent my escape. My strength gave out when pitted against him, and I fell back onto his chest with an *oomph*.

I closed my eyes and looked away. The events of yesterday and last night slammed into me, along with all the unwanted reminders about why I should have left Marcel to his own fate.

"Why are you in my bed?" While my voice sounded hoarse from sleep, the acidic tone I'd intended came across nicely.

"Couldn't sleep," Marcel grunted. His lips touched my hair. The sound reverberated through his chest in a way he knew I found sexy as hell, because I'd once confessed that to him.

Like everything else, it seemed he wasn't above using my truths to manipulate me. He and Lucifer both. Well, and August too. I wasn't sure what it said about me that all the men I had the hots for were emotionally damaged jerks.

I regretted adding August to that list almost instantly because I was supposed to be forgetting him, or at least forgetting my attraction to him. He was Sasha's, just like Marcel was Kat's.

Fucked up as it was, Lucifer was the only one who was mine alone.

That the devil was the only man who I was both attracted to and might trust even a pinch . . . well, if that didn't tell me how screwed my day was to begin with, nothing would.

The banging continued in the background, though it came through as a quiet annoyance as opposed to a loud pounding. I'd added a hole into the soundproofing enchantment that allowed the sound to come through. I needed to hear if anyone was at the door, even if I didn't want them to hear me.

I'd marveled at how skilled Señora Rosara was when she'd set it up for me when I moved in. It never occurred to me to wonder at the reason why she might be so adept.

The naked, collared men from last night probably knew.

At that thought, the last of my cozy feelings vanished.

Irritated with Marcel for disrespecting my boundaries, I shoved at his side, trying to push him off my bed.

He rolled away, but took me with him.

Caging me in his arms, my knees slid between his legs and hit the floor at the same time he did. Face pressed to his chest, stomach to stomach, I felt his stiff cock against me.

Pain shot up my thighs at the impact, and Marcel relaxed his body. "Ow," he groaned. "Was that really necessary?"

"Absolutely." I pushed against his chest and this time he relented, releasing my waist. I twisted to the side, swinging my leg over him, then rolled forward into a standing position. I'd never been the strongest at anything in my life—magic, fighting, any of it. But what I lacked in strength, my genes gave me in grace and balance.

In another world, I might have been a gymnast.

My parents viewed all sports as a waste of time, like playing video games or volunteering. Sure, witches and warlocks were expected to look their best *always*, despite us not having the supernatural metabolism of other immortal species—but when did logic ever win when it came to societal standards?

If we wanted to talk about wasted time, shaving legs would have been at the top of my list. Our bodies grew hair. There was nothing shameful about it. Yet women had been taught to obsess over being as naked as a mole rat. Yes, smooth skin felt nice, but the expectation to be smooth all the time? Piss off. Especially in the winter.

I shook my head, grabbing a sweatshirt from the hook on my door to throw on. A barely there tank top without a bra was little more than a striptease, especially given how chilly I liked my apartment. If it were Piper at the door, I wouldn't bother, but my best friend would never come through the door when she could essentially cross space through the light realm.

With a warded building and only a dozen or so people that knew where I lived, I worked through who would be ballsy enough to wake me.

I stepped out of my room and shot a warning look at Marcel. He lifted both hands in surrender. "Stay put, I know. Dirty secret, remember?"

I rolled my eyes and closed the door. I really didn't want him in there, but I didn't have many options. My bare feet pressed into the hardwood floors as I quietly walked to the front door.

Lifting onto my tiptoes, I squinted through the tiny peephole in the door.

Anders was low on the list of what I'd expected to find, but definitely not the worst person to be dealing with right now.

My fingers fumbled as I unlocked the different devices that were attached to the door, ending with the literal bomb that was strapped to the handle.

He stopped knocking upon hearing the locks turn and waited for me to let him in.

"To what do I owe this early morning *pleasure*?" Sarcasm dripped from my voice, but he didn't grin like I'd expected. I swung the door wide and motioned for him to come in.

Anders wasn't any more an early riser than I was; arguably less so considering he was never responsible for anyone but himself and liked to drink till the wee hours. He thought we didn't know about his little problem.

Maybe the others didn't, but I wasn't stupid.

The guy he bought most of his alcohol from was one of mine and kept me updated on how much he went through. I may have switched out bottles a dozen or so times with enchanted water meant to taste like what he wanted.

Dark circles sat beneath his eyes, the kind of tired lines that immortals shouldn't have etched onto their perfect faces. That could only mean one of two things.

Either he *finally* found Bree and needed my help, or . . .

"Tell me about last night."

He had a soft spot for Sasha, and she, for him. I'd always thought they were fuck buddies and each other's wingmen, but after everything I'd learned about her and August, I'd come to realize there was a lot I didn't know about my friends' romantic relationships.

I sighed and motioned to a barstool.

"Might as well take a seat. I need to brush my teeth and put the kettle on before we have this conversation."

He nodded along, thankfully not as impatient as the vast majority of the people I associated with. I always liked that about him. He was never in a hurry.

If he weren't Ronan's second, I might have considered making a pass at him months ago. But I didn't mix business and pleasure. It was like fire and gasoline. It might be fun for a minute, and the results could be explosive and entertaining for a short period of time, but in the end, nothing good ever came from it.

It only took me a few minutes to brush my teeth and wash my face. I resurfaced from the bathroom right as the kettle whistled.

Perfect timing.

"Can I get you anything?" I offered. "Coffee? Cappuccino with whole milk?" I knew he had a weakness for the fresh stuff I got from my dairy farm. It was about an hour outside of New Chicago. I handled their logistics and transportation into the city, and I stocked my apartment weekly.

"I wouldn't say no to a pour over with some cream."

I smiled. "Coming right up."

I talked while preparing his coffee. There wasn't exactly a lot to say from my perspective. I was only a spectator in the grand scheme of things. I'd coordinated the ritual and brought the supplies to make it happen, but I wasn't actively a part of it. My tea hadn't even cooled enough to drink by the time I finished telling him about taking Sasha to Señora Rosara.

Anders grunted in acknowledgement a few times, but otherwise didn't speak until I was done.

"Where's Marcel?" He took a drink from the pink cupcake-shaped coffee mug and hummed in contentment. Pride thrummed through me. Anders had been around longer than most civilizations. He had high standards when it came to coffee. I liked that I met them and could give him a little piece of joy.

I leaned back, pressing my butt against the lip of the counter so I could face him. I crossed my arms over my chest. "Here."

Anders lifted his eyebrows, turning to glance at the side room off the living room. I shook my head.

He blinked, expression turning skeptical. "I'm not one to judge, but why in the ever-loving fuck would you let him back into your bed after what he did?"

My lips parted. "Is there anyone Sienna *didn't* tell?"

I looked at the ceiling and took a cleansing breath, attempting to ignore all my feelings of frustration over something that was inconsequential at the moment, if annoyingly public.

Anders's lips curled into a sympathetic smile. "Just me

31

and Sasha. We got drunk the other night when Hallie was spending the night with Honor and Orson. It's not important. But if it makes you feel any better, she was raving about cutting his dick off because you deserve better."

Whatever remaining anger I had was snuffed out as a warm sensation spread through my chest. I sighed, deflating myself by blowing over my tea. "We didn't sleep together," I said, even though I didn't need to. Anders came from a place of caring. "I had him take the floor. I would have put him in the side room, but I wasn't willing to risk Mist accidentally seeing him."

"Ah," he hummed, instantly understanding. "That's smart. She might have actually removed his dick and made him choke on it."

I snorted. He wasn't wrong.

"Speaking of Marcel's living situation," I ventured, testing the waters. "Carissa kicked him out. I can't keep him here, but I need to keep an eye on him. Do you think you could—"

"No." He let out a sharp but tired laugh. "Not a chance in hell."

My mouth twisted into a frown as I groaned. "There's literally no one else that can keep him. Piper and Sienna both have kids. It would only be until we get this mess with Sasha sorted out and find my sister."

I stopped arguing my point when Anders shook his head.

"I like you, Nat. I like you a lot. It's because of that I'm not going to say yes and risk an 'accident' happening the first time that cocky shit tries anything." He inclined his head, imploring me to understand. "He did wrong by you. Wrong by Sasha. I get why we need him alive, and why we need someone watching him, but contrary to what you all seem to think, my patience isn't endless. I've been walking a bit of a tightrope myself these last months." It was the closest he'd come to speaking about Bree and whatever happened there.

I sighed, taking a tiny sip of my tea to test the temperature. Warmth suffused my bones, like a hot shower after a long day. A comfortable silence fell over us that neither felt the need to break.

It really was a shame he was Ronan's second and head over heels for Bree. His presence was calming for me in a way I rarely found these days. August had been, but then that fell apart.

"I might know someone that could put him up for a while." It took me a second to process his words after the direction my thoughts had taken me.

"It's gotta be more than Joe Schmo who does your taxes," I said, moving forward to lean my elbows on the opposite side of the counter from where he sat. "Marcel was raised by two cutthroat witch covens. A normal person won't know what to look for or see the warning signs if he is keeping secrets."

Anders nodded, draining his coffee in one long swallow. "The person I have in mind isn't the type to need taxes done. His businesses are off the books."

I cocked my head. "So, a criminal?"

"I didn't say that."

I snorted. "You implied it. Are you sure that's a good idea, with all the stuff Marcel is wrapped up in?" I tilted my cup, swirling the tea around the edges. "I've never met a black warlock as strong as him. He may be broke, but he can trade in magic easily enough."

Anders chuckled, shaking his head. "My man can't be bought. I trust him with my life."

I squinted at him. "Is this the part where I point out you trusted Lucifer once too?"

Anders shook his head, tapping away on his cell phone. A smirk spread across his face mere seconds later when his phone buzzed.

"Good news. He's down to babysit. I'm texting you the address now. He'll be there within the hour, so try not to keep him waiting."

My phone buzzed in my sweatshirt pocket. I didn't reach for it.

"You're not coming with me?" Meeting with people I didn't know was a constant in my line of work, but meeting some corrupt asshole that Anders trusted—for reasons that escaped me—to have him watch over my ex? I wasn't vibing with it. Not one bit.

"I need to watch over Sienna right now. She's struggling, more than she wants to let on." He dragged a palm over the stubble on his jaw.

"Go." I waved him off, running a hand down my face. "I'll handle this."

He gave me a slightly apologetic smile before looking down at his mug and back at the roasted coffee beans that were still sitting out on my counter. "Any chance I could convince you to make me one of these for the road?"

I rolled my eyes and huffed like I was annoyed, even though I was grinning. "Fiiiiine. I suppose it's the least I could do to thank you."

He snorted, shaking his head at my antics. "I spoke to the señora briefly on my way up. She told me to let you know Mist has the day off. Would you like me to have Sienna come get her when she's up? She's not in a place to entertain, but Hallie doesn't understand—"

I held up a hand, not needing him to explain any

further. "That's a great idea. I'll stop by tonight to chat with Mist and see if she'd be up for staying over a few days to spend time with Hallie and take some of the pressure off Sienna. With Marcel potentially coming and going, it's safer that she's not here for the time being, anyway."

He nodded along while I finished making his drink, putting it in a travel thermos instead of the cute glass mug that my adorable goddaughter would steal the second she saw it. Anders came up behind me and snatched it away as soon as the lid snapped shut. He planted a quick kiss on my cheek that was both affectionate and platonic, before turning for the door. "Let me know if there's anything I can do," I said.

"Yep yep." He stopped at the front door, fingers around the handle. "I know it doesn't matter. He's dead now and I don't need to explain myself." I paused while wiping down the counter. "Lucifer wasn't as bad as everyone thought, you know. He might not have been a hero at the end of the day, but he wasn't the evil everyone believed him to be. He wasn't so black-and-white."

"He's gray," I said quietly.

"He was," Anders agreed, nodding along. "I didn't work for him long. Only a few decades, but what I saw . . ." He shook his head, still facing the door, so I couldn't read his expression. "He may have been self-serving, but he was fair. He punished without bias, and he actively condemned true evil. It may not have been enough, but it's still more than any human monarch or ruler did with their fleeting power."

I stared at the spot where he stood longer than I'd realized, contemplating Lucifer's nature and the truth no one wanted to believe. Least of all me.

When I came out of my musings, Anders was gone. The door was closed. No one was there to see my internal debate. To hear the blood rushing in my ears. To hear my heavy sigh as I finished cleaning the kitchen.

No one was there.

But I could have sworn the faintest hint of blood and sex lingered in the air.

NATHALIE

It was cold.

Mornings often were in New Chicago. There was a reason it had once been called the Windy City. This day seemed particularly brutal as we walked beside Lake Michigan, looking for the address Anders had given me.

A glass monstrosity of a building sat right on the water's edge, and it wasn't what I'd been expecting when I was texted an address of someone I didn't know. But if I had to think about it, it made sense that anyone in this city willing to take in another person would also be able to afford it. It just hadn't crossed my mind. I was more shocked that Anders found someone to babysit—as he'd called it—and it was all agreed to via text. Yes, I had a history of taking in strangers, but I also had a gift that let me read people with a touch. I knew what I was getting into. This poor sucker didn't.

Then again, Marcel should be nothing but appreciative of getting to live it up in a swanky apartment on the water. It was certain to be nicer than the room my parents had given him, and nowhere near as inhospitable.

"Must be nice to have friends in high places," Marcel muttered, looking at the five-story glass building.

"You should work on having friends at all," I replied, starting toward the door. "It's not like you can afford to be picky when you're starting at ground zero."

Marcel laughed darkly, like I was being funny and not insulting him.

"I have Katherine."

"She's your wife. Not exactly the same thing." I didn't hold the door open for him as we stepped inside. A young woman with curly black hair and chic glasses looked at me, her expression blank.

"We're looking for—"

"Fifth floor. Elevator is around the corner. Just say your names and it'll take you up."

I blinked, feeling both uneasy and impressed. While it was possible she greeted everyone that way, the address we were given did start with a five, which in these places usually indicated the floor. Which meant she was either told we were coming, or she had foresight and *saw* us coming.

I couldn't get a read on her as we walked past, but I wasn't keen on the possibility of regularly dealing with another seer. I was going to hope that the person we were meeting was simply competent and warned the staff about our arrival.

It's not like I could do much else.

The elevator was little more than a glass box with suspension cables strapped on.

"Marcel Abernathy," he said as soon as we stepped in. The doors didn't close until I added, "Nathalie Le Fay."

They shut instantly, and the world spun.

I wasn't scared of heights. I'd be the first to admit that I

38

had fears—many of them, in fact—but I'd managed to escape that one. And thanks to the complete glass enclosure that overlooked the lake, it wasn't my claustrophobia causing my reaction.

It was the out-of-control sensation that occurred *watching* my feet leave the ground.

My heart started to pound. Sweat accumulated along my spine, beginning to drip down the centerline of my back despite the bone-chilling temperature outside.

"Close your eyes," Marcel said quietly. He placed a hand on the small of my back, stepping into my space. His chest filled my vision before he was smothering me with it.

"Get off me," I snapped, pushing him away as he tried to hold me in what was probably a sweet gesture.

"You're having a panic att—"

"I'm *fine*."

Marcel scoffed. "Whenever a woman says they're fine, it's the opposite. Is it so hard for you to let me help you for even a second?"

"Yes!"

It echoed through the glass box and into the foyer right outside. I stepped out, walking quickly to put distance between us. Marcel sighed, but didn't push it as he followed behind. I turned left as my message instructed. When we got to the end, the door for 513 greeted me. The number was silver embellishments against ebony wood. Elegant. Minimalist. A bit sterile for my liking, but that mattered little.

I knocked on the door without pause, not wanting to be alone with Marcel any longer. I needed to drop him off, speak to the man Anders trusted so much, and then summon the courage to meet with August to get what I needed for Sasha's ward.

A day filled with menial tasks that left me moody and itching to escape. Just another day in the glorious life of Nathalie Le Fay.

Chaos witch. Entrepreneur. Glorified carrier pigeon.

I snorted at my joke as the door opened.

The words that were supposed to come out of my mouth were, "Hi, I'm Nathalie. It's nice to meet you. Anders sent me." It all fell apart and turned to ash on my tongue like kindling that touched flame. What came out instead . . .

"August?"

"Nat." My name was honey dripping from his *deceptively* perfect lips.

"You know this guy?" Marcel asked, breaking the silence, but not the tension. That shit was entirely too thick.

"It's Nathalie to you, or Miss Le Fay," I said once the shock wore off and my mouth could work again. My tone was decidedly less sweet than I'd planned. "Only my friends call me Nat." August's dark eyebrows lifted as he crossed his arms over his chest, his large form filling the doorway.

"I have no desire to be your friend," he said. The dark, husky quality of his voice made my stomach twist in knots. "Glad to see you're on the same page." I didn't miss the poorly hidden subtext.

"This must be a mistake. Maybe Anders got the address wrong—"

I turned to head back down the hall, and warm brown fingers wrapped around my bicep, stopping me. My heart jerked like it crashed into my ribs and suffered whiplash from the impact.

"Anders is my closest friend," August said, dashing my slim hopes that there had been a mix-up. "I could hardly tell him no when he asked if I'd be up for watching a rogue warlock for a friend of his."

"I'm not a rogue," Marcel countered.

"Do you have a coven?"

"I did—"

"So that'd be a no. You're a rogue."

Marcel ground his teeth together. I should have enjoyed seeing someone give him shit. I should have enjoyed seeing him put in his place. Hell, I should have enjoyed seeing August be the one to do it, but that was before . . . Now all I felt was overwhelmed.

I took a slow breath to steady myself and the sudden dizziness made me lightheaded. "I need someone to stay with Marcel for this arrangement to work, not just give him a place to stay. Given this isn't your home . . ." I trailed off, hiding my cringe as I felt both sets of eyes turning to me with intent. "Are you planning to take him with you to Paris?"

"No," August said with a rough laugh that reminded me of what it felt like when his stubble ran over the sensitive skin of my thighs. "My home in Paris is . . . private. I'm relocating to New Chicago for the immediate future. I purchased this apartment as an investment property, but it will better serve me as a place to stay for now."

"Relocating?" I asked dumbly. "Why?"

"The woman I want to be with told me we're just a fling, and she walked out on me. I'm here to show her she's wrong." August smiled, the picture of pure confidence. Arrogance tinged his expression; an air of intensity surrounded him as he leaned over me. In my short, chunky-heeled boots, he towered over me.

I liked that before.

Now I just felt exposed. Boxed between him and Marcel, there was nowhere to hide. No way to blend in.

My chest rose and fell in heavy pants as I fought to control my breathing. I closed my eyes and envisioned myself sitting down in the library with Ann. Her analytical nature gave me the dose of reality I needed to focus on.

"This is a good thing," Ann said. "It's efficient. Marcel won't trust August because of his past with you, and vice versa—plus you don't have to go searching for the incubus. Two birds, one stone, Prime."

She was right. Obviously.

This *was* a good thing.

Probably.

The minute the panic subsided, I found I'd turned myself around when my eyes snapped open and I was staring straight into Marcel's. He was only inches from me, hands wrapped around my shoulders in a grip that was tight but not painful.

"That's it, sunbeam. Focus on me."

"Stop touching me." I jerked, pushing him away and shaking off the infuriating man's grasp. They were both utterly ridiculous. Maybe this could work in my favor, but that didn't mean I would let anyone manhandle me. I stepped back, just enough to be out of arm's length of either of them.

In a classic move I should have predicted, a solid body that hadn't previously been present pressed against my back.

True to his nature, the only thing that could have made this worse was him being here. When we were alone, I'd have to ask if he had a sixth sense about these things. Did he feel me thinking about him? Or was he constantly watching, just waiting for the opportunity to make a big entrance? I could totally see the latter. He was enough of a diva.

"Oh dear," Lucifer said. "Talk about an awkward situation."

I clenched my hands but kept my face blank, showing none of the irritation that made me want to step on his foot. It was like he died just to goad me at the worst possible moments.

"Marcel, meet August. August, Marcel."

Neither of them looked at the other, despite standing no more than two feet apart. Their eyes stayed glued on me, tracking my every movement.

I bit the inside of my cheek and Lucifer laughed, shaking me slightly as he settled a hand on my hip. I wanted to swat it away. Bad ghosts didn't get not-quite-fuckbuddy privileges.

"Marcel is a black witch, August. Anders assured me that I can trust you to keep an eye on him."

"I'm not a fucking convict, Nat."

I wasn't sure what it was that made August's knuckles turn white, but I was certain it had something to do with Marcel's colorful response.

"No," I agreed. "You're an unknown as far as I'm concerned. I don't trust you, and frankly, I don't even really know you anymore. That's honestly worse. At least with a convict, I'd know what to expect."

"That's bullshit, and you know it."

"I thought only your friends called you Nat," August remarked, leaning against the doorway. "Or did I misread this situation?"

Marcel's hands curled into fists and a ghost of his deadly tendrils started to take form. "I don't know who you think you are, Mr. Hot Shot, but I'm the one who gave my fiancé that nickname." August's slate-blue gaze darkened as Marcel continued. "She may let her friends call her that, but—"

"Fiancé?" August echoed, jaw tightening as he stared at me. I could only imagine what was going through his head, given the way I laid into him over Sasha.

"Hardly," I bit out. "We were betrothed. Years ago—"

"I gave you a ring," Marcel interrupted.

"And now you're giving me a headache."

"The feeling's mutual, sunbeam."

Lucifer chuckled again, squeezing my hip a tad tighter. "They're like two studs fighting over a bitch, wouldn't you say?"

My fingers itched.

"Marcel," I said quietly, but with authority. "This isn't the time for a pissing contest. *Your wife* is missing, and she's either a murderer or being hunted by one. Yesterday you nearly killed Carissa in the parlor—which doesn't look great, considering the whole murder thing going around—then you proceeded to lose Sasha in the veil." I glared at him, crossing my arms over my chest. "Due to your involvement, your status is complicated. You could be innocent. Until we get Sasha back and find Katherine, I won't know."

"You can't honestly think I left her in the veil intentionally."

"I don't know what to think, but leaving you to starve on the street isn't an option, as much as I would like it to be. So you're going to stay here and play nice if you want me to talk to Piper about that meeting you asked for, hm?" I nodded once, making my point.

Marcel looked less than thrilled to be put under house arrest when I wasn't his jailer, especially not when it was

44

obvious I had some tense history with his new jailer, but that wasn't my problem.

"When will you be back?"

I sighed in exasperation. "I don't know. I have this thing called a job that I still have to do while cleaning up the mess you, Carissa, and Katherine have all created."

That might have been a low blow I felt a tiny bit bad about. His jaw tensed, lighting a fire in his eyes.

"I don't like being left here without knowing when you'll be back."

"Well, I don't have a better answer for you. I'll be back when I have something. That's the best I've got. What do you want from me, Marcel?"

He glowered. "What do I want?" He pulled his phone out and lifted it. "Here. When I text you, you answer. If I don't receive a response, I *will* come find you—meeting be damned."

I spluttered. "What? No. You don't even have my number."

He smiled and hit a button on his speed dial.

My phone started buzzing.

My lips parted before I could school my expression and snap my mouth shut. I pinched the bridge of my nose, taking a deep breath. "Ignoring that gross invasion of my privacy, you'll do no such thing, unless you want me to have Piper enforce a restraining order with the blood oath."

Marcel didn't twitch.

"Don't care, Nat."

He pushed past August with one dark look of longing aimed my way.

August stepped into the hall, closing the front door behind him.

"I was right," he said softly.

45

"What?"

"He wasn't worth it. The damage. The trust, opening up, everything you withheld from me because of him."

I wish I could say annoyance was all I felt, but the truth was hardly ever so simple. August barely had to look at me for my body to take notice, but when he spoke like this? When he walked toward me without a single hesitation?

My blood turned to fire, threatening to burn my inhibitions to ash.

Sasha was in a magical coma, and here I was, flirting with *her* mate.

Who she'd be bonded to if she woke up.

That thought cooled my desire. The slight frown that graced his lips made it seem like he knew what had caused it.

"He wasn't," I agreed. "But I'm happy I withheld it. I just wish I would've learned the lesson the first time about trusting men who say they know what they want. I knew you were just too good with your pretty words. The two of you have that in common."

"Oooooh," Lucifer encouraged. "That was a good one, little witch. Vicious. I like it."

I tried to inconspicuously sidestep out of Lucifer's grasp. He tightened the hand at my side, making me falter. I really hoped August didn't notice. I'd already revealed too much to Marcel last night when I started arguing with him while Sasha was in the veil. He hadn't said anything, but I had to assume he saw.

"I resent that remark," August said, voice tight. "He and I are nothing alike. He *chose* to marry your twin. I was *forced* to have Sasha as a mate—and I rejected her. Repeatedly."

I shrugged, as if it mattered little to me although I could

admit that was such a lie. It mattered a lot, even though it shouldn't have.

A muscle in his jaw twitched.

"What do you want for this?" I motioned to his door with my chin. "Name your price."

"Nothing."

I blinked a few times, then frowned at him in suspicion. "No one does anything for free."

August shrugged, repeating my gesture in kind—as if my thoughts on it were inconsequential. I guess I deserved that.

"If it makes you feel better, consider it a gift."

"He's good," Lucifer mused. "I can see why you liked him. Sasha too, but they'd be terrible together." I wanted to ask him what he meant. I also wanted to throttle him.

"Watching my ex is a gift?" I laughed humorlessly. "And they say romance is dead."

August smirked. "If you think I did this for any other reason than because it was you asking, you'd be mistaken."

I toyed with the strap on my backpack. "Anders asked you. I never told him about us."

"Like I said, Anders is my oldest friend. There's very little he doesn't know about me."

"He's not lying," Lucifer said. "They go way back. I'm not sure of the connection, but one of the conditions of Anders working for me was that I left the incubus be." He motioned to August over my shoulder.

I replayed the conversation in my head. The way he smirked while texting his "friend." I hadn't thought him capable of playing me like this, attempting to be a drunken fae matchmaker.

"Does he know about Sasha? That she's your mate?"

August nodded. "He recognizes the importance of

choice. Sasha doesn't know me. She feels things a bond tells her to. Things that I don't feel in return. She may think she's choosing me, but she's not."

"How is it," I mused, "that she feels things you don't? You're both bound. It's not a one-way street."

August sighed. He didn't owe me an explanation. Not after I'd walked out on him and refused to go further, but my short conversation with Sasha about him made me horribly curious about his side of things.

"Sasha was a child when I met her." He looked away from me, as if admitting this aloud was difficult. "She was sixteen, and spoiled rotten thanks to the devil's brand of 'parenting.'"

"Hey! Being a single father is hard work—"

I glanced over my shoulder, unable to stop myself from glaring at him. I hoped the look conveyed, *put a sock in it.*

I already knew way too much about his relationship with the twins than I ever wanted or needed to.

"Okay," I said. "So she was a kid. Kids grow up."

"Except I've never seen her as anything but that bratty, self-important, sixteen-year-old that attempted to use her 'gifts' to seduce me and force the bond when I wouldn't bond with her willingly."

I cringed. Using her powers and crossing a boundary like that . . . that was bad.

I wanted to refute his argument and argue she was just a child, like he'd pointed out. But sixteen was old enough to know right from wrong.

"He's not lying," Lucifer said quietly, all humor dropping away. "It wasn't her best moment."

Understatement of the century.

"Did it . . . did she?"

August saved me the mortification of asking and shook his head.

"She might be a powerful succubus, but she still had a lot to learn about using her power. I stayed away after that, and she respected it for a little while, but the bond pushed her into finding excuses to see me. To see if I'd forgiven her."

I licked my chapped lips, swallowing the dryness in my throat.

"You didn't?"

"Actually, I did," he said. "She was sixteen and horny. The mating call is difficult for grown adults to ignore. Forgiveness doesn't mean I want her, though. Even if she hadn't done that . . ." He pressed his lips together, looking to the side, then down at his hands. "I can smell everything, including magic. That also means I can smell how tainted it is."

I frowned. "What do you mean by 'tainted'?"

"Magic corrupts," he said. "The longer it's unbalanced, the more it rots. Its power may not diminish, but the scent . . . It's quite easily the most revolting thing I've ever smelled—and I've been alive since before humans had the luxury of toothpaste and indoor plumbing."

"And her magic smells like—"

"I'd rather sleep in a dumpster than be in the same room as her."

Ouch. It was a harsh truth, but it also wasn't exactly something he could control—no more than I could stop seeing magic or having visions when I touched people. It was a part of him that he would always have.

I felt sorry for him.

Sorry for being given a mate he would never have been able to fall in love with, no matter how lovely she may have been. Sorry for how I'd lashed out without knowing all the details. Sorry that we found each other, because even knowing the truth couldn't change our outcome.

I wanted to ask him what I smelled like. He said his magic chose me. *He* chose me. I could only assume that meant that somehow my magic wasn't tainted. That didn't make much sense when I thought about the line of black witches I'd descended from, but it wasn't like I could test the theory.

I sighed, pulling my backpack around from my shoulder. Dread filled me now that I knew more about their history together. The odds he'd agree to this . . . I had to ask. "Look, I get this isn't what you want since your life would be better if you didn't have to deal with her anymore, but I have a favor I need to ask." I yanked the zipper to the side and grabbed the glass vials Señora Rosara had given me. "I need your . . . fluids."

He hiked a brow. "I'm going to assume that wasn't an incredibly awkward pass at me."

I fought the smirk that threatened to break through. Beneath the intensity and lust and flirtatious glances, I really liked him. I liked his smile. I liked his humor. I liked how I felt when I was around him. I liked how my world felt different with him in it.

And I hated all of it because he wasn't mine.

"Afraid not," I said, extending the container. "I'm assuming Anders told you about what happened with Sasha?" He gave me a tight nod, his hand brushing over mine as he took the glass. A shiver ran through me. A current of electricity passed between us as his fingers brushed over mine. I cleared my throat, pulling away. "Señora Rosara—the witch who's helping us get her back— she said she could use your . . . the connection you have . . .

with her." I sighed. "For the ward that's guarding her body. I know she's not your favorite person—"

August held his hand up to stop me. My dread intensified. I knew he wouldn't do it. Not when he saw her as the problem. I was stupid to think asking nicely would change anything when— "Say no more. I'll do it."

"Really?"

He lifted an eyebrow quizzically. "It changes nothing between her and me, but if I refuse, you won't forgive that. So yes, I'll do it."

My chest expanded and then collapsed in on itself. "There's something you need to know before you say yes." He didn't speak, just patiently waited for me to continue.

Come on, Nat. Rip the Band-Aid off.

"If it works, and she returns to her body, it will complete your bond."

The words rushed out of me like a river overflowing. August tensed. I didn't have to search his face to feel the hesitation. I was soothed yet horrified by that relief and—

"What 'fluids' do you need?"

My lips parted. "What?"

"I've known she's my mate for years and the bond has never pushed me toward her. It doesn't matter. Mated or not, she's not who I want. You are. So tell me what you need."

My mouth opened and closed. Sweat broke out along my palms. "I don't think you understand . . ."

"Have you ever been bonded?"

"No, but—"

"I understand what the norm is, Nathalie, but don't tell me how I feel. I know myself and my magic. Whatever obsessive feelings of love most mates experience, aren't there. I feel revulsion. Disgust. That isn't going to change, but your feelings will. Won't they?"

My mouth was dry again, making it hard to swallow. "I don't have feelings—"

"Bullshit," he snapped, stepping forward. "I'll do this for you, Nathalie, but don't fucking lie to my face. If it was only arousal, your scent wouldn't have spiked with anxiety when you asked me. Your heart wouldn't be pounding like it is because your body recognizes what your head is trying to deny." He hooked two fingers under my chin, lifting it so I couldn't hide my face. "Tell me what you need, sunling."

"Blood, sweat, spit, urine, and . . ." My eyes shot down to his crotch for a brief moment, then I shook my head. A blush crept across my cheeks. It was the epitome of unwise. This could only ever end poorly, and yet . . .

"That will take a minute. Would you like to come inside?"

I couldn't help the small smile from taking form on my lips as I shook my head.

"It's better if I stay out here."

"Is it?" he questioned, conveying disagreement through the tone of his voice.

It sounded like a dare more than it did a question. I forced down the lump in my throat and nodded. "Yes, it is."

August's disappointment was tangible, but he didn't push me on it. Yet, I knew this wasn't the end of it. Not when he'd relocated to New Chicago for me.

Which was crazy to even think. But he didn't just *think* about doing it, he'd done it.

For me.

Peace was stupidly happy and doing a little cha-cha around the kitchen while The Warden and Ann stood shoulder to shoulder, shaking their heads at her ridiculous ass.

"Nathalie," he started, taking a step closer. "There's something I need to tell you."

"Can it wait?" I asked without missing a beat.

He considered my question. "For a little while. Not forever."

I nodded. "Save it for when Sasha wakes up."

"Nat—"

"I can't do this right now, August." I spoke quietly but let the truth of how I felt show on my face. I was tired, on edge, unsure of whom to trust, and struggling with too much weight on my shoulders already. I couldn't do it right now. I couldn't take anything else, even if I did feel bad for him.

"She may not wake up," he said softly. While gentle, there was a hope in his eyes that made me feel like the worst kind of person, because even though he'd give me what I'd asked, I knew he wanted her to stay gone. Permanently. And a small part of me that I loathed and would never let see the light of day wasn't put off by that. That teeny, minuscule part didn't care that it might mean Sasha, our friend, never woke up—because without her standing between us, August and I would be free to explore this thing that I found myself desperately wanting even after everything that had happened.

But she was going to wake up.

She *had* to. I couldn't lose my friend, no matter how much I wanted August. I refused to believe that Sasha would let something like the veil stop her from living.

"She will," I insisted. "She has to."

August didn't agree with me, but he didn't argue with me either.

He dipped his stubbled chin in a tight nod. "All right," he relented. "I'll wait. For now. But I need you to promise me something."

"What?"

"Promise me," he started, leaning close. I licked my bottom lip without thinking. His expression turned hungry. Starving. "You won't let anyone feed from you until we talk."

I jerked; a very familiar sensation of warmth wound around my core. "You have no right to ask for that."

He stepped toward me to close the space and I tried to step back, despite Lucifer's presence holding me in place. August descended, his lips so close to mine they would touch if either of us moved.

"You're right; I don't," he agreed. "But I can't stop trying, anyway. The thought of someone else touching you, tasting you . . ."

He shuddered. Our lips brushed.

I shoved against his chest, ignoring the tingle that ran through me at the tiniest touch. August was a grown man, nearly six and a half feet tall. He wasn't a meathead, but he wasn't lacking for muscle either. Just based on that alone, I shouldn't have been able to make him move. Once you factored in that he was an incubus? It was laughable how weak I was in comparison.

So when he stumbled back, it made my chest hurt. More than a kiss ever could.

Because he didn't have to move. He chose to because *I* wanted it.

August looked away, as if ashamed of himself. "Give me a couple of minutes. I'll be right back."

He retreated into the apartment. The time passed in a blink. I could have ripped into Lucifer, but I didn't trust there to not be cameras, or even worse, someone watching from the other side of that door.

I was still in the same spot, weight on the same leg, when the door opened again. August stepped back out. The scent of sweat from his skin acted like an aphrodisiac. I took the vial wordlessly, placing it back in my bag.

Neither of us moved immediately. What just happened still hung in the air, but I was the one that said *no more*. Not today. Not till Sasha woke.

And if that was going to happen, I had a job to do, and I had to leave.

I started to walk away and paused, only for a moment.

"I promise."

It was barely a whisper. Two little words.

But I made a choice. I just hoped when Sasha woke up, I didn't regret it.

AUGUST

Those two words lingered in the hallway, floating in the air long after she'd left. She walked away, yes, but she'd promised something I never thought she'd give me.

The hope that created sat insistently in my chest.

We didn't have much time before she'd be feeling the effects of the bond as well. I had to tell her soon, and the likelihood of Sasha coming out of the veil was slim.

If she died, a part of my problem was solved. It was unfortunate that she had never let the idea of us go, never moving on to live for herself. That's not a life well spent, and I'd be glad to have that cursed bond dissolved. By that same token, if she died, Nathalie would suffer the loss of her friend, and fuck me sideways, I didn't want her to go through that. Hundreds of years had passed, and I still mourned the loss of my closest friend. Grief wasn't a wound that time healed, it was a hole in the floor you learned to walk around. Being immortal didn't make it easier. It just meant we had more holes.

Nathalie wasn't wrong that nothing was free—especially not in this world. It was true in this case as well, just not in the way she'd expected.

The mate bond with Sasha would never solidify. I didn't care that Señora Rosara said it would. I never *wanted* her as a mate. The spell couldn't make that change. It couldn't make my magic accept tainted magic. I didn't think twice about giving Nathalie what she needed for the ward, but it wasn't for Sasha. It was all for her. My sunling.

So was saying yes to babysitting the little prick sitting in my apartment. The moment Anders sent me that message, it was like I was handed a gift. A guaranteed way to be near Nathalie.

And a means to learn more about her.

I turned around, leaving the hallway and returning to the interior of my apartment. Marcel reclined on the couch with his arms crossed and his feet propped up on my coffee table. My cat was curled on his lap, snuggling up to him like the attention whore she was. Grumpiness settled over me, a feeling that had more to do with my aurae leaving than my traitorous cat, but one of these was reasonable to be annoyed about.

Et tu, Estrid?

Well, if I didn't like him before, I definitely didn't now.

"Now, I know the Le Fays raised you better than this." I cocked an eyebrow, angling my gaze downward and then back to him. "Get your feet off the furniture. And leave your shoes by the door."

Marcel scowled at me, narrowing his eyes, but he dropped his legs to the ground, and my cat darted off, coming to find me despite smelling like the asshole she was purring it up for seconds before. "The Le Fays didn't raise me."

"No?" I walked into the kitchen and poured myself a

cup of coffee while Estrid wrapped her body around my legs. I glared at her. *Traitors don't get tuna.* "That's not what my sources told me."

"I don't know who your sources are, but you're wrong."

I huffed a small laugh, keeping my features neutral. "I rarely am, but okay." I took a sip of my coffee, staring at the boy while he put his shoes by the front door, following instructions like a good little bitch. "So, Marcel-who-was-not-raised-by-the-Le Fays, what happened at the summoning?"

Anders had filled me in already, giving me every detail that Nathalie had shared with him. I wanted to hear it from the source.

"I don't know," he muttered through gritted teeth.

I held a hand up. "You misunderstand. I'm not accusing you of any wrongdoing. I'm merely curious."

"I still don't have an answer to give you. It seemed like it went just fine. No signs of distress. No indication of anything. Sasha just didn't return to her body."

I nodded silently, contemplating whether he was telling the truth or not when he spoke again, this time asking me a question. "I'm sorry. Who exactly are you again? How do you know Nat?"

"Nat and I met recently over an interest in . . . similar hobbies."

He scoffed. "She doesn't have time for hobbies. Try again."

"For the most part, I'd agree with you. She's quite the busy woman, but she manages to make time." I took another sip of my coffee, internally frowning. I needed a new supplier. The beans weren't roasted dark enough for my liking.

"And what's her hobby?" he asked, gesturing to me. "What's *your* hobby?"

I smiled and shook my head. "If Nathalie wants to tell her friends what she does in her spare time, she can."

"Nat is not my friend. We're more than that," he declared, taking the bait and returning to the living room. He refused to sit again, instead watching me and waiting to see what I'd do.

I had no intention of sitting, let alone following him into the living room.

"More than friends?" I repeated, a slightly mocking note in my tone. "You may have been once, but it didn't seem that way to me anymore."

"I wouldn't expect her to share the details of our relationship with you." He looked me up and down. "Whatever you are to her, she doesn't deem you worthy of that information, clearly."

"You're partially correct. She hasn't shared all the details with me, no," I said, leaning against the counter casually. For a brief moment, a smug look crossed Marcel's face. Right before I wiped it right off with my next words. "The time Nathalie and I spend together doesn't leave much room for discussing our exes. That kind of talk ruins the moment, if you know what I mean."

I winked.

Marcel's fists balled at his sides.

"Nat and I have a history together. One that is far more complicated than whatever it is you think you know about her."

"Mmhmm," I mumbled around my coffee, not really caring what he was saying. He was riled up, and I'd barely started. "And yet, she won't let you stay with her. I wonder why that is?"

"She'll come around. You don't know her like I do."

"Maybe not, but I know her now. I know how she feels beneath me. I know how sweet she tastes when her thighs are shaking." A feral grin took over, and my body vibrated with satisfaction when I saw his eyelid start to spasm.

My sunling was so much more than the basics of bodily desire, but if I wanted to get under this boy's skin so he over shared, I had to play to his possessiveness of her.

"You think she'll pick you?" he growled.

"Oh, is she choosing between us? I didn't realize there was an ultimatum she'd been given."

"Like I said, there's a lot about her you don't know."

"I know I didn't fuck and marry her sister, Marcel."

Shots fired.

Me: one. Marcel: zero.

The little warlock rushed toward me, his fingers twitching. A hint of oleander hit my senses as the air stirred with his sudden burst of speed. My curiosity piqued, but I kept it pushed down. That was a question for another time.

I arched an eyebrow and shook my head. "Don't be stupid, kid. You may be a black warlock, but you're outmatched in this fight. Don't punch above your weight class. You won't like it when you get hit back."

Anger flickered in his gaze, but he hesitated. He wasn't as dumb as he looked. "Don't speak about Katherine or *my* sunbeam, when you clearly know nothing about the past you're trying to throw in my face."

There it was again. Sunbeam. He'd called her that in the hallway and the desire to break his neck flooded me. I clenched my jaw, but quickly released it so I didn't give away how much I hated hearing him say it.

He was an absolute tool for calling her that in conversation. I didn't go around calling her "my sunling" when talking with Anders. Why? Because I'd sound like a fucking tool. But I had the feeling he was doing it to goad me as much as I was goading him. It'd almost worked.

I lifted a shoulder, keeping my arms crossed. I didn't want him thinking for one second that he posed any kind of threat to me.

I was old. Experienced. Immortal.

He was none of those things, and he'd do well to remember it.

"I don't know Katherine." I inclined my head, agreeing with him without verbalizing it. "But I do know Nathalie."

"What is that supposed to mean, 'you know Nathalie?'"

Walking over to the sink, I rinsed out my empty mug and washed it, putting it away before looking up and speaking to him. "It means if—and I mean *if*—her choice is between you and me, I'm not worried." Marcel tried his best to ignore my jabs, but he wasn't nearly as experienced at this game as I was. Before he could come back with something, I ended our little banter. "This has been lovely, but I have some work to do. Like Nathalie, I run a few businesses and I'm rather busy. Your bedroom is the third door on your left down the hall. You have an en suite bathroom. Library is across the hall from your room. Don't leave."

Grabbing an apple and bagel from the counter, I saluted him and started to walk away.

"Your manners are lacking," Marcel said softly.

"Are they?" I asked, looking around. "I've been rather polite considering you left dirt on my coffee table and thought it a good idea to charge at me with your little magic fingers there. All in all, I'd say I'm fairly generous."

"You didn't do this out of generosity."

"Obviously." I took a bite from my apple. "Any other

brilliant observations? If not, I'll be in my office. I have a job to do, Baggage."

"Yes, you mentioned you had a job. Twice now." His eyes flicked down to the fruit in my hand. "Isn't it customary to offer your guest something to eat and drink, or has being alone for centuries made you forget how to be around people?"

I inclined my head. "It is customary, yes, and I would have done so had I considered you a guest." My lips tipped up a bit when I could see how my words landed. I waved at the fridge and cupboards as I walked past him. "Help yourself. A *friend* of Nathalie's is a friend of mine."

I didn't turn to look at him, but I knew he could see the Cheshire grin on my face when I glimpsed him in the reflection of my living room window.

six

NATHALIE

"Still nothing?" I asked Sienna as I set the takeout Indian food on the counter. She shook her head, the action devoid of life.

Beside her, Anders sat with his feet kicked up on the chaise. Her head rested on his shoulder as she watched her daughter play in the center of their living room. Hallie was only five months old or so, but her development was closer to that of a four-year-old by this point. Her dark hair was unkempt; Sienna hadn't been brushing it. She wore mismatched clothes that consisted of Slytherin leggings under a fabric skirt and a bandeau top from *Moana*. Her bow and arrows came from her newest fascination with the movie *Brave*. She danced around the room singing "Dos Orugitas" from Encanto, in a surprisingly lovely voice even if she was mispronouncing some of it.

"Where's Mist?"

"She didn't want the day off, so she's with the señora," Anders answered.

"I brought dinner." I said it because I wasn't sure what else to say, or do for that matter. There wasn't exactly a social standard for "your twin sister is stuck in a veil and might never return." Food was a good remedy for most grievances, and the ones it wasn't—it didn't hurt. Especially when Anders was doing a lot of the cooking for them and Hallie. He wasn't horrible. Given he'd had a thousand years or so to perfect his skills, I shuddered to think what his cooking was like when he was younger.

"Mmm," Hallie hummed as she dropped her plastic bow and quiver on the floor loudly. "It smells *yummy*." She licked her lips and started toward the takeout containers. When Sienna didn't move, I took it upon myself to make Hallie a plate.

"What's that?"

"Cheese with orange sauce."

"And that?"

"Meat."

"What kind of meat?"

"The kind you eat."

She made a face, not liking my answer. "I only eat chicken."

"It's chicken." It wasn't.

"It doesn't look like chicken." She pushed a finger into the lamb chunks when I set her plate on the coffee table and went to get her a glass of water.

"And what does chicken look like?"

She twisted her lips as she thought about how to answer. "Chicken's white."

"Not all chicken," I said. "Some chicken is dark."

She narrowed her eyes at me, disbelieving. "Uncle Anders," she said, and it sounded like Uncle Ands. "Can chicken be brown?"

"Mmhmm," he said, looking at something on his phone.

"Are you *sure?*"

Sienna sighed deeply, like our conversation weighed on her. I knew it wasn't that. She was usually the most patient person in the world with her daughter, but two days had passed and there was no sign of Sasha.

"Eat your dinner," she told her daughter. Hallie frowned, then stabbed the lamb with her fork. She lifted it up, glaring at the piece of meat like it personally offended her.

She wasn't usually a picky eater, but Sienna's stress and the lack of Sasha when she'd seen her every day of her very short life manifested in a different way than the rest of us. She was fussier but wilder. She played harder, and cried harder when she hurt herself. She whined at bedtime for an extra story and argued with anything I put on her plate.

"Go on," I encouraged. She took a tentative bite of the lamb.

Her face transformed into a giant smile.

"I like brown chicken!" she declared. Then she ripped a large amount off her fork between her teeth, gobbling it down.

I returned her smile before turning to Sienna and asking, "Would you like me to make you a plate?"

"Not hungry," Sienna said.

Anders frowned. "You need to eat."

She stiffly stared straight ahead. "I'll eat when I'm hungry."

Anders and I shared a look. While she wasn't exactly wasting away, I was worried about what would happen if Sasha didn't wake up for a long time. The deeper Sienna sank into grief, the harder it would be to pull her out.

"I'll make you a plate and you can pick at it if the mood strikes you."

She didn't respond as I placed a small portion of everything on a dinner plate for her and then fixed a larger portion for Anders. I brought them over, handing him his and setting hers on the chaise next to his legs where she could easily reach it if she wanted to eat.

Instead of awkwardly lingering, I packed up the rest of the leftovers and put them in the fridge. There were a few dirty dishes in the sink. I checked the dishwasher to find it clean and unloaded it quickly, reloading the dirty stuff.

"You don't need to do that," Sienna weakly protested. There was no real fight in her words. No true argument.

"I know I don't. I'm choosing to."

She didn't say anything more when I wiped the counter down, then grabbed my backpack. "Thanks for picking up dinner," Anders grunted.

I nodded toward him. "Not a problem. Let me know if you guys need anything."

"Will do."

"Where are you going, Aunt Nat?" Hallie called after me, her mouth still full of food.

"I've gotta get some work done, kiddo."

"Aw," she whined. "But you just got here."

I sighed. "This is really important. Unfortunately, it can't wait." She pouted, not liking that answer. "How about this? If you're a good girl for your mom tonight and go to bed with no fuss, I'll take you to get ice cream tomorrow."

She beamed like I'd hung the moon.

"Deal!"

"Thank you," Sienna said when I opened the door.

I tried to keep the pity off my face as I gave her a tight smile and said, "You're welcome. Hang in there."

I stepped into the elevator and rode it down to the second floor. The walk to my apartment was short, but it

66

was like the last dregs of energy I had left me in the time it took to get from there to here.

I reached for my door, pausing when I noticed the note taped to it.

My fingers snatched it, ripping the tape clean off the painted wood surface without a care for the damage.

I traced the letters, feeling the indent where her pen pressed into the paper.

Not a single trace of magic in sight.

Only one word.

Roof.

I ran back to the elevator, wishing not for the first time we had a stairwell that led to the rooftop. While the ride was short, it felt longer than the longest red light of my life.

The doors slid open, and I hightailed it up the concrete steps to the roof. My body collided with the door, and it burst open.

I probably looked half-crazed, sporting a messy bun and wild eyes, the way I searched the rooftop.

"Excited, much?" Katherine asked. She leaned against the half wall of cement that kept her from falling off. My eyes raked over her, taking in my twin that looked so different from when I last saw her.

Katherine's brown hair was cut short in a pixie style with half of her head shaved. She sported a tattoo on her skull that I couldn't quite make out in the shadows of the early night. Gone were the designer clothes and high heels she'd worn exclusively since we were teens, replaced by a worn leather jacket with patches and torn-up jeans that showed more of her legs than they covered. Unlike the store-bought type that tried to look "edgy," these fit her a tad looser than they should have and long strips of material fell at awkward angles. One of her legs sported a full sleeve, while the other had patchwork tattoos that I recognized as runes for various abilities, like cloaking.

"How did you get into my building?"

She raised an eyebrow. "Your building? Last I checked, Renata Rosara's name is on the deed and she sets the wards."

The implication that the señora let her in here without saying a word to me hung like a bad smell in the air.

"The bomb on your door is a nice touch, by the way," she added, shoving her hands in her jacket pockets. "A bit obvious, but effective. I suppose when it's meant to be a deterrent more than anything, it suits its purpose."

"Why are you here?"

"You've been looking for me, have you not?"

I stepped farther onto the roof and lifted one shoulder in a shrug. "You left a message at the hospital."

She nodded, her boots scuffing against the concrete as she swung one leg back and forth, her heel hitting the retainer wall. "One you misunderstood."

"Uh-huh, is that so?" I crossed my arms over my chest, when we stood only feet apart.

We were born on the same day. Eight minutes and twenty-three seconds apart.

Our faces had such perfect symmetry that even our parents got us mixed up when we pretended to be one another by changing our mannerisms.

That changed the day I scarred half her face horribly.

While I'd created the divide, Katherine shoved a wedge in the crack to blow it wide open.

It was as obvious when I stood four inches taller in my vintage peep-toe heels, tailored black pants that clung to my body, and a dark red vintage blouse with puffy sleeves.

We'd always been different deep down. Now it was surface level, too.

"I'm alive. You need to back off on searching for me, or more people are going to get hurt."

"Is that a threat?"

She rolled her eyes. "Do you need it to be?"

I blanched. "Are you the one killing those people?"

She didn't answer at first, choosing to assess me like she was weighing how worthy I was to hear it. "Yes and no."

My heart seemed to drop into my stomach. I flattened a hand to my chest, wishing I could stop the painful lurch that made me hurt.

"I'm going to need more than that if you plan to walk off this roof."

Katherine chuckled, tossing a handful of seeds from her pocket on the ground. Several crows surrounded us, diving for the food.

"It's cute you think you can stop me."

I wouldn't be the one to do it. All I had to do was reach out over the telepathic link I had with Ronan and he'd be here at a moment's notice. Way back before he and Piper got together, he and I took a blood oath to protect her. Except, because of my weird magic, it didn't quite go as planned. Instead, I gained the ability to communicate with him telepathically.

Katherine didn't know that though, and I kept that secret more closely guarded than the rest of my weirdness these days.

"You're here for a reason, Kat. Tell me what you mean so we can all move on with our night." I wasn't sure whether I'd call Ronan on her just yet or not, but so long as she believed she had the upper hand, she'd keep talking.

Kat looked to the sky like she was searching for something.

"I killed most of them, but it was self-defense. Not premeditated murder."

I deflated slightly, because that meant she wasn't a complete and total monster. Kat and I were a lot of things with *and* to each other. Most of them weren't good. But for better or worse, we were honest with one another.

Not because we always wanted to be, but because we physically couldn't lie to one another. Not with words, at least.

"They attacked you?" I asked slowly.

Katherine blew out a breath, her eyes dropping back to me before nodding.

"I need you to say it."

She released a bitter laugh. "Some of them attacked me. Some of them were casualties because they were going to die either way and I wanted to live."

My brows knit together as I tried to understand what she was saying. "So they didn't attack you?"

Katherine groaned as if I were annoying her. "It doesn't matter."

"Yes, it does." My tone was hard and unwavering. "People died, Kat. They're still dying and you won't tell me why or how or what the fuck is going on—"

"I'm dealing with it," she interrupted. "I can't tell you more than that."

"Then why come here to begin with?" I questioned. "If you're not going to explain yourself, why bother at all?"

Her answer was so simple, and yet the implications were anything but.

"Marcel is dying."

I jerked. Blood rushed to my head. For a few moments, all I heard was the roaring of it in my ears.

"What?" I whispered.

She inclined her head. "He's been dying for a long time. Since we were all teenagers. Whatever is killing him . . . it makes his magic unnaturally powerful, but it's causing his body to waste away. Mother and The Morrigan found a... solution, of sorts. They were giving him what I can only guess was the equivalent of chemotherapy, but it wasn't curing him. It simply slowed down the process. Carissa did it after she died, but now that you two have gone and pissed her off to the point she disowned him, the clock is ticking."

"Back up," I said, shaking my head. "Since we were teenagers?"

The wind screamed as it funneled down the streets of New Chicago and I felt it deep inside me. Katherine nodded slowly. "Soon after you were betrothed."

That was . . . I shook my head.

She was lying. She had to be. Except . . .

"Why did he never tell me?" Katherine shrugged but didn't answer, which made me think she knew. "Katherine," I said her name in a hard tone. "Why did he never say anything?"

She barked a laugh. "I don't owe you anything, Nathalie, least of all my husband's secrets."

I reeled back as if she'd slapped me.

"If you're so concerned about *your husband*, why aren't you with him?"

She smiled faintly at the crows between us and tossed another handful of seeds their way. "I have things to take care of. Things both you and he need to stay out of."

"That's not how this works—"

71

"That's exactly how this works. Marcel is dying and whether you admit it or not, you still care about him. Without Carissa giving him the potion, he has months at best. None of us have been able to find a cure, but I think you can. That memory of yours ought to be good for something, I reckon."

I shook my head, trying to sort through the jumbled mess that she was basically throwing at my feet. "You show up here, admit to killing people, but won't tell me why—"

"I said it was self-defense," she interrupted.

"If they didn't attack you, I don't understand how that could be true, but you refuse to explain it and then drop this on me?" I pressed a hand to my head, closing my eyes briefly to calm my breathing.

"If there's a cure for his disease, I truly believe you'll find it."

I opened my eyes at the sincerity in her tone, then shook my head, at a loss. "He's been dying for *years* and no one said anything. Not you. Not him." Water pooled in my eyes and I bit the inside of my cheek to keep from letting those tears fall.

She looked away, the corner of her mouth tightening, almost like she felt guilt. "I didn't learn about it until you left."

So, three years ago, give or take.

Somehow that made it better, even though I wasn't sure it should have. Maybe my expectations for Katherine were so low that anything above the absolute worst-case scenario was a net positive.

"If he's dying, you should be with him."

The words were both easier and harder than they should have been.

Katherine shook her head. "I can't save him, not from this. Being around him will only put him in more danger."

I pressed my lips together. "So instead you're pawning him off on me so you can run around the city murdering people—"

"Jesus fucking Christ," Katherine groaned. "I'm helping him in the only way I can, by telling you because he's too fucking stubborn to. And while I love belittling you, there's two things we both know are true here." I tilted my head, waiting for her to go on. "You still love him, and while I may be his wife by witch law, he's only ever wanted you. Our parents are gone. You know his secret now. There's nothing to stand between you two but death and your own stupid hang-ups about shit that happened years ago."

I gaped at her. "I've said it before, and I'll say it again. That isn't going to happen. I don't want your sloppy seconds."

Katherine chuckled. There was a darkness in her eyes that wasn't there before. Sure, death clung to her. It always had, but this kind of darkness almost seemed . . . resigned. At peace.

"He's not my leftovers, Nat. I'm gay."

I blanched. Again. "What do you mean—"

"We were married in name only," Katherine said. "I might have phrased it a certain way because I enjoy pissing you off."

Wow. She was a real class act.

"And you decide to tell me this now because. . .?"

Her smile was brittle. "I love Marcel. Not romantically, but I love him all the same. He's the only person I have left —and I want him to be happy more than I want you to be miserable."

That was an improvement over before, so I supposed it was something.

Previously, she preferred my misery. Who said that bitches couldn't change?

"He's going to ask me how I found out, then he's going to want to know where you are. He's spent the last month looking all over creation for you. It isn't going to go over well that you came here and just walked away without even saying why."

"Lie or don't. Up to you." Kathrine shrugged. "He can be pissed at me."

"And Piper? Sienna? Sasha went into the veil to find out who killed those people and she never came back—"

"This really shouldn't come as a shock to you, but I don't care what you tell them."

I huffed. "Piper will hunt your ass down, psychic bond-mate or not—and those runes on your leg may let you stay hidden for now, but how long do you think it'll take the Demon Queen if she decides to come for you personally? When her mate joins her?" Kat's jaw hardened, and I knew I hit home. "You should rethink telling me the full story. Your magic might be powerful, but sooner or later, you'll run out of places to hide. Then what?"

I didn't tell her I knew she was pretending to be me. It's not like it would make her stop, but if she got sloppy due to overconfidence, it could be useful.

Our magic prevented us from lying to one another.

Omitting the truth was another thing entirely.

"I told you, I didn't kill those people in cold blood."

"That's not enough." I shook my head. "Not when I know you've learned how to drain someone's life force to fuel your own magic. Carissa said you lost control—"

"Carissa isn't who you think she is."

74

"Is she the one you're running from?" I asked.

Katherine paused. "No. She's a pawn. Always has been. Always will be. I just don't trust her." That made two of us.

I snorted. "I know she tried to force you to make a baby with Marcel."

She shifted her weight from one leg to the other, watching the crows. "She's dangerous. You should stay away from her."

Like I didn't already know that. Kat may have saved me when we were younger, but she was never subjected to Carissa's particular brand of cruelty. Not until recently.

"I need you to give me a reason, Kat. One reason why I shouldn't tell Piper to hunt you to the ends of the earth for killing innocent people."

Katherine exhaled in a white cloud as her breath chilled in the late fall air. "I can't give you a reason she'll deem good enough, but I can remind you that nothing is black-and-white. I did what I had to survive. No more, no less. As much as you love wearing the white hat, we both know you would do the same."

Tension of a different sort built between us.

She wasn't saying it, but I knew what she was thinking about.

That night. The one that changed everything between us.

The one she never forgave me for, and never would.

I wish I could say I regretted my choices, but I'd do it all again even knowing she'd end up hating me. I guess in that, we really were alike.

Katherine pulled her hand out of her other pocket and tossed something small and gold at me. I reached out with both hands, catching it awkwardly.

"Is this what I think it is?" I whispered.

"Probably."

"The Eye of Parcae," I murmured. The object was no bigger than a quarter in diameter and perfectly symmetrical. Markings that predated living memory were etched into the orb. A language no one knew, but many had tried to understand. A new realization hit me. "It was you." I frowned at the object, then looked up at her. "You killed Faryn."

"I asked nicely first," she replied defensively.

"I saw the body."

Katherine shrugged. "He laughed in my face, so I helped him meet his maker."

"You tortured him and then ripped out his eyes." I lifted my chin, derision written all over my face.

"Don't start with me," she said. "Faryn was a thug that wouldn't have had any qualms selling me in the skin trade if he had the power to do it. I did the world a favor getting rid of that lecherous fuck."

I sighed, pocketing the Eye.

"If you can steal someone's life force with your magic, why bother with the knife and truth serum?"

She smiled, preening that I hadn't figured it out. "Because I didn't want anyone to know I did it. Looks like it worked."

I looked away. "If you went to so much trouble to get this, why are you handing it over?"

"I thought it would help me with my current . . . predicament," she said slowly. "But I couldn't get it to work. Maybe you'll have better luck and it can help Marcel."

I squinted at her. "So this is like, what? A bribe?"

"If you choose to see it that way."

"What other way is there to see it?"

"A gift."

"Right," I drawled. My family didn't do gifts. Nothing came without strings attached. "Any more cryptic warnings or 'gifts' you're leaving out?"

I wanted to ask her about the pictures in the drawer. Ask her why she was meeting with Carissa if they weren't on good terms. Something wasn't adding up, and I knew she had the answers. But there wasn't a chance in hell she'd tell me. I'd be giving up valuable information for nothing when she wasn't even my ally and was potentially acting as my enemy.

Katherine put her hands on either side of her body and hopped up onto the half wall, her legs dangling in front of her. She smiled without humor.

"Just one. Stay out of the veil."

She threw herself backwards, toppling over the edge of the wall. I shrieked in a panic, racing to the edge of the wall. My hands gripped the rough cement as I peered over.

I didn't want to look, out of fear she was nothing more than a red splat against the gray street, but I couldn't stop myself.

Except . . . there was nothing.

No body. No blood. No Katherine.

Just a black feather floating on the wind.

seven

NATHALIE

"I've prepared an agenda for today's meeting."

Ann walked around the ebony conference table, handing each of us a stapled paper packet. I took it from her wordlessly, flipping the page to stare at the dreaded first bullet point.

As she took her seat, Bad Nat sniffed and pushed back on the legs of her chair. The front two came off the ground as she kicked her boots up and got mud on the packet. Given there was no actual mud in my memory loci, it was clearly a purposeful decision meant to piss Ann off.

"We all know why we're here—"

"Okay, first up," Ann interrupted, acting like Bad Nat never spoke at all. "Marcel. The Prime is feeling conflicted over how we should deal with the information Katherine gave us."

Bad Nat tossed her head back and groaned loudly. "No one cares. Marcel is a liar, and he's married to Freddy Krueger—"

"He was our first love," Peace said, her voice rising in frustration. "And Kat's gay. It's a sham marriage, but calling her names is just cruel. Jesus, why do you have to be so hateful?" While my tea-loving, plant-obsessed, smut-reading alter ego was usually the most chill at these meetings, our complicated life had put her under continuous stress. When we'd come to find out Marcel and Katherine were now married and no longer engaged, it tore at an already open wound. Sure, we'd learned it was a fake marriage, but that didn't change the years of pain I'd harbored thinking he chose her over me. Then learning about Sasha being August's mate had blown through the last spoon we had to give.

To say Peace was feeling a little stabby thanks to all the pressure was an understatement.

Caretaker put a hand on her shoulder trying to soothe the fraying emotions that were anything but peaceful and looked at Bad Nat. "Peace can't help her nature. None of us can," she reminded gently.

"I beg to differ," Bad Nat replied. "She feels chaotic half the time and should be named Anxiety. Ann has more empathy than everyone but the servant." She shrugged with a distasteful purse of her lips.

The Warden sighed. "Do you have to do this right now?"

"What?" she said, lifting an aggressive eyebrow. "Point out the facts?"

"Calling Katherine Freddy Krueger is not a fact. It's an insult, and one in poor taste from an objective standpoint," Ann said, pushing her glasses up a smidge on her nose and sitting impossibly straighter. "Furthermore, Peace is chaotic due to the lack of time we've spent on our mental health this last year. Part of which is your fault. As for empathy . . . I don't feel her pain any more than I feel your annoyance. I simply understand the human condition and to achieve desired results, I must take all factors into account—especially emotions."

Bad Nat rolled her eyes. "Kiss-ass," she muttered. It resulted in glares from all around the table. I wasn't sure if it was just me, but she seemed pissier today. More aggressive than even her usual schtick at these meetings. I knew from experience the more we tried to silence her, the louder she fought back. Thinking about that, I went against the grain of how I usually did things.

"Bad Nat," I said, motioning toward her. "You've clearly got strong thoughts. Can you elaborate on why you think we should do nothing about Marcel?"

Her boots dropped off the table and the front chair legs cracked against the hard wood as she righted herself, elbows coming to rest on the table.

"Regardless of the past—which isn't in his favor—we can't trust him. How many ghost summonings has he done?"

"Fifty-six on record," Ann said without looking at her notes. "That excludes most of the last three years, but if we were to use the average per year and adjust for the increase in the preceding two before then, we'd be looking at one hundred and seven."

Bad Nat stared at her, face blank. "That's specific."

"Would you rather I'd been vague?" Ann clapped back. "We remember everything, so I fail to see how willful ignorance could aid us."

"Of that fifty-six we know, during how many of those summonings has he lost someone in the veil?" Bad Nat said instead.

"None," Ann answered immediately.

"That's my problem. He's never lost one, and yet Sasha is in the veil."

"Well, he did say he's never done it with a succubus," Caretaker pointed out softly. She wrapped her hands around a steaming cup of hot cocoa, drawing one leg up to put her foot on her seat and propping her chin on her knee.

Bad Nat scowled. "Magic is magic. They don't have to cast the ritual or *do* anything. They just hover at the edge of death and then come back when it ends. I'm not buying that excuse. We can't trust him. We don't even know if he's in on this shit with Katherine—"

"She said he wasn't," Peace interrupted. "And she can't lie to us."

"She said a lot that could mean multiple things. We'd be stupid to take her word as truth and form a decision on that alone."

"On that, we agree," Ann said, tapping her bottom lip with the pencil eraser. The cut of her jaw seemed severe with the tight bun that kept her hair back. Not a single strand slipped out of place. "She also gave us the Eye of Parcae, which is both good and makes me wonder if there was more motive behind that. Before anyone brings it up, it's on the list and we'll get to it. However, we don't need to simply go off what Katherine told us. Marcel is with August. We can go and question him ourselves."

"And if he goes along with it just to waste our time and try to get her back?" Bad Nat questioned, motioning toward me. The distinction between me and the versions of myself was confusing at the best of times; Bad Nat only differentiated when she didn't agree with the decision.

Which basically meant anytime someone who had previously betrayed me needed help. She had a gift for holding grudges.

"That's my concern as well," The Warden sighed. Leaning forward, she curled one hand under her chin. "I'm not saying Katherine is lying. We just don't know if she's twisting her words. She did it before to make us think they were together. Now she says they're not, and he needs help? That we're the only one that might be able to save him?" She shook her head and the long brown ponytail shook with it. "I have a hard time believing this story, but even if it is true, there's only so much we can do. Committing to this? To trying to cure him from an unknown sickness?" She sighed deeply. "How much are we expected to take on for other people? Where do we draw the line and think about ourselves?"

"Fair point," Ann nodded. "We need to factor in the Prime's emotional health regarding this—"

Two floors above us, a door rattled.

Dust fell from the ceiling as we all looked up.

The entity in there seemed to have a point to make, and didn't appreciate being left out of the conversation.

"I'm worried about her," Caretaker murmured. "It's been a long time. Maybe we should give her another chance..."

"No," three of the five other Nathalies replied. Peace, Ann, and The Warden were all in agreement. I found it discouraging that Bad Nat didn't weigh in. She always had an opinion, and I'd already caught her sneaking around that door once.

"She's likely half mad by now. Letting her out would be throwing a grenade at a situation that needs to be handled with care," The Warden said. Ann nodded along with this. While she often considered my emotions, she preferred methods that removed them.

"But she is one of us," Caretaker said, pushing back gently but firmly in her disagreement about the entity upstairs that was shaking the entire loci.

"She tried to push Ann off the roof last time she was free," Peace said.

Bad Nat snorted. "I can see the appeal."

We ignored her.

"Locking her up isn't going to make her any better at handling herself. It won't teach her anything—"

"*Rage* stays where she is," I said, my position the judge, jury, and jailer when needed here. "Both The Warden and Peace are right. She's a complication we can't afford right now. Between Marcel, August, Sasha . . ."

There were moments I wanted to close my eyes and just disappear. Be like Peace and go into my greenhouse and never leave, or like Ann, who spent nearly all her time in the library. My greatest coping mechanism was compartmentalizing. Avoidance. I grouped things into personalities and locked away the ones I was better off without.

For the most part.

Bad Nat was an unwanted exception.

"To focus on the bullet point at hand," Ann said, steering us away from the topic I wouldn't debate. "Marcel is allegedly dying. While there is a slim chance Katherine found a way to twist her words, it's not logical to assume so. She's been hiding for weeks and only chose now to appear, after he was kicked out. She may not like us, but she cares about him. Which leaves us with one question to consider: what's the worst outcome that we can live with? That this claim was somehow exaggerated, and he tries to rope us back in, which is a headache and waste of energy, or the alternative? He dies, and we did nothing."

Silence settled heavily in the memory loci.

"I'm going to put it to a vote." I leaned back, crossing my ankle over my knee and shifted my weight to one side so I could brace my arm against the rest and fist my hand under my chin. "Peace?"

"We help him," she said in a quiet but sure voice. Her answer didn't surprise anyone, but I nodded still.

"Caretaker?"

She set her cup of cocoa down and took a small breath before releasing it. "I can't stomach the idea that Kat would lie about this. We need to stop debating and start searching."

I shifted uncomfortably. It wasn't her confidence to say so that made me uneasy, but that she chose this reason to do so.

If there was anyone that we would be within our rights to stay away from and not get involved for, it would be him.

Instead, Caretaker was doubling down and ready to go to bat for him.

Which is exactly why I was torn.

"I still think it's a waste of time," Bad Nat said without waiting for me to call on her.

"Warden?" I murmured.

My quiet strength alter ego tapped her fingers in careful consideration. "I don't think it's a waste, per se," she started, lifting her light brown eyes to mine. "I think it's a risk. One we can't afford, not with everything else right now . . ." Her shoulders straightened as she slumped back in the chair. "Peace is struggling enough as it is. We need to put ourselves first sometimes. I'm going to vote with Bad Nat."

"Welcome to the dark side," she chuckled.

"Pass," The Warden said with a roll of her eyes.

"Ann?" I prompted, wanting to finish this meeting up before I got out of the shower. That wouldn't happen if they started a throw down over slights.

"If I were doing an emotional cost-benefit analysis, in this case, I believe more harm will come from Marcel's death than having our time wasted and trust broken. One of these options is annoying, but we can brush it off and have Piper completely separate us. The other, I fear, could have lasting implications . . ." She pointed at Bad Nat with the end of her pencil. "Need I remind you all that *she* showed up after Lucifer died?"

She had a point there. One belligerent, foul-mouthed me was inconvenient but manageable. Two . . . I shuddered. Nope. Not an option.

"So we deal with the problem head-on, which means I need to speak with Marcel."

"Today," Ann pushed. "Katherine said he would have months. The more I know, the better odds there is something helpful in the library I can find."

The Warden sighed. "If we're going down this road, we should probably speak with Carissa and find out whatever it is that they've been giving him."

I inclined my head toward her in agreement. "Marcel first, because I need to know more from him before we go there, but unfortunately, you're right. I really hoped I'd never have to see her again."

"You could always bring Marcel and let him kill her," Bad Nat suggested. "I hear therapy is good for people."

Half the table glared at her and the other half shook their heads.

"Killing people isn't therapy."

"Says who?" she challenged. "Bet Piper would agree."

"Piper is a literal rage demon," Ann deadpanned.

"We've got a Rage of our own upstairs. Let her out and take a new vote."

Ann laughed unfeelingly. "That you think Rage can be

civilized enough to vote shows how ill-prepared and unin-
formed you truly are. If that door were opened, the havoc
she would wreak on not only the loci, but the world, is
nearly inconceivable."

I slapped the table with my open palm. The sharp crack
snapped through the room, bringing them to heel. "I
already said once, I'm not going to debate Rage's release.
She's in the attic where she will remain and if anyone
touches that door, they'll be locked in confinement with
her. *Capisce*?"

Every head around the table nodded except one. The
only person whose agreement I actually needed. Bad Nat
tilted her head at me, a slight smirk forming.

"You think you can rule with an iron fist. That we'll all
be good little Nats and fall in line." I said nothing, because
there was nothing to say to that and to respond in any way
gave her a reaction. The thing she wanted. "One day, you'll
grow complacent. The parts you've hidden will break free."

"Unlikely."

"Unavoidable," she countered. "You've had a hundred
chances to let them out, if not more. You think they were
hard to manage before?" She laughed and the dark promise
in it made me shiver. "We're all going to burn because of
your choice one day. You, most of all."

MARCEL

"That wasn't the agreement!" I shouted. My body shook with barely contained rage. What they wanted . . . what they were going to make me do. I couldn't. I wouldn't hurt Nat.

"Don't take that tone with me, boy," Dolores seethed. "You're in no position to barter here. There was no agreement. You had a choice between them. You chose poorly. You'll marry Katherine instead. It has been decided."

"Five years, I've been betrothed to Nathalie. Five. Why now? I don't want Katherine," I said.

Dolores blinked a few times before laughing coldly. "I don't care if you want Katherine, and I don't care if she wants you. You'll have her. Nathalie has proven to be weak. She's not a bitch worth breeding. Not with a magical line as potent as yours."

My mouth fell open. I knew the Le Fays were horrific. They were shitty parents, and shitty people. Humanity suffered because of witches like them. They'd always preferred Carissa to the twins, and their favoritism was so thinly veiled, I wondered why they even bothered pretending otherwise. As the years passed, it was clear they also favored Katherine over Nathalie. But this . . .

Dolores twisted her lips. "It's settled, then."

"No," I whispered as she began to walk away. She turned, her eyes wide at the one defiant word.

"What did you just say?"

I stood up tall, showing my height and towering over her. "You heard me. I won't marry Katherine. I choose Nathalie. I see her strength. Her worth. What she and I could do together, what we could make . . . you'll see."

I had to play to their skewed beliefs that heirs were what mattered the most. Fuck her. I was going to marry Nathalie. My sunbeam. I didn't care about heirs, or her power, or combining our lineage. I loved her. She was the only one ever meant for me. We belonged together. They had to see that. She was so much more than they realized.

Dolores took a step forward, her magic radiating from her. "If you want to live, you'll marry Katherine. And if it breaks my weak daughter's poor little heart, so be it. Maybe it'll toughen her up some. Unless, of course, you'd rather die a slow and painful death at the hands of your magic. Your tea? The one that keeps you alive? I'll withhold it, and you'll wither away while your magic eats you alive. I'll make Nathalie watch. Every bit that you suffer, she'll suffer tenfold. And when you're dead and rotting, I'll tell her it was her magic siphoning yours. That she was the one who killed you with her own broken powers. She'll certainly blame herself for it. I can only imagine the guilt she would feel. A burden like that might actually kill her."

"That's a lie," I growled. "She'd never believe you."

"Wouldn't she?" Dolores Le Fay was a shrewd woman. Thicker in the middle than in her legs, she wore long dresses that dripped of wealth but were bleak as the woman herself. Her brown hair was streaked with gray and beginning to frizzle with age. Witches usually aged well, but not the dark ones. She was no exception. "You're the one that's been keeping your illness a *secret from her for years. If you tell her now, it'll break her heart even more to watch you die. Then again, I could just kill her myself. Perhaps it would give you the motivation needed to do what those better than you have commanded." Dolores's lips twisted into an evil grin. I tried not to show fear, but she saw through me, anyway. "Oh, and if you tell Nathalie anything, I'll be sure to sacrifice her at the next full moon. Now that Katherine has reached adulthood, we no longer need the spare."*

My body was vibrating. I wanted to lash out. I wanted to end this woman, and I was strong enough to do it. Granted, she was a truly powerful black witch, but whether or not she knew it, my powers surpassed hers. It was my cruelty that could never come close to matching what this coven produced. I fought against the urge. Dolores was only one of the many that held my leash. Killing her would satisfy me at this moment, but I had no doubt Carissa would follow. Every choice I had would hurt Nathalie . . . And I just needed to go with the one that would hurt her the least, even if she didn't understand. I could make her understand, given the time.

Jaw clenched and breathing heavily through my nostrils, I nodded once.

"Your life is in my hands, Marcel, and Nathalie's is in yours. I own you, boy. Don't you forget that."

The door to my basement room where I "lived" during my treatments slammed shut when she exited. I dropped to my knees, barely feeling the rough stone when it scraped my skin and my knees bled. The scent of oleander was overwhelming as I fisted my hair. Dark magic writhed, threatening to come undone.

I'd do anything for Nat. Anything. Even hurt her, if it meant saving her. She'd forgive me one day, when I found a way to save us both. She had to . . .

I wouldn't live without her.

"FUUUUUCK!"
I screamed until there was nothing left in my lungs.

I JOLTED AWAKE, coming back to reality after having fallen asleep slumped over in my chair. Scrubbing my hands over my face, I tried to shake off the dream. A knock sounded down the hall, and the scent of juniper and lilac reached me before I even heard her speak.

NATHALIE

I distracted myself by playing with the wet ends of my braid. The door opened. August's figure filled the doorframe as he swung it wide and took a step forward.

I wish I could say that I kept my calm and cool composure, but the second our eyes locked, I couldn't look away.

His hair was mussed from sleep, falling in wild curls around his face. The stubble on his jaw was longer. Not a beard, but a day or two past shaving that gave him a sexy shadow over his face. His wide, proud shoulders were fully on display thanks to his lack of a shirt. I tried—and failed— not to look at the rest of him.

He wasn't flawless, but he was perfect. Old scars peppered his chest. They were nothing compared to the marks on his back, but he wore them without shame or insecurity. August was glorious to look at. A work of art, just like the paintings he collected. It made me wonder why he always glamoured his eyes.

Were they even blue? Or were they brown? I didn't care either way, but the fact that I'd never seen them bothered me more than it should have.

I didn't realize until he chuckled that I'd been staring far longer than appropriate. "My bedroom is just down the hall," August offered, his voice full of honey and gravel. How he managed to be so sweetly seductive without it seeming like he was trying was beyond me. Maybe it was part of the aurae bond.

Maybe my biology was just responding to the pheromones he put out.

I snorted. It had nothing to do with his gorgeous body and unrepentant self-assurance. Nope. Nothing.

August lifted both hands, mistaking my snort for derision.

"We've been standing here for about ninety seconds, and I can smell your arousal. It was just an offer, sunling. You're tense this morning, and I could do something about that. If you let me."

If I was wet before, I was a frickin' geyser now.

Fuck me.

Yes! Peace seemed to cheer, jumping up and down like the fool she was. She ripped her shirt off and said, *Take me.*

No! Ann reprimanded with equal fervor. *Jesus Christ. Put your fucking shirt back on.*

I swallowed despite my dry mouth.

What I should have said was no. Just no. But when did I ever do anything the easy way? "You know I can't."

He lifted a dark brow. Whatever smartass comment he was probably going to say vanished the second I wet my bottom lip without thinking. August reached for me with one hand, then seemed to think better of it. His fingers tightened into a fist as he pulled back, remembering himself.

"I respect your choices," he started.

"Do you?"

92

The hunger in his eyes was nearly a tangible thing. "Yes. More than you know."

"So moving here, baiting me with this"—I motioned toward his bare skin—"you call that. . .?"

August stepped forward, putting us chest to chest. He bent his neck at a hard angle to stare down at me. "I said I respect them, not that I agree with them. If standing in my doorway and seeing me shirtless is difficult for you, maybe you should consider why that is." One corner of his mouth curved up in a cocky smirk.

I bit the inside of my cheek to stop from smiling back like the flirt Peace was determined we be.

"I was referring to the comments about your bedroom and my—" My mouth snapped shut, not wanting to say it. The word itself didn't have power, but it felt too much like crossing the line to talk about it with August.

"Arousal?" he repeated. His face dipped closer, leaning into the groove of my neck. A deep rumble filled his chest as he drew in a long breath. "It would be easier to ignore if you didn't smell so fucking good." His lips traced the shell of my ear.

I shuddered.

This wasn't good.

"August." I meant to reprimand him, but it came out closer to a plea.

He groaned but pulled away as a door opened and closed in the hall behind him.

"I want to bend you over the counter and spank your ass for denying what's between us while Baggage in there watches, knowing how much he fucked up." It didn't take a genius to guess who "Baggage" was. "I'd finger your cunt until you begged for me to feed from you. Only then would I let you have my cock. Our coupling would be brutal. You'd scream, and you'd love it."

Was I panting or was it just hot in here? My thin sweater suddenly seemed like too much despite the misty fall weather.

"And if I wasn't in the mood to be spanked?" I forced out, my words hardly more than an exhalation. "If I wasn't feeling so submissive? What then?"

August's jaw tightened. His forearms flexed.

"You want the control, beautiful?" he asked, voice taunting. "Want to tie me down and sit on my face so all I can breathe is you?"

My neck flushed. We'd stepped right over the line of inappropriate into downright dirty.

"I won't do that to him," I said quietly.

But gods smite me if I didn't want to.

A different kind of tension entered his body. "And I'm respecting that by not doing those things to you—until you change your mind."

I shook my head. "We can't."

"I hear you," he rumbled. "But it's hard to listen when your body is insisting we *can*."

Didn't I know it? My head wasn't much better, with the all-out riot Peace was fixing to start. She'd stripped her clothes and dumped a water bottle down her front. It pooled on the ebony meeting table where she knelt, arms wide as if in offering. Ann was calling for backup, namely The Warden, because Caretaker was staying out of this one and Bad Nat sure as fuck wasn't stepping in.

I wanted to shake some sense into all of them, but that was easier said than done.

"Nat," Marcel said, appearing in the hall. He tried to step around August's frame, but the incubus didn't shift an inch to accommodate him. "Your *friend* didn't tell me you were here. I'll grab my coat and we can—"

"Not necessary," I said quickly, lifting both hands. "I'll only be here for a few minutes." August chuckled, poorly disguising it as a cough. Marcel glared at him, hands tightening into fists at his sides. My eyes narrowed, bouncing between the two of them. "Is everything here going okay?"

"Oh yeah," Marcel said easily.

"Just fine," August responded at the same time.

"Riiiiight." Their quick agreement despite the tension radiating between them only served to fuel my suspicions, but honestly, if it was just petty male bullshit, I didn't have the energy to get involved. They could work it out amongst themselves.

"Marcel, could you give us the room? I need to talk to Nathalie about something." August phrased it as a request, but the way he stepped to the side, blocking what little of my ex I could see, it was anything but.

"If it has to do with her body—"

My cheeks turned flaming, fire engine red. August noticed immediately. "It's none of your business, Baggage. Learn to read the room."

"Nat?" Marcel said by way of answer, his voice tight. I cleared my throat.

"Now's not really a good time, August."

Marcel snickered and August stepped toward me again, closing the space once more. "Then when?"

I took a deep breath and sighed. "I told you, not till after Sasha wakes up."

"It's been three days. With every hour that passes, she's less likely to—"

"You think I don't know that?" I snapped, more defensive than I needed to be. Instead of getting angry, August put his hands on my shoulders, squeezing them. The tension seeped out of me at the physical contact between us.

"This is important, Nathalie. I need you to make time."

Just like that, my muscles locked tight again. "That's nice." I waved his hands off, batting them aside. "It's not like I have a city to keep running, or that my assistant is drowning in grief over losing her sister. It's definitely not like I'm functioning on less than four hours of sleep a night because I'm doing the work of five people and can't risk outsourcing right now when I don't know who to trust." A hand touched my back, and despite every piece of logic it defied, Lucifer's touch grounded me.

He appeared at my side, and I cast him a sideways glance in warning. I couldn't physically tell him now wasn't the time. It was already weird enough that I silently communicated with him. I didn't need to be drawing any more attention to us.

Lucifer sighed loudly. "Fine. I'll wait in the car. Try not to get worked up. It makes me . . . anxious."

He frowned then disappeared again.

"That's the problem," August continued quietly, his voice calm instead of angry as he tried to reason with me. "Which is why we need to talk as soon as possible. If you're feeling overwhelmed now—"

"Stop."

He did. The first kernel of anger entered his glamoured gaze, but he stopped speaking. "This isn't a matter of simply making time. I don't have it in me. I told you that. If you can't accept it, well . . . honestly, that's not my problem."

His jaw tightened, body going taut despite trying not to.

I moved to the side, handing the reins over to Ann while

The Warden held down Peace, who was throwing a temper tantrum that could rival those of Hallie or Honor.

"You can't ignore this forever."

I snorted. Not a challenge he should issue. He clearly wasn't aware of how well-versed I was in avoidance. "I didn't say forever. I said when Sasha wakes up." August shook his head, as if trying to will something inside himself to not snap and force the subject.

"If you're not here to talk, why are you?"

I lifted a brow. "I thought I was welcome."

"You are, but as you just said, you've been doing the work of five people and barely sleeping. You're not here to let me help you, and I doubt you'd stop by for a social visit, so why?"

Observant. Logical. Ann approved of these traits. She always had. Men who knew how to listen were great, but those that knew how to think and see for themselves were better.

"I need to speak with Marcel about something. Alone."

August closed down, his emotions becoming unread-able. Part of me wanted to tell him why. That I wasn't picking favorites or whatever he assumed, but that I needed answers. The rest of me knew I should let it be. Let him believe what he wanted. Not encourage this thing between us that was already growing rapidly out of control.

"Do you want to go somewhere for this?" Marcel asked, finally shouldering his way past August.

I shook my head. "The guest room or another isolated space would work just fine."

Marcel stared for a short moment, confused and curious about my request.

"Right, follow me." He nodded his head toward the apartment. August stepped aside, allowing us both to pass.

As I went to walk by, his hand wrapped around my forearm. I turned, mentally rallying for the fight this was bound to turn into. But August didn't say anything. He leaned into me and lowered his face to my hair, inhaling deeply.

We were barely touching. Just his five fingers wrapped around my arm. The entry was narrow, but our sides didn't brush. His lips were nowhere near mine.

The quiet moment of intimacy struck me deeply. He let go before I could look further into it, and he turned to walk away. I went the opposite direction, toward the corner where Marcel had turned.

This apartment, while eclectic and with a vaguely old-soul feel, wasn't anything like August's home in Paris. Very few works of art graced the walls, and what was there were paintings I wasn't familiar with. I assumed they were from unknown artists. That didn't make them any less interesting, particularly a piece that hung at the very end of the hall next to the room Marcel walked into.

I stopped before entering, taking a better look. A raven perched upon a stack of books with titles I couldn't quite make out. Beside it, a canine skull was angled so that one of the empty eye sockets was facing the viewer. While mildly creepy and certainly weird, it wouldn't have made me pause if not for one other thing. In the raven's beak was a human eye. Bloody. Raw. The optic nerve still partially attached. The grotesque picture demanded I stare at it.

"Nat?" Marcel said, drawing my attention away from the unsettling yet enigmatic painting. It was only out of the periphery of my gaze that I noticed the band of color around the pupil.

Slate blue.

A shade that balanced itself on the horizon of a stormy ocean and a tempestuous sky. I swallowed hard, not knowing what to think of that. Marcel was an easy distraction, or rather my anger and hurt at what felt like a betrayal was an easy distraction. I'd kept it off my face while August was with us, but now that we were alone, there was no point in hiding it.

"Miss me already, sunbeam?"

"Hardly," I answered, looking around the room. I knew my voice was strained, but I wanted to try to ask the questions I needed answered. Give him the opportunity to tell me. "It looks like you've settled in. It's a nice place. Are you feeling okay? Doing well here?"

"The company is less than desirable. But I do like his cat." He shrugged, dodging part of my question. "It's better than being under Carissa's thumb, but that's a low bar."

"It's also better than the streets," I countered, pointing outside where he deserved to be.

"I prefer your floor, if I'm being honest." He dipped his chin suggestively.

I rolled my eyes, crossing my arms.

"Have a seat," he said, gesturing to a chair.

"I'd rather not." I shook my head, glancing at the room August had given him. It was better than I expected. Spacious. There was a cozy reading chair next to an expansive window that let in a lot of natural light. A modest desk and workspace. A queen-sized bed with a metal frame accented with a white quilt. On the nightstand beside it, six books were stacked—what appeared to be Marcel's current reading material. My attention might have moved on, if not for the title of one.

I'd seen it before.

I'd know it anywhere.

"Nathalie," Marcel said softly, coming toward me and

lifting a hand to my cheek, putting his thumb under my chin so he could turn my face.

"Why is the Le Fay grimoire here?" I asked him quietly.

Marcel's lips pressed together. "You always noticed when things went missing," he murmured after a moment.

"Answer the question."

He blew out a breath that smelled faintly of tea, parchment, and the most subtle hint of oleander.

"I'm researching the veil. Trying to see if there might be something to help—"

"There isn't," I said, utterly assured. I'd seen every page. I knew every word in that dark text. It might have answers, but not to my questions. Nothing in those evil pages could help Sasha.

"How do you know?" he asked. "That grimoire has hundreds of spells."

"Doesn't matter. I want to know how you came to be in possession of it." I tilted my head, taking in the glamour he wore. It covered every inch of his skin. His face. His eyes. He was hiding something he didn't want me to see.

"Took it from Carissa a while ago and never gave it back. When she came looking, I told her that Kat had it, last I'd seen."

I rolled my eyes because of how typical it was. Even as a married couple they still acted like siblings. When one got in trouble with my parents, they'd always blame it on the other. Carissa should have known better than to buy the act since we'd all seen it happen more than once. "I'm not talking about how you got it originally; I mean, how is it *here*? I dropped you off with nothing. Now you have a rather large book, and there is no possible way you could have hidden it in your pants." I paused to open the other doors in the room. "And an armful of clothes you couldn't have carried." I paused again and went to lift the edge of his mattress, muttering a disentangling spell to break the concealment magic I could see. "As well as a notebook that I'm going to assume *isn't* a magical spank bank given the trouble you went through hoping no one could find it—"

"How did you find that?" he questioned, striding across the room to snatch it before I could.

"Doesn't matter," I repeated. Everyone had secrets. He didn't want to share his when they were literally killing him? Fine. He'd die not knowing mine.

"It matters very fucking much," he rumbled. "You've been in here all of one minute and you managed to find and break a concealment spell *I* conjured. Me. Not to be arrogant, Nat, but you shouldn't have even suspected it was there. I'm the strongest death—"

"—warlock in a generation. Yeah, I know and I'm still not answering. Not until you . . ." My words trailed away. There was one short dresser against the closest wall. Papers and pens, books, and half-finished teacups cluttered it. I wouldn't have noticed the thing lying underneath it all if not for the mist that seemed to crawl over the surface like a mirage. I turned to the dresser and pushed the junk aside, removing the teacup saucers and crumpled paper he'd put in it. My fingers wrapped around the gold rim as I lifted it. While Marcel had been using it as a tray, the oblong mirror was not August's.

"What are you doing?" He sighed, acting like I hadn't just picked up a mystport of his own creation. A fine sheen of perspiration had gathered at his temple, peeking through his glamour.

"*Verum revelare,*" I said while glaring at him. The mirror changed to show me a picture of . . . his room. At the Le Fay mansion. I hiked an eyebrow in incredulity. "You made a mystport so you could go back to your old room?" I frowned, my eyebrows drawing together as I set it on the bed. "Why?"

Marcel sighed. "You're doing nothing to satisfy my overwhelming need to know how you discovered that so quickly—"

"Doesn't matter." A saccharine smile lit my face.

"It matters," he snapped, starting to lose his cool. "All of this, you." He motioned toward me. "The way you are now, your magic, you talking to ghosts—don't think I didn't notice that—and don't get me started on the fucking incubus I'm staying with. I feel like I'm in the dark right now when it comes to you, and I don't like it."

A laugh bubbled up my throat. A scratchy, vicious sound that was the closest I'd ever come to laughing like Katherine.

That locked door in the attic rattled dangerously. I clenched my teeth and felt it in my bones. The essence of Rage leaked beneath the door, begging to be released.

She was so close to escaping.

So determined to break free.

Ann and The Warden exchanged a worried look.

Bad Nat cocked an eyebrow, a feral grin curling up her face while she picked her nails with a knife. In a singsong voice, she cooed, "Someone wants to come out and play."

MARCEL

This wasn't going how I'd imagined. From the moment she'd entered, she took control of the conversation in an aggressive way I wasn't prepared for. She found the myst-port. Broken a concealment spell. Nat was closed off and shady and angry, and I didn't know why.

I'd said I was in the dark, and I meant it. Her response shook me. The way she laughed was eerily close to her sister. Emotionless. Detached. Teetering on the edge of rage and madness. I'd never heard that sound come from her before.

"You don't like it," she repeated, mocking me. "I don't care what you like. You haven't earned my trust."

"And whose fault is that?" I growled back, my control almost snapping.

Her lips parted in shock. "Did you just blame *me* for not trusting you?"

"You won't give me the time of day. A chance to even try! You want me to beg? To plead for your forgiveness? I will. I'll never speak to Kat again if that's what you want from me. I'll break the marriage vows. I'll marry you like I always should have—"

"But you won't give me the truth."

"I've already told you the truth," I said. "What little I haven't, you wouldn't let me because you're fucking stubborn and hell-bent on pushing me away. I know I fucked up, Nat. I've said it before and I'll say it every day for the rest of our lives, but I'm not giving up on this."

"There is no *this* anymore," she countered, pointing back and forth between us. "And what I came to discuss has nothing to do with *us* or what we used to be—what we'll never be again."

Her words lashed into me, eroding more of my waning control. "Then why are you here? Are you here to show off whatever magic you're hiding from me? Are you here to flirt and throw yourself at August's feet, then rub it in my face?"

"August has nothing to do with this," she bit out.

"You sure about that? He seems to know you a hell of a lot better than you'd let on." The way he'd goaded me the day I arrived replayed in my mind. The knowledge that he'd felt her. Tasted her. Knew her body. His words burrowed under my skin and enraged me more than I ever wanted to admit, and I couldn't stop it from spilling out of my mouth. That frustration was aimed at her, and it wouldn't help me, but my dumbass couldn't hold it back and I regretted it the instant it came out. She narrowed her eyes at me, her nostrils flaring.

"What do you want to hear, Marcel? You want me to deny it? Tell you I didn't fuck him, and nothing happened between us?" she asked bitterly. "I could. I could tell you that. I could tell you I didn't love every minute of it, but then I'd be no better than you. A fucking liar."

My voice caught in my throat. The way he'd prodded at

me, I had known deep down that he wasn't lying. But to hear her confirm it tore at my soul. I wanted to rage. At her. At him. At the fucking fates who dealt me this shit hand that may very well cost me the woman I loved.

I'd married Katherine out of necessity, but Nathalie didn't know that. It wasn't fair to expect her to keep sitting around waiting for me, but fuck if it didn't kill a piece of me to know the same fucker she'd pawned me off on had touched her. Nat was mine. Always had been. Always would be, regardless of any trysts we might have had over the years. "Any other secrets you want to share with me?"

"It's no secret. You just don't deserve to know what I do in my life. Acting like you have some right to my truths. Fuck you, Marcel." She shook her head. "With everything you've kept from me, you're standing there saying you'll marry me while you're glamoured, refusing to show me what you look like. Refusing even now to tell me you're dying."

My heart skipped a beat. Several, in fact. The room sounded like static and time stood still until blood rushed into my ears and I felt my heartbeat pounding in my head.

"Who told you?" I croaked when I finally managed to speak.

"Doesn't matter," she said again. Those were quickly becoming my least favorite words to hear out of her mouth. "I know now. And if I'm going to help you, I need you to answer my questions. *That's* why I'm here. Now, take off the glamour."

"I want to know who told you, Nathalie." My voice was barely a whisper.

Her eyes began to soften, but the pulsing contempt she held for me in that moment shut it down, the ice returning. "It should have been you to tell me. And you didn't."

"You didn't need to know. It was being handled."

"I was your fiancé!" she snapped, raising her voice. I could count on one hand how many times she'd yelled in the many years I'd known her. "I swore my life to you. My future. And you—" She broke off and looked away, trying to rein her emotions in. "How long? Did you know about it the whole time we were together?"

She crushed me with a look, the anger I had dissipating. What she knew only scratched the surface.

"I didn't know the whole time," I said softly.

"No? Then when?" When I stayed silent, she raised her voice again. "When, Marcel? When did you learn you were sick?"

I closed my eyes and took a deep breath before looking at her again. We were about to go down a path she wasn't ready for. Once we did, there was no turning back. "It . . . manifested when I was eighteen."

Nat stumbled back. "That's when... you've known since we were first betrothed?"

I nodded. "About six months after that was when they suspected that it wasn't just an infection . . . that it might be permanent." She looked away as though she was remembering those years we'd spent together.

"Why didn't you tell me?"

I ran a hand through my hair, knowing she probably felt even more betrayed after my revelation. Things between us were good back then. Civil. Nothing romantic yet, but we hadn't fallen apart. That came later. Now hearing that I'd kept that from her during a time when we did trust each other was only going to rip her further from me. "Because you were fifteen, Nat. We were fucking kids. Even if you always seemed wise beyond your years, it didn't change the fact you were too young. You and I were betrothed, but we were still just friends."

"Friends didn't talk to each other like we did. Friends didn't kiss like that."

"You were older when that part of our relationship started. Don't pretend like you don't remember. I know that memory of yours is solid." She may try to believe we were in love then, but my Nat was three years younger. She was a child and I barely deserved to be called a man when we'd been betrothed. While I'd had passing flings, she hadn't even kissed a boy before me. Those early years, her inexperience, her innocence, her age . . . they were both blessings and barriers for us.

"I remember," she whispered. "I kissed you on your nineteenth birthday. You certainly didn't seem to mind it then when you pushed me up against the wall. Didn't feel like kissing *a friend*."

I sighed. "I kept my distance. Yes, you were my betrothed, but I was older than you. I didn't want to take advantage. You couldn't consent—not really. Not when it was Dolores who signed you away to me to begin with and didn't ask permission, and frankly, I didn't want that shit on my conscience. You were fifteen when I found out. There was a chance we'd never even make it to getting married if this sickness took me. I didn't want to dump all of that on you. I didn't even want to face it myself."

"You could have told me when I was older. Why not when I was seventeen? I was old enough to consent then."

She had me in a corner. I knew where she was going with this. I remembered it all too well, but she was turning everything around. "Don't do this, Nat. That's not how it was."

"I was old enough to fuck, but not old enough to share your secrets with?"

"Goddammit, Nat," I growled. "It wasn't like that, and you know it. Don't come here and act like I manipulated you into sleeping with me. I'm not like your asshole family. I didn't use you, and I never regretted anything I've shared with you. You were my best friend, but you know nothing of what happened."

"Because you never told me! You told my sister though, didn't you? Was that before or after you married her? For all your bullshit lies and claims of love, you couldn't even tell me you're dying? Everything you do is a betrayal. A lie. Everything." She laughed and a hint more madness crept into her voice, as if after everything, this would be what broke her. "I hate you for it. I hate that I fell for you. That I fell for any of it."

"I couldn't tell you! Your fucking family would have killed me, or they would have sacrificed you!"

Silence swelled between us as my words settled over her.

"What?"

"You want to know my secrets, Nat? Your mother had me by the balls. I married Katherine, or they stopped giving me the treatment. There you go. And you know what? I refused. Do you hear me? I told your bitch mother no. I *chose* you."

"You told Dolores no?" The shock on her face was real. No one defied that family. Certainly not its matriarch.

"For all the good it did me, yeah. I was blackmailed no matter which way I turned. If I told you I was sick and being forced to marry your sister, you were dead. Dolores said she'd kill you on the next full moon. So I did what I had to do to survive. For *you* to survive. I kept my mouth shut and

married Kat. I've been trying for years to make you understand without endangering you—to earn your forgiveness.
You refuse to listen to me when I try."

"My mother died ten months ago." Still stoic. Still a
roadblock. I bared all of this to her, and she went for the
argument, trying to find holes in my story.

"And Carissa controls me now. Or she did. The deal still
stands. The executioner's ax just passed on to her."

"She can't kill me even if she wanted to. You could have
told me."

I shook my head. "Carissa has been looking for an
excuse to hurt you for years. I wasn't going to give her one. I
don't trust that she wouldn't find a way when she's got the
Ouroboros Coven. You were all that ever mattered to me.
Kat may have married me, but she didn't want it any more
than I did. I'm not . . . I was never meant for her. We both
agreed on that." I wouldn't betray Kat's secrets. This was
about mine, and mine alone.

Nat chewed on her lip, glancing at the dresser where
the mystport was. "I don't want to talk about my sister. I
want to know about this potion."

I huffed a humorless laugh. "I just told you everything
and you have nothing to say about it?"

She returned her gaze to me. "I'm just . . . spent. I can't
process all of this right now. I don't have the spoons to deal
with it. I need to know about what they're giving you so I
can try to replicate it. That's what I need to focus on. I can't
do that without knowing what kind of illness you actually
have."

I didn't know what "spoons" were, but it wasn't difficult to figure out based on context. It was her available
energy. Everything was draining her, and this was no differ-

ent. She was hanging on by a thin thread, and this entire conversation was making it worse.

I sighed, wishing I could take away her pain. "They never told me what kind of illness it was. I don't think they knew."

She cocked her head, exhaling her annoyance through her nose. "Even now . . ."

"It's the truth, Nat. You want to talk about lacking the spoons? Same, sunbeam. Same. The cat's out of the bag, but you still won't tell me who told you. Me? I have nothing to hide."

"An anonymous tip, Marcel. That's all you'll get from me." She waved her hand, signaling me to continue. "Go on. If they didn't know, how did they start treating you?"

Anonymous tip, my ass. Kat and Carissa were the only two alive who knew about it, though Nat proved she had other tricks up her sleeves I hadn't been expecting. I knew better at this moment. It wasn't about what I wanted to know. I couldn't make it about me right now. No more than it already was. "Trial and error, mostly. Some attempts did absolutely nothing. Some made me terribly ill for weeks."

"How sick?"

"Well, I felt like death on a Monday." Feeling pretty close to it now.

Her brows pinched together in thought. "I have no memory of you being that sick. Just common colds. A case of the sniffles here and there."

"Of course you don't remember it. We hid it. You were about seventeen when they found a potion that worked well enough. I'd take it every two months, and it'd knock me on my ass for about a week."

Realization shone in her eyes. She'd pieced the timing together quickly. "You were gone every two months . . .

You'd said you were on trips representing the family at other covens."

I inclined my head, confirming her guess. "And in reality, I was down in my basement prison on the brink of death, waiting for whatever potion your mom concocted to work."

Her lips pressed together, and she nodded a few times absentmindedly. "So you need it every two months? When was the last time you had it?" My features softened, and her face fell. "How long has it been?"

"Thirty-two days . . ."

"That's—"

"I have to take it once a week now," I said softly. Her lips parted. "I can push it a week and a half sometimes, but the recovery is harder when I do."

"What happens to you when you don't have the potion?" she asked, but the hesitation in her voice told me she didn't want to know the answer. She needed to ask, but she feared my response.

"My magic begins to destroy my body from the inside out." I lifted my jaw, knowing exactly what was coming next.

"Take off the glamour, Marcel," she murmured, her voice shaking.

I shook my head. "No, you don't need to see what happens. There's nothing that you can do."

She laughed bitterly, taking a step toward me. "You know nothing of what I can do."

Fair point. The way she'd entered my room and blown my mind proved her statement. Still . . . this was different.

"Your family couldn't find a cure, Nat. If the most powerful coven in the world couldn't, what makes you think you can?" She glowered at me, and I held my hands up in surrender. "I'm not trying to be an asshole. I've been searching for a cure too. For years. And I've got nothing."

"Show me." Her jaw clenched and her fists tightened at her sides.

"I don't—"

"Dammit, Marcel, take off the fucking glamour!"

I sighed loudly and closed my eyes. What was the point in hiding it now? Dropping the glamour, I waited. She gasped and when I opened my eyes, I saw the woman I loved struggling to comprehend what was happening in front of her. All the fury she'd had moments before had vanished.

I knew what I looked like. I'd seen it in the mirror for eight years, and I was nothing compared to what she expected. I waited quietly as she took me in, following her gaze as it trailed over my body. Unnaturally dark circles curved around my eyes. My skin was a morbid combination of deathly pale and aggressively flushed, the grotesqueness of it accentuated by the thin sheen of sweat that coated me. Her perusal halted, focusing on my arms.

"What is that?" she managed to choke out. Her voice was breaking. Tears formed, threatening to spill over, but she couldn't stop looking at the patches of my skin that flared bright red, like a light had been shoved just beneath the surface. The sound of her voice said she knew the answer, but needed confirmation. It didn't make sense. It took two years for us to figure out what that symptom was. How could she know in an instant?

"It's my magic." I swallowed thickly and the power pulsed beneath the surface. "It's trying to break free."

"Holy shit," she gasped, her chest heaving. "You're really . . ."

"Dying?" I finished for her. "Yeah. I am." She choked on

a sob, the reality of it hitting her. Her body wobbled and I stepped forward, wrapping my arms around her shoulders and pulling her into my chest. Resting my cheek on the top of her head, I whispered, "I'm sorry, sunbeam. I never wanted you to see me this way."

For a thousand nights I'd wished to hold her again. To caress the silk of her skin and feel her warmth against me. To breathe in her scent. But not like this. Not because she saw me withering away.

She looked up at me, tears streaking down her face, brown eyes wide and focused on mine. My gaze dropped to her mouth, and I couldn't help what I did next.

Leaning down, I pressed my lips to hers. Nat inhaled sharply and tensed, but just when I thought she'd pull away, she leaned in. Fisting my shirt in her hands, she pushed herself up on her tiptoes, opening her mouth to me. Our tongues met, the kiss deepening as I drank in every bit of her taste. Her smell. Her touch.

Nathalie groaned, tilting her head to give me better access as she deepened the kiss, wrapping her hands around the back of my head, threading my hair through her fingers.

I cupped her face, holding her to me as tenderly as I could. There was a hunger in the way her lips moved against mine. A desperation for what hadn't been shared between us in far too long. I missed it. I missed her. The way she drew me in told me she missed it too, even if she denied it.

The low rumble in my throat vibrated against her and I nipped at her bottom lip with my teeth before devouring her again. Her hands trailed down, nails skimming my neck and then over my collarbones.

Her hands froze in that spot, landing in a place that

used to have a much thicker layer of muscle. I wasn't emaciated, but I had leaned out more than she expected. My body struggled without the potion. She felt it then. The way the bone was more prominent than it had been before. She pulled away. Not just from the kiss, but from the embrace. From my arms. From me. Glancing at my shoulders, she shook her head. "I shouldn't have . . . not when you're . . ."

"I don't regret any moments I've shared with you, sunbeam. That includes now," I said, repeating my statement from earlier. I hadn't wanted her to see me this way. Not for my vanity or peace of mind, but because I wanted to spare her this pain. Too late. It was written all over her face.

"I know." The words were barely audible. She chewed on her lip, a frown forming between her brows while she began walking backward to the door, turning to reach for the doorknob. "Carissa knows what's in that potion. I'm going to find out what it is and put an end to this."

I forced a smile. "She'd rather die than tell you."

"We'll see," she whispered as she walked over the threshold. Turning to me slightly, she said, "Do me a favor."

"Anything."

"Don't die while I'm gone."

I nodded once, my face grim, and then she shut the door.

I couldn't say the words to her. I would have done anything for her, but that was a promise I couldn't keep.

I had countless spells at my disposal. I had years of study and mastery. I had powers greater than any witch or warlock in a century. And it didn't fucking matter. I didn't possess the one thing I needed.

Time.

eleven

NATHALIE

"Get your shit together, Nat." I gave myself a much-needed pep talk as I drove back to my apartment building.

I couldn't shake the image of Marcel's dying body out of my head.

I'd never be able to, no matter how much I wanted to erase it. It was no different from every other detail in my life.

It was burned into my mind.

Forever.

A torrent of emotions tumbled through me. The Nats of the loci were just as shocked as I was. Ann stood by, her expression grim and filled with concern. Caretaker broke down, falling to her knees next to Peace as they both dissolved into a mess of tears. Even The Warden sat on the floor next to them, taking on an unusual duty of protecting: she was trying to soothe them. It didn't stop her from watching Bad Nat like a hawk.

I hadn't planned on letting that all out. Bad Nat had been egging me on while I fought with Marcel. Her cutting words started to drown out my more reasonable selves. She reminded me of all the hurt and pain he'd caused and how damn good it felt to let it out. Rage pounded against her cage, and Bad Nat watched with a salacious smile on her face. Just itching for the moment that door cracked down the middle and I finally let out the piece of me that no one ever needed to see again.

She was so close.

All the hurt and betrayal were wearing me down.

All the lies and the deceit had poked holes in my armor.

But even Bat Nat was left speechless when Marcel removed his glamour.

What I saw . . . the way his magic writhed beneath the surface? It was violent. Potent. Like nothing I'd ever seen before, and I'd seen the essence of magic my entire life. The patches of skin where his power was starting to break through burned brighter than fire.

Worse, I saw fissures forming. Lines across his face and his arms that were beginning to split apart, like a cracked vase waiting to shatter into a million pieces.

All the fury and anguish that was fueling my attack vanished.

For all my years of being mad at him, any actual hate I felt was merely surface deep. Shallow. Pain disguised by an easier emotion. Seeing him like that . . . I didn't want him to die. It reminded me how much I'd loved him at one time. That in some fucked up and inexplicable way, there was an infinitesimal part of me that still did.

Everything I'd been told was a lie, and yet somehow not.

The circumstances were, but the feelings weren't. The actions hadn't changed, but the reasoning had.

I couldn't make heads or tails of it, and my thoughts were careening out of control.

To make matters worse, the way August looked at me when I stormed out of his apartment ripped into my tender and fragile heart. He'd seen the hurt I was in, and I was in no shape to pretend otherwise.

"Nathalie, wait," he called, grabbing my arm to stop me as I burst through the front door and headed straight for the elevator.

"What are you doing in the hallway?" I turned my head away, unable to school my features. I didn't want him to see my face. The brokenness. The tears.

"You started yelling. I wanted to give you privacy."

Shit. *I squeezed my eyes shut. "How much did you hear?"*

"Enough," he said quietly. "Are you okay?"

"Nope," I murmured, tugging away. "Being hit in the—"

"Did he hurt you?" His voice darkened as it cut off my words, and I snapped my head around, coming face-to-face with him.

"No," I said firmly. The last thing I needed was him going in there to pick a fight and defend my honor. "Being hit in the gut with everything I learned is a bit much right now, and I want to be alone. I came for information, and that's what I got."

"You're sure you're okay?" August looked at my face, trying to read me with his glamoured eyes.

"Yup. My family has a way of reopening the scars of healed wounds."

August's lips twisted in thought, and he glanced back at the door, uncertain.

"Leave him be. Marcel didn't do this," I whispered, feeling the pads of his fingers press into my skin. "The Le Fays did."

He dipped his chin once, then placed a hand at the back of my head, pulling me toward him. Pressing his mouth to my forehead, he left a gentle kiss, then released my arm, rubbing over it softly. "I wish you'd let me in, sunling."

I shook my head and opened my mouth to speak, but he pressed a finger over my lips to shush me.

"*I know. You don't need to say it.*"

I wanted to let him in. I wanted to throw myself into his arms and cry out my pain and scream in my frustration. I wanted to let him be that safety net for me. I wanted him to be mine.

But he wasn't.

My cell phone ringing made me jump. I'd been so lost in replaying everything that I wasn't even entirely sure how I'd made it to the shop.

Distraction like that was dangerous, and carelessness wasn't going to get me anywhere. I couldn't keep my head on straight, and that needed to change.

"Your phone is ringing," Lucifer said.

"I know." I blew out a strangled breath. He'd been uncharacteristically quiet during the ride, or maybe he hadn't been, and I was so deep in my thoughts I hadn't even heard him.

"Still ringing," he muttered while I threw the car in park. "I'd be happy to answer for you if they could hear me. Alas . . ."

I grabbed the device, swiping to answer when I saw the name on the screen.

"Rafael," I said politely. "What can I do for you?"

"Nathalie," he crooned, his silky voice coming through the speaker with pristine clarity. Incubi had honeyed tones even over the phone, and it never ceased to amaze me. "I hope you're well, love. I'll keep it brief. I know your time is money. I wanted to set up a meeting. There are some matters we need to discuss in private."

I glanced at Lucifer, and he shrugged. "At least it's not

Isadora calling. If I have to listen to that cunt talk down to you one more time—"

I lifted a hand to shush him. Lucifer paused and arched a brow.

I hummed in response to the incubus leader on the other line. "Let me look at my schedule for a moment." I mentally turned to Ann so she could give me my agenda for the coming week. As I got out of the car, I gestured for Lucifer to come. In my loci, Ann peered over her glasses with a look that said "not a chance." "Rafael, I'm full this week, but perhaps at the end of next week we can have a call—"

"I'm afraid it's rather urgent, Miss Le Fay. If it weren't, I wouldn't be asking for an in-person meeting, I assure you."

I groaned internally. "Of course; what's it about?"

"A jasmine supplier of yours is trafficking more than just plants. Several of my clan manage those logistics and deliveries, and the situation was brought to my attention. I know how much you value your businesses and the wellbeing of your employees and customers. I wanted to make you aware straight away. Another shipment is due in three days, so you understand my desire for urgency is for your benefit." I pressed my lips together. *Shit*. This didn't sound good. One more thing to add to the long-ass list of things going wrong. "I'll keep it short, of course. Dinner tomorrow night? You have to eat, correct? You can kill two birds with one stone."

Walking up to the door of the shop, I spotted Piper inside speaking with Señora Rosara. My heart jumped into my throat. "That's fine, Rafael. Tomorrow. Please text me the time and address. See you then," I said in a rush and hung up.

I quickly strode to where they were standing and didn't

even bother to politely interrupt while I stuffed my phone in my pocket. "What's happened?" I blurted out. "Why are you here?"

Piper frowned. "Nice to see you too, Nat, but bring it down a notch."

I glared at her, then took a second to think about their demeanor.

They stood casually. No emotions or looking as though Sasha had been lost. I shook my head. "Sorry. It's been a long morning. Day? I don't even know what time it is anymore." I scrubbed my hands down my face. Piper pressed her lips together in an awkward smile while rubbing my back.

"I understand that more than I ever thought I would," she muttered.

"Right," I said, hooking my thumbs into the back of my jeans.

"Checking up, I assume?"

She nodded. "The señora and I were catching up."

"Any changes?" I asked, looking at the witch.

"No progress on her body. The vessel is stable," she began, and I internally cringed. I appreciated her clinical assessment for its calm and straightforward delivery, but talking about Sasha like that made it feel cold and unfeeling. Of course, that was my own fear leaking into logic. "However, there's a shift around the edges of the wards."

A sharp inhale escaped me. "And what exactly does that mean?"

"I believe she's testing the boundaries, pressing against the magic to get back into her body. She's near," she said, nodding her head. "I feel her presence, but I don't know what's stopping her from returning."

I exchanged a glance with Piper, who pressed her lips

together and raised her eyebrows, shaking her head slightly. "I don't know."

Señora walked around the counter of her shop and pulled out a box, setting it on the glass top and pushing it toward me.

Looking down, I frowned. "That's a Ouija board." She could see the confusion on my face. I'm sure anyone looking could—I wasn't trying to hide it.

"Obviously."

"And you're giving me this because . . .?"

"You have a connection with the veil," she answered. "Call to her. She might answer. You may be the key to guiding her back."

"That's a child's game. Made by humans," Piper pointed out, raising an eyebrow in disbelief.

"These don't work," I added with certainty. "They aren't real."

Señora glared at me. "Says who?"

"I . . ." The words halted as I considered her. She was being serious right now. "Communicating with the dead, accessing the veil . . . black witches covet that. They'd use any means necessary. If it were this easy, why don't they use them?"

"Donkeys know more than your family," she answered in Spanish, and I couldn't help but laugh at the slight. "The covens were too narcissistic and narrow-minded to think outside the box. You just dismissed it as easily as Piper did, and you were never bludgeoned with the stupid stick like the rest of your coven." She pushed the box toward me again. "Call to her, Nathalie."

She was right. None of them would have ever considered something so simplistic. I hadn't. I didn't think the señora was screwing with me, not at a time like this, and so a tiny bit of hope made my heart flutter.

Scooping up the box, I held it to my chest. "I'll let you know if she answers," I said, and the señora inclined her head while she reached for another object behind the counter, then handed it to Piper.

"As requested," she said.

"This is it?" Piper looked at the pulsing teal-colored orb with skepticism. "It looks like a soccer ball. Orson can control time . . . You're positive it'll put them on the same sleep schedule?" she checked, unsure.

"If you don't want it, then give it back."

Piper reached over and grabbed it before the señora could retract her offer. "I want it."

I pressed my lips together, suppressing a smile. The twins loved to sleep on opposite schedules. Still. Even though they aged quite quickly, it didn't change the fact that opposite sleep schedules with two kids was a nightmare—especially when those two kids had impressively dangerous powers. Piper, Ronan, and their guardians all had their hands full.

I questioned telling Piper about Kat for a moment, but then second-guessed myself. What exactly was there to tell her? Yes, I saw my sister, and she was cryptic as fuck when answering my questions. Yes, my sister had murdered some people, and I didn't know why, but it also wasn't what we'd thought, and I believe her. At least I thought I did. It all sounded laughable when I played it out in my head. When I had more to report, I'd let her know. As it stood, I figured it would just stress her out over nothing.

"Payment can be delivered. I expect it by the next new moon," Señora said sternly, raising a brow.

Piper looked at her with tired eyes. "If this works, I'll give you *the moon* if you want it."

"I believe you would," she chuckled.

I waved to them and headed to the door so I could go to my apartment. I had no idea what payment they'd agreed on, but I wasn't asking. I'd get the information from Piper later. Having already told Señora Rosara I wouldn't inquire about her slave-cats, I thought it best to not ask questions.

"Sasha, are you there?" I repeated, the scratchiness of my throat making my voice sound gritty.

"Nothing is happening," Lucifer muttered. Again.

My nostrils flared in annoyance. "I know that," I said through clenched teeth. "I have eyes too."

For six hours, I'd called to Sasha and moved the planchette, waiting for her to take control of it. With an audible sigh, I let go, rubbing my eyes. Exhaustion made them dry, and my vision was starting to blur.

"Maybe you should take a break," Lucifer suggested.

"I can't," I mumbled, and shook my head in defiance. "It moved once. She has to come back."

Half an hour into my first attempt at using the blasted Ouija board, the planchette moved away from my fingers. My heart caught in my throat, and I'd taken my hands off of it, letting it go where it wanted as it was being led by an unknown entity. Even Lucifer had muttered, "I'll be damned." But it stopped halfway to the word *Yes* etched at the top left of the board. Then nothing. Not a damn thing for the next six hours.

"You're exhausted, you haven't eaten, and you're

grumpy. The instruction notes in the box said you're not supposed to do it while angry," he said, chastising me. "Now you're tired *and* hangry, which is probably very much against the rules."

"Those are human instructions and they're stupid." I didn't even know why he bothered reading that garbage. "Stop telling me what to do."

"Someone has to," he said, shifting his position next to me. "You tell everyone else what to do, but you don't take any of your advice for yourself."

"No one asked you," I snapped, then I pinched the bridge of my nose. "Maybe you're half right."

"Half?" he asked, cocking an eyebrow.

"I'm *hungry*," I admitted.

"But I'm wrong about you being grumpy and tired? Riiight," he drawled, and I glared at him.

I got up brusquely, went to the kitchen, and opened a storage container on the counter, eating two homemade protein bars. It wasn't dinner, but it was something. He let me eat in silence, knowing it was wiser to let my blood sugar stabilize before I did a séance and tried to stuff him into a bottle or something of that nature. I'd threatened that a few times, as well as salt.

I wouldn't do it. Probably. I didn't want to say it out loud, but most of the time I liked having his company. Whatever we were was . . . safe. I wasn't sure if that was the right word, but it was the closest thing to it. I was the only one who could talk to him. For once, it didn't feel like a guy could fuck me over. I just had to be careful. He'd tricked me into our bargain, but I wasn't letting my guard down like that again.

I grabbed my thermos of water and came back to the board, sitting cross-legged next to him. Again, we waited to see if Sasha would answer. Two more hours passed, and the planchette didn't move on its own.

He sighed. I tried to stifle my yawn—and failed miserably. My back ached from sitting for so long. My neck was stiff. Turning and stretching did nothing to ease the pain anymore. Even my jaw was sore from the tension.

"You should get some sleep, little witch."

"I can't."

"You can," he argued. "You're choosing not to."

Frowning, I shook my head. "She moved it, Lucifer. She almost answered. I have to keep trying. What if she's moments away from finding us again?"

"Did you know people used to think you could summon a demon with this? What if you make a mistake in your exhausted state and do the unthinkable and summon me?" I rolled my eyes. "I wonder if I'd return to the living realm with my clothes on," he mused.

"You're an idiot," I mumbled and yawned again, loudly. It took my breath away, and I swayed.

"Nathalie," he whispered, his voice gentle and not at all seductive or playful. "Sleep. I'll watch the board. If she comes back—if it moves—I'll wake you up."

I shifted my gaze between him and the board. "Maybe I'll just rest my eyes for a minute," I said, feeling my body's desperation for sleep tug at me.

Lucifer moved to sit behind me, putting himself between me and the couch, stretching his legs out on either side of mine. I leaned my back into his chest, and it felt as solid as any living person's. Like he wasn't a ghost. I could feel him, and it was so real, I could damn near feel the imagined body heat. Connection or no connection, that wasn't possible. I knew my mind was playing tricks on me. Fatigue was making me delusional.

Tilting my head back, I rested it on his shoulder, turning into his neck. If someone walked in and saw this, they'd think I was possessed. The thought made me chuckle.

His cheek came to rest against the top of my head, and the safety and comfort I felt in that moment was hard to explain. I didn't have much time to dwell on it. He grazed his thumb over my arm, and darkness consumed me as I was cocooned in the devil's warm embrace.

twelve

AUGUST

I shifted and tried to ignore the tightness in my chest. My suit was tailored to my measurements, but it felt tight and uncomfortable, restrictive in all the wrong places. But it wasn't. My nerves were just slowly roasting over an open fire with every tick of the clock.

Two minutes till seven.

I moved again and swallowed the remaining brandy I'd ordered fifteen minutes ago. I was early, more than early, but given the circumstances and the private area I'd booked, I didn't want to risk Nathalie arriving first.

I knew some of the most intimate parts of my sunling.

Yet I didn't know if she was perpetually early or late. Did she procrastinate? Or was she type A to the point of scheduling ahead and arriving early so she could set the meeting on her own terms?

Another minute passed. The wait was killing me slowly.

At seven sharp, I heard heels clicking against the concrete flooring. The gait was smooth, but a little uneven. There was a little more weight distributed to her left foot than to the right. An old injury was my suspicion, but I wasn't sure. I just knew the tempo of her walk because I'd heard it enough times when she was leaving me.

The thought did nothing to quell my nerves as Jean Paul, our server and someone I considered a friendly acquaintance, pushed the curtain aside. My breath froze in my lungs, body stilling like a statue as I took her in.

Black-and-white checkered twill pants shaped her legs, making them appear even longer, accented by black oxford heels. I had a thing for her in heels. It didn't hurt that she wore them frequently. Then again, I was pretty sure I had a thing for her no matter what she was wearing.

Nathalie wore a black blazer and light makeup. Mascara and eyeliner by the scent of it, and apple-red lipstick. Her chocolate brown hair was pulled back in a simple French twist, but several strands had slipped free in the wind, now framing her face. Cheeks pink from the cold and her cell phone in hand, she didn't notice me right away.

Her thumb flew across the screen as she tapped out a reply that made her brow furrow. When she finished, she clicked the button to close the screen and lock it.

"Apologies. I'm handling a few crises at the moment—"

Her voice broke off when she lifted her head. Eyes wide, lips parted, she stared in shock. I ordered a bottle of my favorite wine and dismissed Jean Paul before she recovered. As the red velvet curtain fell shut behind her, the pink in her cheeks steadily darkened to an angry crimson. I sighed, having known this was coming.

"Before you lay into me—"

"Where's Rafael?" she demanded. My brother's name on her lips made the magic tense, coiling with unreasonable jealousy. Rafael was happily mated. He was thrilled to be able to help me with Nat, making me promise to bring her by for dinner once we worked things out. Rajvi had chimed in from the background about how lovely she was. How smart. How perfect she'd be for me.

Little did she know, I was already well fucking aware my sunling was perfect.

I wasn't the one who needed convincing.

But I didn't tell them that, because even though I called in a favor, the last thing either of us needed was my brother and sister-in-magic putting their noses in our business.

"Home, I imagine." Her eyes narrowed when I shrugged. "I'm not my brother's keeper."

"Brother," she repeated, before letting out a shaky laugh. It was quiet, uneasy, and just a fraction unhinged. Concern overwhelmed me. "You don't look much alike."

"We're half siblings," I said, watching her closely.

"Of course you are," she sighed, looking away. "Be sure to let him know that next time he tells me something is urgent, I won't be going out of my way to accommodate him."

She started to turn, and I jumped to my feet. The chair scraped against the floor. "Wait, please."

She paused but didn't turn back. Her form shook. "I don't have time for this. I told you no, and you went behind my back—"

"You didn't give me a choice."

"So it's okay for you to take mine?" she shot back, spinning around and marching up to me. Her chest heaved and gold flecks started to glint in her eyes, as they did under powerful emotion.

Anger. Lust. Hurt. Desire.

"Unbelievable." Nat shook her head. "You know, I

thought you were different. I knew I shouldn't. Every experience with men has taught me that you all lie and manipulate to get what you want. For once, I just wanted it to be different. I wanted *you* to be different."

She was going to walk out of here and never give me a second chance if I didn't give her a reason to stay. As she twisted to leave, I grabbed her wrist and snapped her back to me. She hit my chest with a thud, her free hand splaying against my right peck. Brown eyes big and wide, her lips parted in shock once more before inhaling indignantly.

"I *am* different." Unable to help myself, I leaned closer, inhaling her perfect scent. Jasmine and lilac. Raspberries and juniper. Her shampoo smelled like one thing, but her magic another. Sweet, but not sickeningly so. Floral with a touch of earthiness. Like a breath of spring.

"You're doing a bang-up job proving it," she deadpanned. I resisted the urge to grin at her because she wasn't flirting. She was pissed. I might find it cute simply because I was calmer when she was near, but I wouldn't find it so appealing if she stormed out on me again and started really avoiding me.

"I've never lied to you. I told you it couldn't wait, and it can't."

"You also told me you'd wait for Sasha to wake up."

If I disliked my brother's name on her lips, I hated my mate's even more.

"I've given it three days. Her odds of survival are under five percent at this point. I can wait indefinitely. *This* can't." Her eyes dropped, trailing down my body to where we touched, my hand firmly holding her wrist, her fingers splayed on my chest. "Just give me dinner. Hear me out so you at least have all the facts. I know the timing is shit, and you've got so much on your plate right now. I don't want to add to it . . . but you deserve to know."

Her eyebrows drew together a fraction. She bit the inside of her cheek, eyes sliding away from me. "Dinner. That's it. Nothing more."

I nodded once, releasing my grip on her wrist. It took everything I had in me to step back and pull out her chair for her, when even those few feet of distance were too far.

Nathalie watched me as she dropped her backpack on the floor beside the two-person table. Next, she slipped her blazer off, revealing a silky white blouse that was just this side of see-through. At least for my vision. My jaw hardened as she lifted her brows, waiting for me to comment. I kept all thoughts to myself.

What a woman wears isn't my business, even if I want it to be. Even if everything in me screamed she was mine.

Nathalie deserved more than some controlling asshole that tried to cover her shine so he could hoard it all for himself.

I took my own seat after pushing hers in. Jean Paul reappeared with the wine.

"Ready?" he asked in French, eyes flicking between us.

"I think we need a moment," I answered back in the same language. "She hasn't gotten a chance to look at the menu."

Without touching the thick paper in front of her, Nathalie leaned back and crossed her legs. "What type of wine did he order?" she asked in perfect French, surprising me.

"Your favorite, *mademoiselle*. 1982 Petrus Pomerol."

Her eyebrows lifted, skirting over to me in interest. It wasn't a well-known bottle. Half the reason I came here was because they were the only place in the city that had it, and they didn't put it on the menu due to its rarity.

Nathalie slowly turned back to Jean Paul. "*Gigot d'agneau pleureur.*"

Yet another thing they didn't put on the menu, but would make for the right price.

"Bœuf bourguignon," I said, handing him my menu. He took hers as well, and she gave him a slight smile. It dropped away once he walked out.

"You know French."

"And?" She leaned forward to take her glass of wine. Inhaling its bouquet, she twirled the glass stem between her fingers.

"Your family isn't French, but you have an accent like it's your first language."

She angled her head. "I spent a summer there when I was seventeen and picked it up quickly."

"A summer?" I questioned. "Not even the best linguists can learn, retain, and master a particular accent in that time."

Nathalie shrugged, unbothered. "I have a good memory." A hint of amusement made the corner of her mouth tip, like she thought that was funny somehow.

"Aren't you full of surprises," I said quietly.

"You have no idea," she replied, smiling around the rim of her glass. I'd learned in my research that she was younger than I'd originally thought due to her nature. It was as hard to believe then as it was now that she wasn't in her thirties, at the very least, when I observed how she carried herself. Age didn't grant maturity, but I'd never met a twenty-three-year-old like her.

"Do you come here often?"

She lifted a delicate shoulder and her silk blouse

shifted, revealing another inch of olive-toned skin. "You could say that." The slight smirk was back, making me certain there was more to her answer.

Nathalie's coyness simultaneously frustrated and turned me on. I wanted to know her deeper than the flesh, but she wasn't making that easy with her evasive answers.

"What does that mean?"

"What did you bring me here to tell me?"

I sighed. "Straight to the point tonight, I see."

"You've never been one to waste my time with games. I don't see why you'd start now."

My teeth gritted at the backhanded compliment. "This isn't a game for me."

"Then what is it?" she asked, canting her head. Red lipstick smudged her glass, and I couldn't help envisioning it making a mess of my cock. I was already half hard just being near her, and the thought turned it from mildly annoying to uncomfortable.

I leaned forward, elbows on the table. "Is it so difficult for you to believe that I want to know you?"

Any false amusement she wore faded into uneasiness. Her eyes darted to the side, narrowing a fraction, before coming back to me. "You shouldn't."

"How much do you know about aurae bonds?" I said, leaning back. If we kept going down the route of should and should not, we'd end up arguing about Sasha again and the last thing I wanted to do was bring her to the forefront of this conversation. Her mention would be inevitable, but now was not the right time.

"A bit," Nathalie said, setting her wine down. "Your kind have mates and auraes. Your mates are pretty much the same as every other breed that has them, but you can have more than one aurae."

I nodded. "Many of my kind do. Forever is a long time, and to incubi and succubi, variety is the spice of life. For most."

"I know the aurae bond is largely responsible for your population. Out of all the immortals, you reproduce almost as fast as the vampires because of harems."

"The aurae bond . . . is rather particular. Mates can be anyone, but auraes have to have similar magic, reproductive compatibility, even chemistry." I waited for a response, but she didn't give one. "No one knows the whats and whys of how a mate bond is chosen, but for incubi and succubi, our *magic* chooses our aurae. It considers criteria most people would give almost anything to know when choosing a life partner."

Nathalie sighed. "If you're trying to sell me on the bond, you're wasting your time. It doesn't matter, anyway." A troubled expression pinched her face for a split second, but she didn't specifically bring Sasha into it. "Even if I wanted to undergo the process, which I don't, this wouldn't be the time."

That was my opening. I'd been trying to figure out how to ease into it, but she cut to the chase before I had a chance.

"I know . . . but it's too late for that."

Nathalie froze, a subtle frown appearing. "What do you mean, 'it's too late'? The bonding process usually takes more than a month." So she did know some, or had done her research at the very least. I tried not to get my hopes up by thinking that action meant she was interested.

"Usually," I agreed with a dip of my chin. "Ours triggered the second time I fed from you."

Her face paled visibly, far from the reaction I wanted,

but it wasn't unexpected. Slowly, she started to shake her head. "That can't be right—"

"I can feel it, Nathalie."

"How? Are you sure? Maybe it's Sash—"

"Don't say it," I snapped, anger bleeding into me. "Don't tell me it's her. It's never been her and to suggest I don't know the difference is absurd. This is about us and the bond we have already started making." I needed to be patient. To lead her like a horse to water. If I tried to make her drink, she'd run. But it was fucking hard to keep my cool when her go-to was always that cursed succubus I wanted nothing to do with.

"The spell—" Nat began shaking her head slowly. "Even without the spell, I can't do that to her. I can't," she broke off, letting out a sharp breath. Her eyes flicked to the side again, narrowing.

"It's already started. My magic is . . . restless. The morning you left I had to fight myself not to chase you. I went to Anders because I didn't know where else to turn. I've never bonded before . . ."

"To anyone?" Her cheeks flushed again, like she was embarrassed to have asked that.

"Not a soul."

She closed her eyes and pressed the heels of her hands to her temples. "Then how do you know the process has started with me?"

My jaw tensed. I didn't like her questioning my feelings on the matter. Questioning me. That level of irrationality was part of the problem, though. "I won't lie to you, Nathalie, but if I answer your question honestly, it will scare you. I'm trying my very best to remain in control, but I can assure you there is no doubt in my mind what is going on right now."

Nathalie huffed. "That's a cop-out answer. You want me to believe you? You need to explain, because 'bond' implies both directions and I don't feel anything."

If I thought her insults hurt, they were nothing compared to her dismissal.

It wasn't her fault. This situation wasn't her fault.

But the monster my magic made me wanted to show her exactly what she claimed not to feel.

To bend her over the table and dump the ridiculously expensive bottle of wine all over her delectable body just so I could lick it off.

My cock twitched. It and my magic were in agreement here.

If my attempts to be the good guy didn't work, perhaps letting her glimpse a hint of the monster would make her realize the severity of the situation instead.

"I feel like I can't breathe when you aren't here. Like I'm suffocating under intense pressure and the only way to ease it is you. Your scent. Your touch. Those sweet little moans you can't deny me." Her pupils dilated, chest flushing with desire. Nat didn't want to believe she felt anything, but her inhibitions were low where I was concerned. If I played my hand right, I had little doubt she would let me bend her over this table. The inclination was strong, but first we needed to have a real conversation without Marcel in close proximity. "I'm starving, which is nothing new for me, except I shouldn't be after I fed from you. My appetite has grown. I'm insatiable. Irritable. My magic rides me day and night to track your scent across the city until I find you, and every second I don't, I feel myself losing this battle. The need to be near you, to touch you, to learn everything about you—it's visceral and all-consuming."

She picked up her glass, probably so she'd have something to do with her hand, fingernails tapping the glass nervously. "That sounds like an obsession."

"It's worse," I said, unable to help the gruffness in my voice when her arousal perfumed the air. "Obsessions fade. They burn bright then pass. This . . ." I shook my head. "When the bonding process starts, the umbra feels it first. We call it the courting period. The desire to be near you turns to physical pain if denied. Our appetites become nearly unending. Some umbras cannot be away from their auraes without losing control of their magic. Others become possessive to the point of murder."

I expected her to show a hint of fear. To look at me with disgust. The apathy I got was somehow worse. "Aurae bonds can be broken," she said quietly. "They don't have to form. It may be . . . difficult, but with distance the bond will fizzle until neither party feels it."

Her talk of ending it, letting that delicate thread between us unravel and snap . . . I was glad I wasn't holding my wine. I would have shattered the glass. Hell, I would have crushed the table if not for the white-knuckled grip my fingers had on each other.

"I don't think you understand the impact attempting to deny this will have on you," I said slowly.

"It won't kill me." She shrugged stiffly.

"Your emotions will become unstable, the less time you spend with me. Your hormones will fluctuate rapidly, going from incredible highs to dangerous lows. At first, you'll simply miss me. Then you'll begin to crave me. The more the bond threatens to break, the worse the symptoms will get."

Nathalie pressed her lips together, watching the dark red wine swish around her glass as she twirled it between her fingers. "Temporary sacrifices," she said after a suspended moment. "I can speak with the señora and see if there's anything to offset the hormones. As for the rest of it. . ." She shrugged, and my teeth threatened to crack. "I'll survive."

I shook my head. "You're not listening."

"Invalidating me because you don't like my decision isn't a great way to win a girl over."

"It would be easier to believe you if not for the fact you already can't help yourself the second I touch you. What are you going to do when I no longer have the self-control to respect this distance you're so insistent on? What will you do when the fervor hits—because it will—and your skin is literally burning for me? When your pheromones become the only drug my body desires and I will do *anything* to get to you?"

She swallowed unevenly. Her chest rose and fell faster than before. Her pulse started to race. Sweat and other delectable scents started to overwhelm me.

I groaned.

Her heart skipped a beat, pulse jumping.

"You make it sound worse than mating madness," she rasped, voice thick with things she shouldn't be thinking about.

"For some, it is. For some, it's not. I have a feeling, based on how easily we entered it, ours will be incredibly difficult if you choose to dissolve the bond." I didn't want to guilt her, but I couldn't lie. Once her decision was made, there would come a point where I would be so intent on finding her that I would have to be physically restrained, or worse. I wouldn't say that. Not when she was struggling so much with the idea of Marcel dying and Sasha never returning. It wouldn't be fair to play that card, despite its truth.

I'd lived a thousand years, and the anhedonia that

consumed me wasn't so obvious until she stumbled into my life. If she didn't choose this . . . I'd give it her mortal life, but odds were, I would follow her into death. I'd realized that I couldn't live another thousand years this way, waiting until another bond potential I actually wanted were to come about. One lifetime was enough for many people. I'd lived more than ten, carrying with me a soul-deep apathy I only ever rid myself of the moment I encountered her.

I wouldn't force her to choose us.

But I'd kill myself before living the way I had any longer.

"August, I—"

Whatever she was going to say didn't come out. The velvet curtain swept aside, and Jean Paul returned carrying our meals. He set them in front of us and checked if we needed anything. I shook my head, too focused on the conversation at hand, but Nathalie turned on the charm.

She smiled like he made her day, thanking him enthusiastically. The hand he dropped to the back of her chair made my fingers tighten around my fork. He leaned over, gushing about the import they'd just gotten in and how Sean was so grateful.

Who Sean was, I didn't know.

"Of course," she said in French.

Jean Paul laughed, leaning in to kiss her cheek.

The fork bent around my fingers, thinning in sections that threatened to break. They both glanced over at me.

Jean Paul flushed, apprehension appearing for the first time.

"*Monsieur*, I didn't mean—"

Nathalie patted his arm reassuringly. "I've got this one. Give Sean my love, will you?"

Our server nodded, making a hasty retreat. The second the curtain dropped, her pleasant smile disappeared.

"Who's Sean?" I asked tightly.

She lifted both brows. I half expected her to refuse to answer. I should have known she'd never do what I expected. "Our chef." She motioned to the meal before us.

I knew that my jealousy was irrational. Insane.

I knew this.

That didn't stop it.

"I believe this is one of those moments you were just telling me about. Possessiveness?" She didn't say it cruelly or with anger.

I nodded. "It's difficult to watch you put on a mask and smile at strangers when things are so strained between us."

"Would you rather I wore a mask around you?" she asked, sounding genuinely curious.

"No," I sighed.

One side of her mouth curled up. Sad or amused, but definitely not happy. "Rafael owns this building. He rents it to Sean, who is married to Jean Paul. They live in an apartment above the dining room." She looked up, then back to me again. "The years following the Magic Wars were hard on everyone. They were running a skeleton crew and approaching bankruptcy. They were going to lose the restaurant. So I offered them a deal. Within sixty days, I became their supplier for every single meat, produce, and wine that's served. I personally negotiated in Bordeaux for the wine. I visited vineyards throughout the French countryside to test the soil and see the product myself, so I could best gauge who the safest choice was. I've been to farms and butchers on their behalf, and when they couldn't make their rent to Rafael, I financed them. They've catered events for me. Aided in fundraising and awareness for passion projects I've had over the years. They're that rare breed of people who managed to hold on to religion despite all that's happened. I've been to Passover at their house and met their children, and when those kids were old enough, I secured them apprenticeships that have put them on track for respectable, well-paying positions that can afford them security in an incredibly unstable world. You're probably wondering where I'm going with this."

I did, but I wasn't going to interrupt. This was the most information she'd ever voluntarily offered, and it was everything to me. Color filled in parts of my incomplete picture of who my sunling was.

"There are hundreds of Jean Pauls and Seans in my world. People that I've helped in some way. That I've saved from poverty or prison or even certain death. I don't do it for the thanks. I do it because underneath this mask is someone who's seen the worst parts of humanity. My oldest sister has tried to kill me repeatedly. My twin married the man I loved. My mother stole my will and used me for a ritual that killed millions of people, and I've recently learned she would have killed me years before just to teach someone else she deemed more worthy a lesson had they not complied with her demands. I've been beaten, bullied, and emotionally harmed since I was a child. Those things don't go away. I will never forget them, and it seems that the older I get, even shittier things about my past get uncovered, so that's fun." She stabbed at her food with a fork and popped it into her mouth, groaning in delight. "Point is, I help people because I hated the world I was born into. The prejudice. The violence. The abuse. Sometimes I can't help but wonder if it will never end . . ." Her eyes glazed over for a moment, as though she had traveled far away, and I wondered what she saw in her memories. "I can't change my damage, but I can stop some of theirs. I can fix their problems. I can train people to be better than they were before. I can help them grow, so that when they're able to, they can help someone else. I can give them a smile even when all I want to do is scream, because that's how you do it. You become the change you want to see."

"That's selfless."

She snorted. "I'm filthy rich, so don't give me too much credit there. I'm just a businesswoman with good intentions. I can empathize with them, even if underneath it all I'll never be the person I present to the world. I can't. . . ." She wanted to say more but stopped herself. "I've been this way for so long now that it's second nature to slip on the mask for people, but the truth is, it's exhausting. You have no idea how many times I wish I could put my phone on silent and just *be*. Read something other than reports and forms. Garden in my greenhouse while music blasts. Cook for enjoyment instead of necessity because no one else in my life knows how to. Hell, I'd settle for some decent sleep if I could manage it. The point is, smiles might be pretty, and my words might be nice, but allowing myself to be that —the ugly, messy realness—it's what I truly crave."

Her chewing slowed before she swallowed, then took another drag of her wine. My own meal sat completely untouched. "Then why are you doing this? Why are you fighting me? I could be there for you; I *want* to be there."

"You know why," she said slowly.

My reaction was visceral.

My frustration, palpable.

"My magic will not accept her, Nathalie. Neither will I. There is no spell that can change that. If I can move on, so can she. You're mortal right now, but if you were to accept the bond, you'd live as long as I will. You wouldn't age. In time, she would come to grips with it," I insisted.

If she came back. *If* she returned, no matter what that witch claimed, our bond wouldn't be completed. It would never be completed. *If.* Five percent wasn't great odds. Nathalie would mourn Sasha and feel guilt over it, but as long as it was my shoulder she cried on and me she confided in, I knew we'd get through it.

Nathalie sighed in exasperation. "Have you considered that whether or not what she asked is fair, whether or not I want *this*, it makes me a shitty person if I were to say yes when I knew she wasn't okay with it? That it would hurt her?"

"What about you?" I asked her, my voice tight. "What about how much you're going to suffer because of her? One day, she could find her own aurae. Ten years. A hundred. You don't get that luxury as long as you're mortal. What happens when she moves on and it's too late for us because you put her first?"

Her lips parted.

Every other question, she'd had an answer for. Every other part of the discussion, she could refute. This wasn't something she'd considered. I could see it in her hesitation.

Out of everything I'd said, it was that one inevitable truth that got past her defenses.

"And if she doesn't?" Nathalie asked quietly. "If I were to take that gamble, and that's assuming I was willing to go through with the bond, what happens when she's fully mated to you? What if you're half right and you don't accept her but that bond is irreplaceable for her? Now I get however many hundreds or thousands of years knowing how miserable she is, while I'm—" She stopped speaking, and it pissed me off more that she cut herself off from saying it.

"Happy?" I questioned, lifting a brow. She pursed her lips, glaring at me.

"You're awfully confident in forever when you hardly know me."

She was saying it to piss me off more, and it worked.

"You want to do this again, sunling?" I leaned forward, then shoved my seat back. I stalked around the table and stood behind her before she had the chance to move.

"What—?"

I clasped her shoulders, stopping her from getting to her feet by using my body to hold her chair exactly where it was. My fingers kneaded the knotted muscles with ease. Nathalie groaned.

"We already know I can do wicked things to your body that make you see stars." My voice dropped to a lower octave, the tone I used when we were alone and I had her chained to my bed.

"Arrogant," she grunted.

"Is it?" I asked. Leaning down, I followed the shell of her ear with my lips. "If I were to unbutton your pants right now, how wet would you be?"

Her chest flushed, and this angle gave me a direct view of her cleavage, pushed together by lacy white strings that scarcely deserved to be called a bra. My thumb slipped over her collar, pressing into a particularly sensitive muscle where her shoulder and neck met.

Nathalie twitched, moaning despite the teeth she had buried in her bottom lip as she tried to keep the sound in. Blood welled on her skin. The coppery scent was laced with jasmine.

"That's just cruel," she said, sucking in a haggard breath. "Using my body isn't playing fair."

"Why? Your scent fucks with mine. I've been hard since you walked in here."

"I can't control that."

"And those noises you're making?" She made another one, and it took all my self-control not to pull the chair out and sink to my knees at her feet.

"I'm trying." She was. She really was.

"I'm trying to control my hands," I said, pulling all the tension from her. The aphrodisiac that I naturally produced worked to help her relax.

She turned her head to glare at me. Hunger consumed her irritation as I hit another sensitive spot that made her jolt, hips flying into the edge of the table. The table shook and the bottle of wine shifted over the edge. Glass shattered as it topped over.

"This is wrong," she groaned. "Gods, if Sasha knew—"

"If she knew, and she loved you as much as you clearly do her, she wouldn't stand in the way."

"She can't help it."

"Stop saying that," I growled roughly. I threaded my fingers through her hair at the nape of her neck, maneuvering her head to look at me fully. "You're only lying to yourself because you recognize what she's asking is wrong. I hold the other end of the same bond that she does, and I have no desire to be with her. I never have. Anders *lost* his mate, and he's in love with someone else now. People choose differently all the time. They move on. They reject the bond. Some of them even end up finding another mate. So get the idea that you denying this means she'll get what she wants in the end out of your head. Your refusal and telling me no cannot make me be with Sasha. *I. Don't. Want.*

Her. I didn't before you. I don't now. I still won't even if you choose to sacrifice us. There is no world where she gets me as a mate. Not even that spell can make me choose her."

I didn't know how to stress it enough. I could understand what she was saying, thinking, if perhaps Sasha and I had ever been together. But this desire to be a good friend and martyr herself in the process was the thing that was truly wrong here.

Nathalie took unsteady breaths. "If I choose you, I'm choosing a man I barely know—"

"Tell me to stop."

"What?" Conflict warred in her expression.

"Tell me you don't want this."

Her lips parted, but the only sound that came out was her labored breathing.

"Tell me you don't want *me.*"

She swallowed hard, body shuddering.

"I . . ." Nathalie's chest heaved roughly. Her gaze dropped and my fingers stilled.

"You want me to stop? To walk away?" I released her and stepped to the side faster than she could blink. I flipped her chair around to face me with the toe of my shoe. Placing my hands on the armrests, I leaned forward to bring us face-to-face. "Tell me with a straight face that you don't want me, and I will walk right out that door. I'll put the distance between us you keep claiming we need. I'll have Anders do his best to keep me away. I'll let the bond unravel . . ." It killed me to say this. To offer this. Especially when there was no way I could hold to it of my own accord. I'd quite literally have to get him to lock me up so that I couldn't go back on my word. For her, I would. But a piece of me would die in this restaurant. "If you *truly* do not want this, say the words. That's all you have to do."

146

A choked, anguished sound slipped past her lips.

"It doesn't matter what I want—" she started.

"*Tell me.*" The hard edge to my voice could have cut. I didn't want to force her hand, but over the course of dinner, one thing had become increasingly clear to me above all else.

She would sacrifice herself if she thought it would save her friend.

Nathalie was selfless to a point I'd only ever seen once before.

She wouldn't choose her own happiness until I made her understand that choosing herself wasn't the same as dooming Sasha. Nathalie wasn't responsible for the succubus's choices, including her decision to not move on. That decision lay with Sasha alone.

Only when I separated the two would I get an honest answer.

"I . . ." she started again, opening and closing her mouth. Pink crept across her skin. She tried to look everywhere but at me. "I can't."

My mouth slammed over hers. We met in a clash of teeth and tongues. I kissed her brutally, putting every ounce of my frustration and want into it. She met that hardness stroke for stroke, her fingers sliding through my hair to rake my scalp.

I groaned, and she swallowed it.

The armrest squeaked and threatened to crack under my lethal grip. I jerked away, both of us panting hard.

So much for respecting her boundaries.

I scrubbed a hand down my face and stood to turn away. My control was rapidly slipping the more of her I touched. Tasted.

Fingers fisted in my shirt.

I stilled, turning my head. Nathalie got to her feet, using me to pull herself up. She put her other hand on my waist, fingers hooking around my belt. Then she used every bit of strength she had to pull me back to her.

The conflict in her eyes was dead.

"Don't you dare walk away from me," she growled, stretching up on her heels. She pressed her lips to my neck. "You started this. Now finish it."

thirteen

NATHALIE

My blood burned for this man.

Sure, he was hotter than a statue of a Greek god, but it wasn't his looks that caused that desire within me. While a pretty face and lickable abs went a long way in getting someone's attention, it didn't make me obsess this way. Long for him. *Need.*

Being in the same room together was torture.

I could feel his eyes on me. A look so deep and intense it pulled me inexorably closer, leaving me with little hope I could ever push it away. It burrowed beneath my skin, to the point that any attempt to rid myself of it was painful.

Sharing the same air was torture.

Beautiful yet piercing as it invaded my lungs like poison. It touched my skin. My pores. My lungs. It made me want more while simultaneously pulling me into its depths. That's what made it so dangerous. I could drown in it, in him, but it had no right to feel so good at the same time.

His touch was pure agony.

Whether it was the briefest stroke of his fingertips or

the rough palm of his hand splayed across my ass, August's touch was a torment I'd never known. More than lust. More than love. I'd felt both in copious amounts, but nothing ever made me want to combust on the spot quite like he did. I couldn't even blame it on him being an incubus because I'd been with his kind before. The oils their skin produced may be a potent aphrodisiac, but it didn't make my head spin in the best way possible.

All of this made the tension between us brew like a perfect storm.

As much as I may respond to him—his body, his scent —I prided myself on self-control. Growing up the weakest in my family, with a demented older sister hell-bent on making sure I didn't live to adulthood was a lesson in self-control. There were times I'd wanted to scream at her, or cry from the pain, but any reaction at all would have only made it worse. I wanted to hit her back, to hurt her like she did me, but even burning with rage, I learned to bury it and smile.

Sometimes I wanted to make bad choices as much as the next person. But my brain couldn't tune out the consequences. It was stifling, but it also meant I rarely made mistakes.

Which was how I knew the horrible, ugly truth.

I cared for August entirely too much.

For all my self-control, I couldn't deny myself.

And regardless of what happened with Sasha, I wouldn't be able to pretend this was a mistake. I made the choice.

Even knowing I would struggle to live with it.

"Nathalie . . ." he groaned as I unbuttoned his shirt with slow, almost lazy hands. I was desperate for him, but it was my mind that sped up instead of my body.

I neared the hem, humming under my breath. My heels made me tall enough that I could lean forward and kiss the pulse of his neck. So I did.

His muscles were tense as I ran a hand down his hard chest, then pushed him lightly. He stumbled back into his chair, legs spread, arms loose on the cherry wood rests, but jaw tight. I cocked my head, striding forward easily to climb on his lap. I straddled him with a knee wedged to either side of his hips. Our bodies pressed together, chest to chest. August's breathing was heavier than I'd ever seen. His hands gripped his chair, making the wood crack.

"Touch me," I urged, reaching up to unclip my hair and let the French twist fall.

"Are you sure?" he asked. His voice came across quiet and husky, tinted by anger.

I frowned, my lips centimeters from meeting his, like it was the first time all over again. "I wouldn't be sitting on your lap if I wasn't."

He didn't uncoil.

If anything, my breathless reply made the darkness in his gaze churn, like raging waters that couldn't do anything but react to the storm.

"If I touch you, I won't be able to stop myself from feeding."

I purred, kissing the corner of his mouth. "I never said you couldn't."

The low growl that rumbled through his chest made my core tighten painfully.

"Our bond will strengthen," he said through clenched teeth. "If I fuck you, feed from you, any of it—"

"Do you want me?" I interrupted him.

He narrowed his slate-blue gaze. "You know I do."

I nodded. "Do you want to bond with me?"

A pucker formed between his brows, the hint of arrogance transforming to confusion. "Yes, more than anything."

I nodded, running my fingers through his hair. "I want you, but I don't know if I can bond. Especially if . . ." *You bond with Sasha too.* The sharp edge of frustration came back twofold on his face, but I didn't let him speak. "I know that it's either growing or weakening every minute of every day. If I do nothing . . ." I shook my head. "I need time, but we don't have that. So instead, I'm asking for right now. This moment. Not completing the bond is a future problem that will suck for both of us."

The shadow in his eyes made me shiver. I had a feeling that was a massive understatement, but the last thing I wanted was to rehash that particular topic.

"No strings attached," he muttered, unable to keep the dissatisfaction out of his voice.

"Not completely," I said. "I won't lie and promise you something I haven't been able to really consider. It has far-reaching implications . . ."

"Then why give me this?"

I licked my bottom lip, wetting it. "I want *you*. I want *this*. I'm already guilty, whether I act on it further or not. If . . . I'll have to talk to her about it no matter what." Something Ann had no qualms about saying, even though every other version of me was on team August. Well, Peace, Caretaker, and The Warden were. She was tired of us putting everyone else first and thought he was good for me. Bad Nat . . . I could never tell what she was thinking if she wasn't saying it. Her oddly quiet but watchful gaze made me nervous. Truthfully, there was a lot of fallout involved if Sasha came back and bonded to August immediately like

Señora Rosara suggested would happen. In the meantime, my heart wanted what it wanted. "If I'm going to suffer the punishment, I'd rather commit the crime."

August clasped my hips, dragging me forward, then back. He guided me over his already-hard cock. I wished I'd worn a dress right about now.

"I'm not sure if being viewed as a crime is a turn-on or if it just pisses me off," he remarked dryly. Despite his apathetic words, he started to remove my blouse.

"Why not both?"

A smirk dragged up one side of his fuckable mouth. "All right, sunling, we'll do this your way." He lifted me suddenly and my head spun from the sudden shift. Dishes hit the floor a half second before my back thumped into the table. August undid my blouse and then yanked it wide. He pulled back to stare at me, his glass of wine in hand.

A shuffle sounded as the curtain that separated our room from the restaurant was pulled aside. "Is everything all right, *mademoiselle*?" I turned my cheek as a flustered Jean Paul burst in, then paused just as quickly. His eyes went wide, a blush creeping up his neck.

"Leave," August barked in French, his voice hard and unyielding. Jean Paul turned on his heel, sporting the tiniest of smiles as he did. He and Sean always insisted I didn't get out enough. That I worked too much. Enjoyed life too little.

They would be gossiping in the kitchen about this for weeks.

"We'll take dessert to go!" I called after him.

The curtain fell closed and August's shaking form drew my attention back to him.

"What are you laughing at?" I demanded, breathing

harder when he set the wine down. With warm, callused hands he removed my heels and set them aside—out of the puddle the bottle of wine had made.

"You," he said roughly. "Your sweetness. Your shame-lessness." Next, he undid my twill pants and slid them off, folding them over the back of his chair. I expected him to go for my panties next. He didn't.

"I have no reason to feel shame."

August nodded, putting one closed fist in his mouth and biting it as he took in the pristine ivory undergarments. "No, you shouldn't."

I kicked out a foot, curling my toes around the edge of his pants. I tried to tug him toward me, but he didn't move except to grasp my heel. Gently lifting it to his face, August kissed my instep then nipped at my ankle. I moaned.

Desire filled me, smearing the thin cloth that covered me.

Under different circumstances, I might have felt embar-rassed by my reaction. By the severity of it.

August bent my leg, placing my foot on the very edge of the table, then repeated the action with the other. With my center on display, he picked up his wine and admired the view.

"I'm not in the mood to be toyed with tonight."

His beautiful eyes flicked from my wet panties to my face and back. "What about a little game?"

My interest piqued. "What kind of game?"

August grinned. Leaning forward, he lowered the glass and angled the lip toward my body. I froze as wine touched my navel, pooling in the slight dip of my stomach.

"You better not stain my panties with that. I'll never get it out."

They were expensive, laughably so, but I didn't actually care.

August leaned forward, face only inches from the thin scrap of lace between my thighs. "I won't do anything. You on the other hand . . ." He inclined his head in a cocky grin. My chest rose and fell in heavy pants.

He blew softly on the heat between my thighs. My body jerked instantly, and the wine started to dribble. August tsked.

"Strike one," he murmured, licking the dark red stream from the top of my hip bone to my navel. The roughness of his tongue on my sensitive flesh made a shudder roll through me.

"Strike two." He almost sounded disappointed at how badly I was losing this game. Another drop escaped, this time heading toward my panties in a slow descent.

August let it get right to the edge before blocking it with the tip of his tongue. He licked and kissed and nibbled as he followed its path back to the tiny pool of wine.

"What happens on strike three?"

He grinned up at me. "I dump the contents of this glass on your weeping cunt and see if it tastes as good as you."

My thighs strained.

"Hardly seems like a strikeout," I sighed.

"Your panties will stay on."

I swallowed hard. Core throbbing. Jesus Christ, I wanted this man and his filthy mouth.

Two fingers brushed along my inner thigh. They toyed with the edge of my panties, rubbing in the stickiness before slipping inside. He ran them through my folds once before shoving them into me. My core contracted.

Every drop of wine spilled.

Down my stomach. To the side. Toward my breasts.

Deep crimson liquid colored my skin and August grinned victoriously.

"Strike three, beautiful."

He poured his wine on the lace, staining them beyond saving.

I didn't care.

August ran his hands under my ass, pulling it up a few inches off the table. My bottom half became weightless, legs flailing as he brought me to his mouth.

Nothing prepared me for the way he sucked at my core with my panties still on. Nothing compared to his wicked tongue as it snaked around the edge, cleaning every damn drop from my pussy.

My legs quaked again as an orgasm built rapidly.

He took the strip that covered me between his lips and sucked.

I moaned like a dying woman, my skin heating to a fever pitch.

"August." His name was a plea on my lips. One he thoroughly ignored.

I was so close to tipping over the edge, I could see it.

Then he dropped my ass back on the table and slid his hands to my sides. His fingers twisted in the material of my panties as he shredded through them.

"What are you—"

"I will break this table if I fuck you on it." He stood straight, and pulled his chair closer, and then sat back down. I sat up in shock as he unzipped his trousers, my ruined panties still in hand. His cock jutted up in the air, long and thick with dark veins that seemed to throb more every second I looked at it.

"Come here."

His quick, sharp words acted as a spark to my skin, jarring me into action. I slid toward the ground, and he put his feet right where mine were so I didn't step on the glass. Rough hands grabbed my waist, steadying me as I lifted a leg to one side of him, then the other. I reached for his shoulders to steady myself.

"If it's too much, you snap your fingers. Understood?"

My brows drew together. Understanding clicked right as he shoved my ruined panties between my parted lips.

The scent and taste of my arousal coupled with the rich wine was erotic and overwhelming. August grabbed my hips once more, then impaled me on his cock.

I felt I could split in two, but would die a happy woman if I did.

He took me rough, using strength I didn't possess to fuck me at a speed that made my head spin. Even with the room moving and my body struggling to tell up from down, my core wound tight as a fist around him.

Cocooned between my legs, our chests brushed one another, skin growing slick all over. Sweat trickled down my spine, flinging off me from the sheer power August used to hammer into me. Brutal and unyielding, he took my body to new heights, tethered only by him.

I sensed movement over his shoulder. My chin lifted, eyes flicking up for only a moment.

Lucifer leaned against the wall. The room was tiny, so he wasn't more than a few feet away. He was dressed in a suit, arms crossed, one leg bent. He was the picture of an apathetic model. The unfeeling angel.

If not for the gold light in his eyes that burned.

It moved like liquid and shone like the flames of a fire. Burning. Ravaging.

He made no move to stop us. I knew he wouldn't, not

when he stepped out during dinner to give us the room. It was oddly considerate.

Him present, watching us fuck? Less so.

But for some reason it didn't bother me as much as I thought it would.

He was dead, after all. I was his anchor to this world. His . . . little witch. No one had to know the complicated nature of our relationship. I never had to question the feelings I had or didn't, because it was impossible to truly have anything with him other than this weird, messed-up sense of protection that he gave me.

I don't know when it happened, or how, but Lucifer went from the demon that haunted me to the man in the shadows that watched over me.

"Eyes on me, sunling," August demanded.

My attention shifted, drawn back to the man between my legs. I could feel the devil's heated stare as August pounded into me, his hips rolling and thrusting like a man trying to throw me off him, even though his arms kept pulling me back.

"Just because I don't want the entire front house to hear you scream for me doesn't mean I don't want your all. You keep those eyes on me when you come on my cock. Nod if you understand."

He didn't slow, which made it harder to nod without my head bouncing like a bobble toy. August smirked then got to his feet. Before I knew it, he had my back pressed into the brick wall. Right next to Lucifer.

The change in angle was everything when he rotated his hips, grinding against my clit with every thrust. Water filled my eyes at the intensity of it all.

My legs shook from the need to get off.

I was so close . . .

"Come for us, little witch." Lucifer whispered the words in my ear, lips brushing against my skin, tipping me over the edge as my orgasm ravaged me. "Let me see you shine like the fucking sun."

LUCIFER

Golden light illuminated the room.

It was as if someone took two drops of pure sunshine and put it in Nathalie's eyes. Her magic was stronger than she thought, but it never relieved itself outside of her most intense moments.

Extreme anger.

Extreme pressure.

Extreme lust . . .

My little witch became the sun itself when she let herself unravel. That she did it for me, at my command, was everything.

Her legs shook where they locked around the incubus's waist. Her chest arched forward, head tipped back. Sweaty strands of chocolate brown hair clung to her face and neck.

My hands clenched with raw desire and jealousy. That was a new one for me. I'd never had someone I felt possessive over before.

The incubus had been with her several times now. He had tasted her magic and the sweat on her skin. Felt the embrace of her thighs as her tight pussy wrapped around him and then swallowed her cries of pleasure. It was all that I wanted, and soon it would be within reach.

Because I knew the truth that my little witch was trying to hide.

She wants me too.

The sounds of their rough fucking fell silent as he thrust into her one last time. His forehead pressed against hers, intimate and sweet despite the way he took her. On one hand I approved, because if anyone deserved to be fucked like an animal but treated like a queen, it was her. I just wished I was the one doing it to her.

Ten months of being dead and thousands of years that were so forgettable I couldn't remember them had changed me. Changed my priorities.

Ten months of watching her struggle and sacrifice for everyone else around her changed my perspective.

I may be her familiar, but Nathalie was *mine*.

She may have feelings for the incubus and her ex, but they would never fully be hers. Not like I was.

They had ties to others, and her past, scarred by cheating, would make it impossible for her to fully surrender with them. But not me.

As much as she struggled with my lack of morality, she wanted me.

That was enough.

Nathalie wanted to be put first, even though she didn't ever do it for herself. She wanted someone that would choose her, heedless of the odds or what they'd sacrifice in the process. She didn't like to admit it, but my little witch didn't want a good guy.

She thought she did, but what she needed was a villain. She needed me.

I may not have her love yet, but in time I would. August

would make a mistake, whether it was now, in five years, or when Sasha returned. He'd ruin his chance, just as Marcel did before him. With any luck, the warlock's sickness will have taken him by then, leaving me to comfort my little witch. To become her anchor. Her world.

Nathalie's eyes flicked toward me every few seconds as they dressed. Her tongue darted out to lick her bottom lip, still hungry for more. The incubus was right that the bond had begun to affect her. She may not want to believe it, but I watched her at night when her skin grew feverish and her thighs became slick. I heard the husky moans that came from her parted lips as she pushed her fingers into her panties and tried to put out the fire that raged in her.

She'd had dirty dreams for months, but over the last few days they seemed to never end. She spent more time trapped in lustful fever dreams than not. It was beginning to show in the circles beneath her eyes.

If I thought she'd let me help her, I would have.

But she hadn't been ready yet.

I had to play my cards more cautiously the closer we came to Samhain. While she'd kissed me and even fell asleep in my arms most nights, she also hadn't let it go beyond that.

"I want to spend the night with you," the incubus said, buttoning up his shirt. His eyes never strayed from her mostly dressed form as she tucked her shirt into her checkered pants and finger-combed her tangled hair. I longed to wind it around my fist while I took her from behind.

My incorporeal muscles tightened with impatience. I pushed it away, forcing myself to relax.

"What about Marcel? I doubt Anders will want to watch him all night."

"It's fine," he lied smoothly. "Anders owes me a favor." No, he didn't.

I was tempted to tell her the truth, but something made me pause.

"Are you sure?" Her brows pulled together. "I know how much he struggles to be around him."

August shrugged. "He knows where I keep the good booze. I have a feeling I will have paid him handsomely for his time by tomorrow."

Her lips quirked up in wry amusement. "As long as they're both in one piece, that's all I care about. Marcel has a tendency to push buttons."

The incubus smirked. "You don't say?"

She snorted, then giggled. "Shit." She lifted a hand to her lips. "I'm sorry. I know he's not always the easiest. I shouldn't be laughing when you're doing me a favor—"

He lifted his hand, smiling at her. "It's fine. Truly. Annoying as Baggage can be, I'd rather him be with me than making things harder on you."

She stared at him with fucking stars in her eyes. I tried to squish the little green monster by reminding myself that he may get these parts of her, but I got the other side. The ugly side. The cruel side. The devilish side. The honest side.

I wanted all of her, but I'd already obtained the hardest parts first. She held nothing back except her heart where I was concerned. Even that was beginning to give. It was only a matter of time.

Days.

"Come to my place," Nathalie said slowly. I jerked as if struck by lightning. She never invited anyone back. Marcel was only allowed under an extreme circumstance. She'd never invited someone outside of her small group of friends. Not her sister. Not her fuck buddies. Not the nice

KEL CARPENTER & AURELIA JANE

old lady down the street who was actually an information broker I'd hired back in the day, but who she thought was just the sweetest nana to the gang of orphans she took care of. Not those same orphans who straight-up adored her for bringing them treats every week, so they never stole from her or let anyone else fuck up her car. No one.

Except this bloke apparently.

The sooner Sasha returned, the better. I'd love nothing more than to have Nat all to myself when the fervor hit.

"I'd love that."

I'm sure you would.

I wanted to say it, but my little witch didn't like it when I spoke my mind about her underlings. Especially the ones she fucked.

Normally, I wouldn't care if she liked it. I still didn't, really.

Except she gave me the cold shoulder when I did. Her silent treatment, while juvenile, was effective. She thought she was training me like Pavlov's dog, using her time and attention as my positive and negative consequences.

What she didn't realize was that I was choosing to give her what she wanted. Just like she'd given me what I desired, even though she didn't know it yet.

"Let me go pay Jean Paul for . . . ugh." She glanced back at the ruined meal and shattered plates. "Dinner. And the dishes. I'll meet you out front."

He stopped her with a touch to her arm. "I'm the one that arranged dinner, and ruined it. Let me."

"I feel like it bothers you that I pay for things," Nathalie said in a guarded tone. I couldn't even call it feminist sensibilities. She simply didn't like being on the wrong side of a debt. Money was how her parents controlled her for years. Sometimes she associated other people buying things as the same thing. Not that the incubus knew that.

"It does."

I smirked, shaking my head. He was making this easier than I thought he would.

"Not because I'm emasculated by your success," he added after a moment. She squinted her eyes, hesitant. "I don't want you to think I'm with you for your money. I might not be the 'Rockefeller of New Chicago,' but I can afford to take you out to dinner and then some."

"I've seen where you live. I don't think you're mooching off me." Her stiff shoulders slowly uncoiled as a coy grin tugged at her lips. "You hardly ate. Let me buy dinner tonight. I'm sure you can find a way to make it up to me."

He gripped her waist, pulling her back against his chest. One hand tugged her hair aside so he could run his jaw up the column of her throat. "Does eating you for dinner and dessert count?"

She chuckled, a husky sound. Sultry and rich with authenticity.

"It's a good start."

"A guy might start to worry you're only with him for his dick."

"Your tongue is great too. When you do that little thing to my clit . . ."

He groaned. "So it's my expertise you're after?"

She hummed for a moment, staring off into space. "It would be so much easier if that's all it was." He paused, sensing the shift in her focus.

"I'll wait right out front." He kissed her farewell, and she gave him a half smile. As he strode through the thin tapestry acting as a barrier to the rest of the restaurant, Nathalie turned to me.

Her eyes were soft, but her features were tight.

"Give me tonight."

I feigned nonchalance and lifted a brow. "I can hardly stop you—"

"Give me tonight *alone*."

I wanted to say no, but the desperation behind her plea made me pause. I gave her a truth instead. "I can't be away from you for very long physically. It becomes . . . painful." An understatement.

It felt like I was dying all over again.

Like my soul was being smothered.

She didn't need to know that.

"Oh," Nathalie whispered. "I didn't realize—"

"I'll stay away for tonight. Someone has to watch the board to see if Sasha answers."

Guilt followed by gratitude crossed her face. I'd said it partially to see how committed she was. Unfortunately, the answer was more than I'd hoped she would be.

"Thank you," she whispered, taking a step closer to me.

I kissed her forehead, mentally preparing myself for the rough night ahead. As long as I stayed in the apartment it wouldn't be too bad.

"Enjoy your night, little witch."

I stepped away to turn and gesture for her to lead the way out. She clasped both sides of my face instead, pulling me back to her. Her small breasts pressed against my chest as she kissed me with more feeling than I could even remember. Her wine-stained lips were soft and seeking. She didn't take it as far as I wanted to. The taste she gave me acted more as a tease for what was to come.

I pulled away a second before she could, just to leave her wanting—as I was.

She wouldn't understand it the same. She couldn't,

when she wanted three men and I only wanted her, but the taste of another on her lips wasn't as awful as I would have thought.

On the off-chance August managed to not fuck this up, I could think of worse people to share my little witch with.

After all, the only way to truly have her—to own her—was if she let me.

I wouldn't get in between her and the others. That would only backfire. Better to let them dig their own graves, or not.

Either way, she'd be mine in the end.

AUGUST

Nathalie lay beside me in her bed, tucked into the crook of my arm. Her breathing was steady, but I knew she wasn't asleep. She should be, after all we'd been doing since we got back to her apartment.

I got the distinct impression that she didn't ever bring anyone home. Not because of what her apartment looked like, but because of how she treaded carefully around entering the building and leaving the elevator. Her eyes had shifted to the door across the hall from her, and she looked like the teenager sneaking a boy through her window.

There was also the matter of a bomb wired to her door, so it was clear she didn't welcome guests. That suited me just fine. It meant she wanted me here. It also meant we'd be left alone.

We'd barely crossed the threshold before stripping each other's clothes off in a frenzy. We didn't make it beyond the kitchen counters before I'd hoisted her up there and then buried my face between her thighs. There would never come a time when I'd have my fill of her. I made her come two more times before we found her bedroom and fucked until the gray light of dawn greeted us.

My thumb grazed her hip softly, caressing her skin while I was lost in thought.

The smell of sex was heady, but it was *her* scent that filled the room and enveloped me, settling over my body in a way that didn't entirely make sense. It was enticing and drove me into a place so feral I had constant difficulty controlling myself. I wanted my hands on her, always. I wanted to kiss her. I wanted to be inside her. Every moment that I wasn't felt like torture. That, I expected. Simultaneously, her scent had a bizarrely calming effect. It was this gentleness that burrowed under my skin and made me crave the depths of her being. The deep. The tortured. The ugly. All of it. Somehow, it felt like contentment. At least it did at this moment. Because she was mine, and mine alone.

For now.

She could still refuse the bond. She could walk away from me. Away from us.

The unwelcome intrusion of that thought made my insides twist, and my chest rumbled.

Nathalie tilted her head up, her amber-brown eyes meeting mine. She trailed her fingers over my stomach. "Penny for your thoughts?"

I curled my arm around her tighter, not wanting to share where my mind had taken me.

"Is that all you have to offer? A penny?" I cocked an eyebrow, glancing down at her.

She smacked my stomach playfully. "I think you've taken *plenty* of the other things I have to offer."

"I haven't taken your ass yet," I countered with a grin, and she sat up quickly.

"Well, that turned around faster than I expected it to,"

she said, laughing. She arched her back, stretching her arms above and releasing a contented groan. Turning her head to glance at me over her shoulder, she grinned. "Also? You're changing topics with sexual innuendos to avoid answering whatever was on your mind."

She was right on the money, reading me like an open book. I wasn't used to someone so easily calling me out. I liked it.

"You like my innuendos."

"I like a lot of things about you, that included."

I rubbed my fingertips over the skin of her back, not wanting to lose contact with her. She shifted her body, throwing a leg over my hips to straddle me, and my cock twitched, feeling her welcoming heat. I moved where I held her, settling for her thighs, gliding my hands up. Her breasts pressed into my chest as she leaned down to kiss me, and I wrapped my arms around her, hugging her closer.

"Someone is hungry for more," I mumbled, nipping at her lips and covering her mouth with mine. Her stomach growled loudly, and her eyes flew open in surprise to meet mine. I chuckled, smiling broadly. "Very hungry, apparently."

She let out a raucous laugh. "I don't think that has ever happened before."

Smacking her ass, I kissed her and said, "C'mon. I need to feed you before I devour any more of you. We still have those desserts we left on the counter."

Even if she'd wanted to argue, another loud growl spoke for her as she chuckled. Climbing off of me, she walked to the bathroom, turning her head slightly to say, "Give me a minute and I'll be right out."

I kept my eyes locked on hers, never breaking contact. It made for an awkward walk as she glanced at me over her shoulder, but I wanted her to know how much I loved looking at her. I wanted her to feel desired, even if she was just in the next room. A tiny smile graced her lips as she shut the door.

Tossing the blankets aside, I searched for my pants, but realized they were strewn somewhere between the front door and the kitchen, so I headed there.

After I slipped them up, I filled up the kettle, flicked it on, and found the to-go bag of desserts Jean Paul had packed for Nathalie, as requested. They, too, were on the floor, having been dropped haphazardly.

Her kitchen was remarkably organized. Everything had its place, and items and canisters were identified with clearly marked labels. Finding her loose-leaf tea and a strainer was effortless. After I arranged the desserts on the countertop and prepared us both mugs, I walked toward the living room to take a moment and see what Nathalie was like at home.

This was her safe space. Her place of rest. It was private. Which meant it was tailored to her, and not to someone else. Not to some perception of who she was. Not that mask she wore for others.

Her apartment was surprisingly modest for someone so wealthy. It wasn't small, but there wasn't the extravagance one might expect. It was personalized and homey. Quaint, in the sincerest form of the word.

I shifted my hands into my pockets as I moved through the main living area. Her couches were plush and inviting, with soft pillows and textured fabrics. She was tactile, it would seem, and I made note of it. Her furniture had clean lines, but was not what I would have classified as modern. A Ouija board sat on the coffee table, its planchette resting on top. It struck me as an odd choice for a centerpiece.

Glancing up, I saw what looked like a study with French doors, and I headed toward it. A worn but comfortable-looking reading chair fit into the corner. Several books lined a shelf, and I read their titles. All romance novels. The spines were well-worn and creased, clearly read many times over. I now had an overwhelming desire to go through each one and know what she loved about them. Making a mental note, I perused another shelf of items that looked personal. Nathalie didn't have a lot of knickknacks that I could see. She didn't appear to collect "stuff." She kept things for a purpose, whether it was functional or had emotional value. That much was clear.

Teal-painted frames held pictures of her and her friends. My mood soured for a moment seeing Sasha in them and I pressed my lips together, shoving her out of mind. I didn't want to think about her. Not ever, and especially not here.

Moving on, there was a large mason jar sitting on a shelf, and in it was what looked like shards of old glass. They didn't have a pristine or clear quality, and appeared to have been old when the glass was broken. A small, tarnished silver heart-shaped box rested near it, not having been polished in quite some time. A sheathed athame had been placed nearby on a purple velvet cloth. I didn't know the stories behind the items, and while some of them were unusual, that wasn't what had caught my attention the most. It was the single piece of art adorning the walls. Hanging next to the shelf was a grotesque watercolor I wouldn't expect to see amid the warmth of this room.

The gray-blue creature centered on the canvas was bent back at an unnatural angle. Streaks of reds were brushed into the body with purpose. Cloaked figures shadowed themselves in the background, while indiscernible entities teased at the being that was the focal point.

"It's a Dali. Not a well-known piece," she said quietly, leaning against the doorframe with her arms crossed, wearing nothing but an oversized T-shirt. "But I imagine you already knew that."

I did. What I didn't know was what it was doing here.

"It's rather dark compared to the art you have in the living room." Beautiful, serene landscapes and calming still lifes accented her other walls. This was different. Grimmer than I'd have expected. And in this room, which seemed to be intimately her space, it made me want to know why.

She hummed in response, understanding that I was asking for more without my having to voice the question. "They're his interpretation of the furies in *The Divine Comedy*. Reminds me of my family."

No doubt she noticed the surprise on my face when my brows shot up. "This? How so?"

"My sisters and I, specifically. One of whom I need to pay a visit to tomorrow, despite every desire not to. I thought the last time I saw her was, well, the last time. But now . . ." Her eyes met mine, wearing a look of concern as though she'd said too much, but I inclined my head for her to continue. "I have some questions I need to ask her. Time-sensitive ones, unfortunately, as that house is a place I'd rather not be."

"I'll go with you." If she didn't want to be there, there was no way I'd leave her side. Not unless she forced me.

"You don't have to do that. It's about . . . things you may not want to be around for."

It was Baggage. He and Sasha were the only reasons she'd tread so lightly with me, but there was an inflection in her voice when she was talking about her ex. I didn't like it. Him, or her feeling like she needed to hide what she was doing because she feared my response to it. We'd need to work on that.

"I know I don't have to. If it involves you, I want to be there." I jutted my chin toward the wall. "What about this painting in particular reminds you of them?"

Nathalie sighed, walking closer to the painting. She angled her head while gazing at it, not making eye contact with me. "There were three furies, and in Greek mythology, they were sisters. The first was Megaera—the jealous one. For Dante, she represented evil deeds. The second was Tisiphone, the avenger of murder, and she represented evil words. The third was Alecto—and she represented evil thoughts."

I studied her features, staring at her while she focused on the painting. Nathalie had left out the meaning of Alecto, telling me exactly which one she found to be like herself. Just because I knew the answer didn't mean I wouldn't ask. "And Alecto was . . .?"

She smiled at me knowingly, glancing at me from the corner of her eyes. "Unceasing in anger." Turning to address me, she added, "But I imagine you already knew that too."

"I know a lot of things." Curious that she found herself to be the fury defined by rage. There was so much about her that I had yet to understand. She'd opened up more than I'd expected, and I wasn't going to push my luck. The tension in her voice was enough to tell me what she had already said was hard enough. I eased my arm around her waist, pulling her close to me. Bringing my lips to the shell of her ear, I murmured, "But I like to hear your voice."

"Is that so?"

"You know it is. And while I want to hear more, I said I

was going to feed you, and I'm a man of my word." Her body trembled against me, and I held her tightly while nipping at her neck and lifting her off the floor as I started walking to the kitchen.

Setting her down on the countertop, I remained standing between her legs, letting them straddle each side of me. Her hands grazed down the sides of my arms, her nails tickling the skin of my biceps.

She was teasing me. Testing me, perhaps? It was maddening. Touching her. Scenting her. Being so close to her set my nerve endings ablaze. My cock strained, wanting to be buried in her heat all over again.

Instead, I grabbed the plate of desserts and pulled it toward us. As I cut a piece of opera cake with a fork, Nathalie looked down and her eyes lit up. When I took her chin between my finger and thumb and brought her attention back to me, her brows furrowed. "Don't ever come between me and dessert. It won't end well."

I chuckled. "I wouldn't dream of it." Lifting the bite to her mouth, her lips made an 'O' when she realized what I was doing. Of all the things we'd done together, and of all the dirty words we'd shared—none of them made her appear shy until this moment.

"Oh, you meant literally," she said, and I nodded in confirmation. "I can feed myself, you know."

"Never said you couldn't. That's not what this is about."

"I . . ." She trailed off while I held the fork suspended. Her gaze flicked to the living room, and I didn't know why, but the faraway look unsettled me. Like for just a moment, I'd lost her.

"Eyes on me, sunling," I told her, and her attention snapped back. Glancing at her mouth, I inclined my head. "Now open up."

Her hands gripped the edge of the counter, and she did as I'd asked, her lips wrapping around the cake as I pulled the fork away.

She groaned and closed her eyes, letting out a noise of satisfaction as she chewed. I fed her every bite on her plate, leaning in to lick the final crumb stuck on her lip after she'd finished. Her stuttered breath made me chuckle.

"Why are you laughing?" she asked, her mouth hovering near my own.

"Because I never thought I'd have to compete with cake, but those sexy little moans you made while eating it makes me think I have my work cut out for me."

"I never thought I'd be turned on by you feeding me, so I guess we both learned something new."

I wanted this from her, and so much more. I wanted to learn and share these things with her. She'd said no strings attached, but this felt like anything but—and the aurae bond didn't give a shit about perimeters. I feared separating myself from her in any capacity, like at any moment she'd realize the intimacy of our situation and tell me to leave, since this time she couldn't walk away.

"Don't move," I said, stepping away from the warmth of her body to get her teacup from where I'd placed it on a warmer. My very being screamed the moment we lost contact, but that demand eased when I rested between her legs again.

She looked up at me in disbelief when I set the drink beside her. "You made me tea?" Her voice had lost its sultry, flirtatious tone. She was genuinely shocked.

"Does that surprise you?"

"Honestly? Yes and no. No one makes tea for me. I'm not sure anyone even knows how I like it."

"I'm familiar with quite a bit of what you like." She

tucked her bottom lip between her teeth, and it did wicked things to me. "What's the reason you're not surprised?"

"If anyone was going to, I'm not that surprised it'd be you."

"You're not used to someone trying to take care of you."

"That's not what I said." When I pinned her with a glare, she smirked while picking up the mug and blowing over the steam. "But not entirely wrong."

"I get the impression you don't want anyone to take care of you."

She sipped carefully before sighing, clearly pleased with how I'd done. "It's . . ." She paused for a moment, considering her words. "It's hard for me to let someone do that."

"You're letting me." I took a drink of my own before setting the mug down. I had a feeling the reason why she didn't let her guard down was sitting at my apartment at this very moment.

Her lips twisted in a bit of a smile, and she placed her hand on my cheek, pulling my face closer so she could kiss me softly. My body craved turning it into something more —but that's not what this was.

Nathalie was giving me a brief moment of vulnerability, and I would happily accept it.

Something in my chest ached terribly, wanting this to be our reality. Standing in the kitchen together. Intimacy. Sharing a bed with no inhibitions. I couldn't help but wonder if she would ever give this to me without reservations, or if this would be the one night I'd hold on to until she left this world.

The thought made me growl, and Nathalie mistook it for something different—which worked out just fine. Again, she didn't need to know the direction my thoughts had turned.

Breaking the kiss, she leaned back, a coy smile gracing her lips. Reaching down to my untouched cake, she scooped some on her fingers and held it out for me to eat.

"Open up," she said, repeating my statement earlier, even using the same tone.

I cocked an eyebrow at her, but I obliged, taking her fingers into my mouth and scraping my teeth over them, leaving behind an absolute mess on her hand. She wasn't kidding when she groaned earlier. The cake was remarkable. But that's not what made a low rumble escape my throat. It was Nathalie herself. She was otherworldly. The way she tasted, the way she looked at me. Everything about her.

While she scooped another bite onto her fingers, my hands traced her inner thighs, finding the warm heat of her cunt, and I shoved two fingers inside and curled them. Her body jolted as she gasped, holding the cake out for me to take from her again. Short little sighs escaped her, and trembling moans punctuated every thrust. Closing my lips around her fingers once more, I pulled my hand out and held the two fingers up to her.

Without hesitation, she twirled her tongue around them, licking them clean.

I came undone, but so did she.

With a hunger that couldn't be ignored any longer, I threaded her hair in my hands to bring her mouth against mine. Grabbing me in the same way, she used one leg and dug her heel into my back, bringing me closer to her. We devoured each other like it was the first time.

The striking combination of her sweet arousal coupled with sugar and cake was mind-blowing. Everything should have a hint of her taste. I took her bottom lip between my teeth, rasping over it as I pulled away from the kiss, leaving my mark when I let go and rested my forehead against hers.

"Not that I don't want to take you twenty different ways before the sun rises, but we only have a few hours before morning. You need to get some rest, sunling."

"I don't want to," she admitted, breathing heavily while she entwined her sticky fingers in my hair. "I feel like if I fall asleep, I'll wake up and this will all be gone."

"I don't know what's going to happen when we wake up, but I'm here with you now, and I'm not going anywhere." I couldn't even if I wanted to.

Nathalie nodded with her eyes closed; her brows pinched together while she did so. Pulling me closer, wrapping her legs around my waist and pressing herself into me, she whispered, "I know."

The tremor in her voice stabbed at my soul. She wanted me to stay, yet not. I could hear the confession laced in the way the words came out strained.

It didn't matter. I had her now, and I wasn't letting her go.

I carried her into her bedroom, kicking the door shut with my foot.

We kissed, fucked, and reveled in each other like we were on borrowed time.

Maybe we were.

sixteen

NAT

My knuckles flexed against the steering wheel. I shifted in my seat, trying to ignore the two very male gazes locked on my face. August sat beside me in the passenger seat, completely at ease despite the way his presence filled the car. Larger than life. In the backseat, Lucifer had manifested in the middle seat with his legs splayed and elbows braced against his thighs. He leaned forward, his head settling between the front seats.

I could practically feel his breath against my skin now.

Samhain had come.

The dead were as close to the living as they would ever be.

And I was driving straight to the worst of both worlds.

The Le Fay manor had been built on a graveyard of witches. They didn't move the bodies. They just laid the foundation with them in it. Any workers that died were buried in the walls. The floors.

Katherine used to tell me that it was just a ghost story Carissa made up to scare me.

Now I had enough experience with death magic to know better.

That house wasn't just evil. It was built on it; steeped in it. If evil was a tea, that's where its plant would grow.

But Marcel was dying.

So headlong into evil I walked—or drove.

A cold sweat broke out on my arms when I flipped on my turn signal and slowed to a crawl. I turned onto the mile-long driveway. I could have sworn that the air itself changed when I did. Like we'd crossed some sort of invisible barrier.

"It'll be okay," August said quietly. He reached for my hand, but I brushed him off, shaking my head.

I wanted to lean into his comfort. To let him be my protector. My safe space. If there was anything my family taught me, though, it was that the only space that's truly secure is my own mind.

Especially here.

If anything, he needed me to be his safety net. Carissa may be magicless, but she would tear him apart if she could.

Kat's warning from the balcony came back to me.

Carissa's not who you think she is.

I'd asked myself a hundred times what she meant by that, but every Nat in the loci came to the same conclusion as me.

We didn't know.

That was scary, because there wasn't much that I didn't know.

Even less that I couldn't find out.

The car rolled to a stop, farther from the house than was probably called for, but I didn't want to be here. Stopping was subconscious. The desire to leave wasn't.

KEL CARPENTER & AURELIA JANE

I put the car in park and sat there for a moment.

"Nathalie?" August said, concern coloring his tone.

"Hm?" I answered, not looking away from the stone creatures that leered over the edge of the roof. Red eyes seemed to glint with malice.

Rough fingers touched my chin, turned my face away from the decrepit manor, and forced my eyes to meet his.

There was a hardness in his expression I didn't expect.

"She can't hurt you anymore."

Most people who said that to me would find I'd nod along and not argue. It was easier to give platitudinous responses that put others at ease.

August wasn't just anyone. Those responses felt like lying.

"Physically," I corrected instead. "You should know, she's going to say things to . . . turn you against me. She'll try to drive a wedge between us."

"There's nothing she can say that would do that."

My eyebrows drew together. "You don't know that."

"I do," he said, the picture of utter assurance.

That he could remain so unflappable in the face of uncertainty both attracted me to him and made me want to shake him. There wasn't much point in the latter, or the former for that matter.

"I've done things. Terrible things."

"We all have."

Such a simple statement.

Its meaning, anything but.

I wanted to ask about his terrible things. I wanted to walk into the shadows of his mind and shine a light on them. I wanted to know them and know him, but it wasn't the time or place for that.

"Perhaps," I said, not wanting to argue. "Don't let her

get to you, at least not until we're leaving. Carissa is psychotic, but she's brilliant. If she sees any reaction at all, she'll find a way to manipulate—"

He kissed me.

Lips gentle but insistent, he stopped the loop of anxiety my brain had started to enter with a single touch. My muscles relaxed instantly, the tension draining out of me.

I kissed him back, licking the seam of his mouth. He groaned, letting go of my chin to slide his rough hand over my jaw and around the nape of my neck.

We shouldn't be doing this. Especially here.

But August was a quick learner, and he'd found my weakness.

My mind may be strong, but the thing I craved above all else was *touch*.

Mentally, I was always equipped. Years of abuse followed by teenage hormones and lust changed something in me, or maybe it was always there and growing up just unlocked it.

I was a physically affectionate person by nature. Not an addict, but I craved it all the same. Hugs. Caresses. Massages. Sex.

I wanted it all.

When I was a child, emotional abuse became physical abuse. Anger directed at me became a candle that wasn't lit when I went to sleep, set aflame in the middle of the night and then knocked over—a half-assed attempt at getting rid of me. My own fear became a dark room that smelled like mold and mothballs, where hunger pains became second nature because Carissa would threaten to do awful things to me if I left the basement before she told me I could.

Feeling anything was dangerous. Reacting was dangerous.

Then Marcel came.

He taught me that emotions and touch were okay to feel together. That they could be good. Better than good. Touch could mean love and safety. Sex could mean passion, an outlet for things too extreme to express otherwise.

His wicked fingers and persistent mouth and hungry cock became a sanctuary, as crazy as it was.

But then he ruined everything. I learned a hard lesson.

Love wasn't safe. Emotion wasn't safe, not where touch was concerned.

It belonged in my mind and was given to people that earned it. Platonically. So that I never crossed that boundary again.

Touch was a physical refuge I could still find with strangers. It wasn't about them. It was about me. It was about sensation. Feeling, but not *feeling*.

Touch lacked emotion.

Love was only emotion.

Together they ripped me apart, but separate? It worked for me.

But August was using one to get to the other. He was pushing me to merge the two again. He didn't have to say it when he kissed like he did.

Like I was air, and he was the fire that burned for me.

His tongue licked mine, then twined around it.

He unfastened my seatbelt with his free hand and pulled me toward him. I broke the kiss—or tried to. He didn't make it easy. Repositioning me on his lap, August maneuvered my legs to either side of his thighs. My core pressed against him, tender from the night before but not enough to stop the wetness from coating my panties.

It hurt so good.

He gripped my hip, bringing me forward at an angle as he used his stomach muscles to contract and grind into me.

Fireworks exploded in my mind and a needy moan filled the car.

It took an embarrassing amount of time to realize that sound was coming from me.

August groaned. "You feel that?"

I tilted my head back, staring at but not seeing the roof of the car. Black touched the edges of my vision. "You know I do."

I felt his lips curve into a smile as he kissed my throat, not missing a beat while he maneuvered my body like an instrument against his.

"I'm going to tell you a secret, and you're going to keep grinding this sweet pussy against me." It wasn't a question.

"What if Carissa sees—"

"Do you care what she thinks?"

Good point. "No."

"Then it doesn't matter if she sees or not. This is between me and you."

And Lucifer.

Who had been oddly quiet for the entire ride here. I didn't lift my head because if I saw that look in his eyes, the one I knew so well . . . *No.* I wouldn't look.

But that didn't mean he wouldn't.

Knowing his eyes were on me while August handled me this way made my blood heat. Fire burned a trail up my torso and neck, flaming my cheeks.

"Sasha blackmailed me into finding Katherine," he stated. I froze, tension snapping tight in my muscles. It was only his superior incubus strength that kept me moving the way he wanted. We pressed together; my slick core still covered by my pants tracing the hard outline of his cock.

My orgasm was just out of reach, but also just a hair too close to walk away.

That I was doing this with him after—

August pulled my hair to the point of pain and gave my neck a sharp nip that would leave a mark.

I shuddered.

"Pay attention, Nathalie." He used the same voice that he did in the bedroom and I was fucking gone.

If there was an afterlife, or spirit equivalent to hell that we didn't know about, I was going there for this.

"I didn't know it was Katherine yet. I wasn't aware you had a twin. I'd only just met you when Sasha came to me talking about dead bodies and life forces. She gave me a picture and told me to track the person it belonged to."

It didn't take much to put together the timeline. This would have been right after they took me to the alley–when I put together that the timeline of Kat's disappearance overlapped with our mysterious serial killer. Or at least the bodies being found.

"This isn't exactly the conversation I wanted to have while doing this," I said, managing to make my voice impassive despite the way my body was shaking.

"I know, but it's important." He kissed my neck, sucking at the spot he'd bitten.

My lips parted, an aching moan escaping.

I was close, and he hadn't even removed my clothes.

I really was way too far gone for this man.

"More important than me getting off?" I questioned dubiously. He chuckled. "Do you know what the people I talked to said when I showed them the picture?"

"Hmm?" I grunted, only half listening.

So close . . .

"They called you a murderer. Said you make deals with

people like Faryn Lightseeker. That you'd sell your soul for the right price."

I recoiled.

My jaw dropped, eyes snapping open.

"What the actual fuck?"

August wasn't grinning now. He stared intently. Despite the horrible turn of the conversation, I found my attention split between wanting him and needing to know more. It repulsed me.

I shouldn't be turned on after hearing this.

Maybe I'd done such a good job that my body now separated physical touch away from my feelings so well that it didn't matter anymore.

It would explain a lot.

I should probably see someone about that. Too bad all the money in the world can't buy time for me to actually go to therapy. Then again, there were pocket dimensions that existed outside time. Maybe there was a way for me to hit pause. I told Ann to make a note to look that up, at which point she gave me an exasperated sigh. It was her way of saying, *"Sure. With all this free time I have. It's not like I'm already trying to save your ex and research an ancient object of great power."*

She may have had a point.

August kept talking. "Those were the things people said —when they thought you were Katherine. Then I figured out you're a twin, and it was the other one Sasha was after. Would you like to know what was going through my mind before I'd pieced it together?"

My lips parted.

Did I?

Yes.

No.

Crap.

"What?" I crossed my arms over my chest, leaning back as far as I could in the cramped car.

"I wasn't sure who you were—the woman who gave back to the city her family destroyed, or the one who terrorized it? I had no idea, but I didn't walk away from you then. I couldn't. Even if the rumors were true, I knew there was more to it. I was all in, and I didn't know half the things I do now. That was before the bond started to form. Before I tasted you. Before I fucked you—"

"You should really see someone about that," I deadpanned. "Professionally, I mean. I should too since I seem to attract crazy like flies to shit. I wonder what that says about me?"

August chuckled, leaning forward to rest his forehead against mine.

"Maybe it's you that makes us crazy. We see you and can't help ourselves."

I smiled wryly, arching an eyebrow. "Smooth. Next, you're going to ask if it hurt when I fell from heaven."

He threw his head back and laughed deeply. It rolled through him and touched me. I shook my head in begrudging amusement.

"I hate to break it to you, but you're no angel, sunling."

I smacked his chest, barely holding back a laugh. "Hey! You're supposed to be 'wooing' me, remember? Telling me how I'm so great that you ignored me being a potentially crazy, evil bitch—"

August kissed me but just when I started to melt for him, he pulled back. "I knew you weren't a crazy, evil bitch. I'd already tasted your magic. I knew you were an aurae bond for me. My magic never would have chosen someone tainted. You're perfect for me as you are. No angel would be."

I swallowed hard.

"You know, you could have just said it didn't matter. Laying all that on me while working me up is just cruel."

"I did tell you. You didn't understand, so I made you. I know what your family is like. I did my research. I also know how I feel about you, and there is *nothing* anyone can say that will change that now."

I dropped my arms. My skin pebbled with goosebumps everywhere we brushed, even with a dress shirt between us. A couple inches of distance somehow made it more intimate than if I'd been pressed completely against him still.

I believed him. I did.

I also knew everything Carissa might say, but there was one thing I wouldn't want him to hear from someone else. Regardless of what happened to us. Of what happened today.

"Not even murder?" I told myself I didn't feel guilty over it, but could that really be true when I still felt the need to ask?

August didn't hesitate. "No."

"I mean like murder, murder. Not self-defense."

I looked away, wanting to slap myself upside the head for that one. I may as well have said I killed someone. Then again, that was what I was trying to say, wasn't it?

"I don't care."

The truth shone in his slate-blue eyes. My brows drew together in confusion and concern.

"You're not even going to ask what happened or how?"

"Do you want me to?" he countered, voice still thick with sexual tension but holding it at bay. This was a serious conversation.

"I . . ." My voice stalled. "I just don't understand. Aurae bond aside, I'm a murderer and it still chose me. Don't you question that? Don't you want to know what happened? If it was even justifiable or not?"

He nodded lightly, resting both his hands on my hips and squeezing them softly. "I want to know everything about you. I want to know your likes and dislikes. Your dreams. Your nightmares. I want to know what makes you, *you*. But you haven't been ready for me to push and I'm trying to respect that. So do I *want* to know? Yes. But I don't need to, because whatever the story is won't change what I feel. I'm not walking away from this, Nathalie. Not until you make me."

"It could have been a child. You'd still want to be with me? A woman you barely—"

"Finish that sentence and see what happens."

I swallowed hard, wanting to push him. I knew where it would lead. To sex. Right here in the driveway with Lucifer watching. I'd feel better . . . but it would only be a distraction.

"Let me rephrase," I said, my fingers toying with the buttons on his shirt. "Why would you be with someone like that?"

"I know that things seem far more black-and-white at your age," August said. He spoke quietly, but his voice was deep. His fingers slipped under the edge of my shirt, making my skin flush. "Murder isn't the worst thing out there. Far from it. I grew up during an age when people removed hands for stealing a piece of stale bread. Murder was as common as dirt. Everywhere you looked people were suffering or dying, or both." August shook his head, as if trying to clear a past he couldn't quite forget.

My lips parted. Two questions vied for priority, both

wanting to be asked. The thing was, one was already answered.

"You've killed before." Because only a murderer would say that.

"Yes."

I opened and closed my mouth. For him to admit it in a manner so blasé . . . Did that mean it was a long time ago? Or were there so many it didn't mean much to him at all?

Despite his utter confidence in me, this conversation was making me question everything I knew about the man I'd crossed lines with.

"Do you feel better?" he asked when I didn't speak.

"Yes. No." I sighed and looked down, smoothing my hands over his dress shirt. "I'm happy you don't think I'm a monster. That would really suck after . . . everything."

"But?" he prompted gently, sensing there was a lot more I wasn't saying.

I took a deep breath, organizing what I was going to say before I word-vomited it like I did the whole murderer thing.

"I'm not you. I need to know more," I said honestly. "I need to know when and why and how. I need to know if they deserved it, if your ends justified your means. I know that I'm young compared to you, though you haven't given me a number—it's easy enough to put together that you're at least several hundred years old." He dipped his head in acknowledgement. "I'm not against murder, for the record. Kinda hard to be when my best friend used to hunt witches. I'm not necessarily for it either. Taking a life isn't as easy as breathing for me, and I can't accept it being that way for the person I'm with either." I shook my head, trying and failing to avoid locking eyes with Lucifer. He sat back, his golden gaze locked on me knowingly.

"I'll tell you anything you want to know," August said, running his hands up and down my thighs teasingly. "But be prepared, you won't like everything you hear. My story isn't a nice one, not even for the times I lived in. You might find parts of it hard to . . . stomach." He kneaded my hips gently.

"I'd rather know who I'm getting into bed with."

August nodded slowly. "What will you do if you don't like the answer?"

"I . . ." The words fell silent on my lips.

Like a deer in the headlights, I froze.

Would I leave? Would I stay? I hadn't even talked to Sasha yet, and may never get to—but that aside, this was a question I'd asked myself for months.

The way it was worded was different.

The reason was different.

Would I bring Lucifer back if it saved more lives? Would I play god? Would I cross lines myself that I deemed uncrossable for others?

I'd told myself no. I swore it up and down.

Bad Nat had laughed at me, because she knew the truth.

No matter how or why I asked myself where I stood on moral ground, I'd come to the realization that I didn't want to say yes, but for something I wanted enough, I would.

Things weren't black-and-white in my world.

So far from it.

"I don't know."

It was the best I could settle on, and it still tasted like a lie somehow. I wanted to be good, and sure, if he was some sort of closet Delphine LaLaurie or Jeffrey Dahmer then I'd run for the hills and sic Piper on his ass for good measure.

But I had a hard time believing that whatever he has done could be that bad. That *he* could be that bad.

"Then we should talk soon," he said solemnly. "Before the bond winds any tighter. If you were to walk away now ..." He paused then shook his head. "We should talk, but first, we need to get what you came for."

The change in subject was hard to interpret as anything other than avoidance. My mouth twisted into a slight frown. "If I were to walk away now?"

August opened the passenger door and helped me off his lap, quietly contemplating his response. Lucifer followed us outside the car where the dry cold made my skin tingle.

"I'd rather not say."

"I'd rather you did."

August sighed and his muscles bunched in agitation as he shoved a hand in his pocket then surveyed the empty woods. "You deserve the truth, but sometimes it's hard to give it to you when I know you're always half a foot out the door."

Ouch.

It was a fair critique, but I hid my wince, nonetheless.

"I'm working on it. We're not exactly two random unattached people here—"

"That's the problem," he said suddenly. "I'm *very* attached. August, the man as you know me, respects you and your decisions. I can logically see why you're struggling even though I'm not. Your feelings are important to me. August the incubus? He's not such a gentleman. I've tried to explain before, but maybe I'm not being plain enough. In the same way I don't care what Carissa, or Piper, or Sasha thinks about this"—he motioned between us—"I don't care about any consequences of us being together. Just that we are." He leaned forward, towering over my slim form. "My magic isn't soft or seductive like most of my kind. It's passion in its purest form. Brutal. Obsessive. Unyielding. It wants you—now, at night, every day, in my bed or my arms. When you leave the room, it pushes me to follow. When you leave my vicinity, it wants me to *hunt you down*." He ran a hand over his jaw then mouth, troubled by his own admissions. "My magic and I have been at odds as far back as I can remember, but now, for the first time, we're both wanting the same thing. *You*. And every second together, every touch, every feed—our bond winds tighter and I fall deeper into this."

Speechless.

Turned on but terrified.

That second one was reasonable, expected even—if I were terrified of him. Except I wasn't.

I was terrified of how much I liked that. Terrified that I was falling just as fast, as hard, as carelessly as he was.

"And if I walked away . . ."

Darkness gathered in his slate-blue eyes like storm clouds preparing for the hurricane of a century. "I've barely been holding on to my own control where you're concerned. I worry that might be the point where it will snap and I can't stop myself or my magic."

Silence spanned between us.

He was right that he'd been telling me in not so many words that his control was already shaky. The thing was, more than a small part of me wanted to see it unravel.

Strings held me back. Attachments. Morals.

I wanted him to cut those strings for me. To take the choice away so that I didn't have to make it. And in that admission, I knew what I needed, what I wanted, and what I was going to do about it.

"You might find this hard to believe, little witch," Lucifer cut in. Cool eyes that glowed with liquid gold and intense passion regarded me. "When you live long enough that you see your world and everyone you know evolve or die, *again* and *again* and *again*, it changes you." His impassive gaze raked over me like the coals of a furnace, yet somehow remained cool. "Immortals that find something —*or someone*—they want aren't going to let it go lightly. That is something both the incubus and I have in common, though he has misplaced guilt about it. No matter what you've done or will do, we're yours. We won't abandon you like your beloved Baggage—or leave you for anyone or anything else."

My lips parted. August gave me a quizzical expression before glancing down where his arm grazed Lucifer's chest. He frowned, as if struggling to understand.

That he could feel Lucifer in some way spoke to how strong the devil was on Samhain when the veil was so thin.

August sighed. His next words stunned me.

"Who is he?"

I locked up, my muscles tensing. "Excuse me?"

"The ghost that's been lurking," August said, lifting both eyebrows.

"I do not lurk," Lucifer argued. I rolled my eyes before I could think better of it, then froze. *Ah, shit.*

"I—he—how did you know?" I stepped back from them both, crossing my arms over my chest.

"It's not my first Samhain. Far from it. I know what it feels like when a ghost is this close to our realm."

I narrowed my eyes. "You said 'him.'"

The corners of August's lips curled with amusement. "That part was a guess. I'd been starting to wonder if you could see them because of how you'd respond at times,

195

looking at things that aren't there. Reacting to comments out of character. Then he stepped into me and you did it again."

My brows drew together. I smoothed a hand over my still-damp hair.

"I see."

"Who is he?" August asked again. This time I heard something different in his tone that I missed the first time. Possessiveness.

"You assume he's anyone," I said vaguely, stepping away from the car. I never thought I'd voluntarily go toward this mansion to get away from another situation, but fate did love to fuck with me.

"I *am* someone," Lucifer muttered, keeping stride with me. "The devil, as you love to remind me. *Your* familiar. The demon of desire—"

"I've seen the way you look at him."

My feet tangled. I pitched toward the ground, my ankle twisting in my ballerina flats. A strong arm grabbed me, halting the fall.

Sin and sex washed over me.

The coppery taste of blood along with something floral filled my senses.

My back pressed against a hard chest, leaving my face to stare at August who stood opposite me.

Shit. Shit. Shit.

Apparently now that the cat was out of the bag, Lucifer was done pretending he wasn't here—even if I was the only one that could see him.

August cocked an eyebrow, looking me over from head to toe. The hard edge had returned to the muscles in his jaw. "He would have been a powerful supernatural being in life to have so much ability as a ghost," August remarked coolly.

"Try demon," Lucifer said smoothly.

"He was something, all right," I muttered.

August wasn't pleased. Fair enough.

But he still had no idea who this particular ghost was and something told me he'd be infinitely more displeased once he did. Although whether Lucifer's identity or me not telling him would piss him off more remained to be seen.

"You're avoiding," August said, crossing his arms. "Why?"

I sighed. Unfortunately, I had a feeling not answering would be the worse crime in this case. After all the shit I'd given him about not saying he had a mate, he would have a reason to be upset that I failed to mention my kind-of-dead-familiar that also kissed me on occasion . . . and liked to cuddle. Also he read me smutty books.

Ah, crap.

Yeah, this one was on me.

"Hiding me like your dirty secret?" Lucifer whispered in my ear. My skin flushed at the sound of his voice, so close to such a sensitive part of me. "I'd be offended if I wasn't used to—" It was literally the sound of all my filthy fantasies come to life given his vast and sudden improvement in the narrator department.

I scrubbed a hand over my face, wishing I could wipe the warmth from my heated skin. "It's not as simple as seeing ghosts," I said. "That's not a power I have. This one —he's different because I killed him."

Lucifer snorted against my shoulder, his nose running along the length of my throat. "You didn't. Not really. The Morrigan and her underlings are responsible for that. Carissa. Katherine."

I tried to ignore him in favor of August, whose confusion was turning to suspicion. If he did his homework on me when hunting for Kat, he would have learned a few choice things I suspected.

"Are you trying to tell me you're being haunted by the—"

His revelation was cut short by a door slamming.

I twisted around, my neck cracking from how far I bent it.

Standing on the porch, looking her age instead of the old hag she'd been these past ten months, was none other than my least favorite sister.

I was so shocked by her appearance, I almost didn't notice that she wasn't wearing her usual sneer.

She was crying.

Uncontrollably.

"Why can't I remember?" she sobbed, falling to her knees in the same powder-blue dress I'd last seen her in. That was over a week ago.

Ah, hell.

seventeen

AUGUST

I stared at the spot next to her that hummed with power.

Physically, he wasn't there, but I could have sworn a faint trace of gold magic like glitter shone for a second, illuminating a large male form wrapped protectively around her.

My own possessive instincts needled me.

I shook my head, purposely unclasping my fists. Touching her in the car got me worked up. My magic was already pissed off at the distance between us. Piecing together that she had a ghostly admirer wasn't helping things. I already knew I'd have to share her with Baggage, for however long he lived. Learning there was another contender for her affections who wasn't so mortal had my magic seething with possessive fury.

The appearance of her sister was anything but welcome.

Not that I could say that out loud when Carissa was technically the person we were here to see.

I ground my teeth together, my jaw tensing under the pressure. Nat flashed me a sympathetic glance, lips parted and glistening. They were still a touch darker than her natural color from us kissing. I wanted to rewind time and do this morning differently, starting with asking about the damn ghost she had feelings for.

Carissa's weeping rent the air. Her putrid desire magic stank like cat piss. My own recoiled in further agitation, lashing out at the first smell. I squeezed my fist, straining to hold it at bay.

"Why?" Carissa screeched. The scent of urine increased as her voice broke. The hoarseness seemed to ripple through her power, cracking the windows flanking the impressive entrance.

"I don't understand." Nathalie spoke slowly. Not soft, but without any of the aggression I was fighting off.

"My memories!" Pain and despair muddied her otherwise pretty features. "They're not gone. It's like they're twisted. Covered . . . I only get flashes. You were there. You and Marcel . . ." Her erratic behavior stopped as she went unnaturally still and narrowed watery red eyes at Nathalie. "You did this," she spat. "You and that *boy*. I told Mother we should have put him down like a rabid dog. His sperm wasn't worth keeping such a treacherous piece of shit alive." Carissa continued to rant, convincing herself of a narrative neither Nat nor I knew anything about. "She insisted Katherine held his leash, but I knew. *I knew*." She started to spiral into a muttered cycle of repeating herself that Nathalie was quick to put a stop to.

"What exactly is it that you think you knew?"

Carissa's head snapped up. The action was inhuman and put incredible strain on her neck. If her mind wasn't entirely broken, it would be soon.

"Just a matter of time until he snapped. Wedding and

witch law be damned." Carissa scowled with a mad sort of hatred.

"Why would he snap?"

The older woman glared, eyes dead apart from that single spark of hate that seemed to be the only thing keeping her alive. "*You.*"

"Me?" She hid her confusion well, but this was the first question that wasn't her leading her sister along.

"Men are controlled by their cocks. It's why they aren't fit to lead. To rule. Did you know The Morrigan used to sacrifice male witches at the age of ten if they couldn't show restraint with their magic? She'd bleed them dry and allow the coven to reabsorb their power, further strengthening the female line." She smiled cruelly. "I voted to do that to Marcel. The Abernathy line is all but extinct, anyway. We would have just been speeding up the process. If only they knew then that keeping him alive would be the downfall of our house." I knew the ritual she spoke of. I was in France when those rumors started. Whispered tales of the horrible deeds that went on in the Le Fay family.

I wasn't sure if they were true. I'd made a point to avoid black witches for most of my very long life. The Morrigan included.

"You're wrong," Nat said. She was stiff and unsympathetic. The scent of lilac and jasmine perfumed the air. "The Le Fay house ended when you decided to use my body and magic to kill the devil. Like always, you're just looking for someone else to blame and punish. Except there's no one to blame for this but yourself." She motioned to Carissa and then her own head, making the universal sign for crazy.

Carissa's face blanched before contorting into a rictus.

"How dare you!"

It was the only warning she gave before a harsh command formed on her tongue in Old Gaelic.

A curse.

Not to kill, but to torture.

To break the mind instead of the body.

I moved to my aurae's side in an instant. That same sensation of a ghost passing through me occurred, but I ignored it in favor of focusing on the witch in front of me. I summoned my spirit magic in the form of wraiths.

Their appearance released the seal on the pressure building inside me, giving me an outlet less likely to upset Nathalie than killing her sister outright.

After our conversation about murder and other morally gray things, I didn't think that would go over particularly well, even if it was deserved.

Wraiths made of spirit and rage formed a wall in front of us, moving forward to converge on the twisted sister.

But my efforts were for naught.

Like flipping a switch, a light came on.

Gold magic as bright as the beating heart of the sun eclipsed *everything*.

If I had looked through biology instead of magic, it would have blinded me. Instead, the scent of raspberries and juniper flooded the air alongside the lilac and jasmine. They swirled together into a scent that made my mouth water and my cock go hard. I couldn't control my response as gold washed over us.

Nathalie had mentioned that her magic protected her.

I knew she wasn't as weak as she seemed to think. Not when her eyes turned into twin suns when she came for me. Not when a wind that shouldn't exist lifted her hair when she rode me.

Weak supernaturals didn't have physically visible magic.

In fact, very few had magic strong enough to see at all.

That alone told me my sunling had a skewed view of herself.

For a witch, she used magic very little in her day-to-day life. I didn't care. I wasn't with her for her magic any more than I cared about her money or name. I just assumed that she preferred to do things the harder way out of a subconscious avoidance.

I knew there were sides to her I hadn't seen yet.

Pieces from her past, from Baggage, from her ghost— but I was not expecting this.

Nothing could have prepared me.

A tidal wave surged from her body like water through a crack in a dam. Gold painted her skin, her clothes, her hair —coloring her in the likeness of an impassive god. Neither angry nor pleased, she wore a stony, neutral expression as she wielded power like I'd rarely seen before without ever making a sound.

That was another sign. Or a warning.

Witches needed words to cast.

Their spells came from centuries of magic users before shaping and training their bloodline's innate power through speech. Only a handful of witches I'd encountered through history could cast without speaking.

Including Nathalie.

She thought herself weak . . . but I was starting to wonder if the truth wasn't further from that lie.

If she might be so strong of mind and power, she suppressed it all beneath a calm exterior in her effort to be what her family and friends wanted.

If she'd buried that power so deep that she didn't even

realize it was there anymore, until she needed it.

Cold touched me as her magic made contact with the wraiths. A single speck was all it took for my own blue and red magic to be eaten away. Like blood on a white cloth, it spread. Gold consumed them one by one, faster than a blink.

Fear settled deeper inside of me. Not because of her, but *for* her.

Her magic had reacted faster than I could process. Faster than any mortal was capable. Which meant it was acting on an instinct that shouldn't exist. With only her thoughts and feelings as a guide. She was influencing it at best, and completely unable to control it at worst.

Because her magic had a mind of its own. *Like mine.*

And magic that could think for itself was dangerous.

That thought was the only thing running through my mind when the golden wave touched something midair, halfway between us and her sister. It traveled along that invisible force, creating an outline of what I could only assume to be her sister's curse.

I'd never seen one before. While I could scent magic, I couldn't see it. Until now. Until hers.

The curse took the form of jagged, deadly edges and spider-like threads. It billowed up the stairs to the very top, where wicked words had been vomited from Carissa's lips.

The gold dusted over her skin.

Time sped up, snapping back into place.

"This is exactly what I mean," Nathalie said in a bored, flat tone. "You spew hatred at everyone and act like an impulsive child—all emotion, with no rational thinking." Her golden gaze swept over the other woman shrewdly as she walked past me, then stopped to angle herself *between* Carissa and me.

She was trying to protect me.

That's what elicited the sudden change in her.

My heart warmed and cock stiffened, but I ignored both those things to step up beside her. I lifted my hand to her nape, silently offering my support.

Carissa shook like a leaf in a hurricane, speechless and wide-eyed at the power that held her captive.

"Have you forgotten the same witch law you love to spit at me; the lessons in hospitality? It would be within my rights to kill you for attempting *sguir* on me."

Just as quickly as it had unleashed, the golden aura she exuded blinked out of existence. The only tell that it was there to begin with was the way her eyes still glowed, as if brimming with so much power that it shone through the windows to her soul.

Carissa collapsed to her knees, gasping for air.

"Go fuck yourself," her sister spat. "I remember the lessons."

Somehow, she found it within herself to still be a spiteful cunt despite the circumstances.

"Then why would you do that? I don't like the word stupid, but that was incredibly stupid." She shook her head, not quite in disbelief but frustration all the same. "Even if I didn't stop you, August would have attacked you and possibly killed you for it. What curse could be worth that?"

I would have.

She spoke of it so calmly, but I knew it wouldn't sit well if I had. Nat could be angry with me later, as long as she was alive to be angry.

Not a shell of a person that resembled the wretch that was Carissa Le Fay.

"I guess you have powers you can actually use, after all. Shame. I was going to enjoy playing with you." Carissa Le

Fay pulled herself up to a kneeling position in her unwashed dress with dirt and dried blood smeared on her face. Tear tracks marked her pale skin beneath the filth. Her hair was greasy and matted. Yet, she sat with her back straight and head held high like she didn't just have a complete mental break and hadn't tried to curse Nathalie.

The way my sunling wasn't responding to this sort of behavior made my hands ball into fists.

She was used to it. This level of mistreatment was her norm.

I knew things were bad, but there was bad and then there was this.

Insanity.

Rage suffused my veins.

It's her show, I reminded myself. *She'll never trust me again if I lash out just like she accused that bitch of.*

While true, it didn't stop my temper from rising.

"You used me to open a portal to hell. Did you really think I would put myself at your mercy again?" Nathalie snorted once, but her amusement was false. A mask so that Carissa didn't see how deeply she hurt her with her words. "You really have lost your goddamn mind."

Glares.

Silence.

We stood there for over two minutes while Carissa stewed. It was a power move, waiting for her to break first, and the correct one, it seemed.

"Why are you here?"

"Answers," Nathalie replied, tipping her head. "I know Marcel is dying. What were you giving him?"

Her nose wrinkled in surprise, confusion, or distaste. I wasn't sure which but suspected a combination.

"I didn't 'give him' anything."

Nathalie didn't betray her emotions by tensing. No. On the contrary, her expression of neutrality was impenetrable. "The potion. Elixir. Whatever you want to call it. I know you were healing him just enough to keep him alive. I need to know what was in it, and anything else you might know about his condition."

Her eyebrows dropped low, furrowing. "I already told you, I wanted him dead. Our mother was the one trying to keep him alive and dependent on us, but I never learned what was in the potion because I didn't—and don't—care."

"Wow. That was good. I almost believed you," Nat said dryly. "But I don't like having my time wasted, and my schedule is quite packed today. So last chance, are we doing this the nice way or not?"

Carissa's temper surged again, ready for round two. "I'm not lying to you! He can walk off the tallest building for all I care. Hell, give me the chance and I'll push him—"

"August," Nathalie said softly.

"What do you need?"

She lifted her chin, sad faraway eyes exhausted in a way that went beyond the last few minutes or weeks. It spoke of years of abuse. Years of pain. She was hurting so much for someone that deserved so little.

"Can you . . . persuade her?"

I hesitated. "You won't like the effects of that."

"I know."

Part of me withered. She knew what persuasion entailed. For me to use that power on her sister would create such an intense desire for me that Carissa would say or do anything I wanted.

"There are other ways to get answers," I said quietly.

She nodded almost absently.

"For most people. Le Fay witches are subjected to a

series of trials as children that make us immune to most things. Poison. Truth serum. Tracking. I won't be able to use an object or potion on her. No spell will work either, and I refuse to physically torture her. It's a line I can't cross."

I wanted to offer to do it but something told me she'd see that as almost as bad. Like consenting to letting me hurt Carissa for information somehow made her the same. It didn't, but I wasn't going to push her. How she handled this situation was her choice. I'd offered my support, so I was along for the ride—even if I didn't like the destination.

"What makes you think persuasion will work?"

Nathalie turned away from me to look straight at her sister as she said in a voice that was loud enough to be heard, "Carissa's mind is already weak and she left some holes in that part of it so her partners could, uh, control her. She likes to be taken by force. Consensual non-consent, if you will." The woman in question stilled. Something other than anger touched her expression. It smelled like fear.

"How do you know that?" Carissa asked in a hushed tone.

Nathalie smiled with bitterness. "You've done nothing but hurt me my entire life, so I did what any intelligent person would. I've watched you." Nathalie moved closer and squatted down until their faces were only inches apart. "I know how you like your tea, and that you always sleep on the left side of the bed. You're superstitious and won't step on a cracked sidewalk, which is also why you rarely go downtown and never travel by foot when you do. I know that you can't get off with only one partner unless you have the illusion of being forced. There's nothing wrong with CNC when done right, but you didn't do it right, did you? Between consenting partners it's one thing, but you don't have that kind of trust in anyone. So you used your position over the men of the Pleiades Coven to get them to agree to being drugged and used by way of an oculus charm." She trailed one manicured fingernail down Carissa's dirty cheek. "Your methods were questionable at best, but that's the least of what you did, wasn't it? When those you were taking advantage of got transferred and the warlocks sent to replace them weren't so willing, you took your debasement a step further. You invited them to practice dark rituals with you under the pretense of teaching—only to drug them with tea and then use them without permission. That's rape." Nathalie shook her head in disgust. Her hand dropped away, like she couldn't bear to touch the other woman for even a second longer. "You didn't get away with that for long. Mother caught you and transferred them to cover it up. I regretted I wasn't able to get them out sooner, but I couldn't overplay my hand. There's a certain amount of caution needed when moving pieces in such a deadly game. I'd have been killed if they'd figured out how much I really controlled. You. Mother. Several prominent witches that Lucifer's death happened to rid me of. I suppose everything has a silver lining if you look hard enough, hmm?"

Carissa was nothing short of stunned. Her parted lips were dry and cracked. Eyes wide with disbelief.

"A whisper here. A dropped hint there. People are predictable in their patterns. I have an entire lifetime of information I've cataloged on you. If I want you to bend, you'll bend. If I want you to break, you'll break. So here's the thing: what I want from you, I will get. You can't stop me. It's far too late for that. You can't hide from me, because I know everywhere you might go. In the end, the only real choice you have is how easy or hard you make this. So, what is it going to be, Carissa? Are you going to bend, or make my friend here break you?" A dangerous sort of calm seemed to have hold of Nathalie as she waited for the inevitable answer we both knew her too-stupid-to-live sibling would give.

Carissa reared back and spat viciously, coating Nathalie's face in her disgusting scent.

"Do your worst, cunt."

Nathalie sighed, not letting slip even a sliver of the anger I was literally seething with.

Slowly and methodically, my aurae stood tall on her wedged heels and pulled a tissue from her Mary Poppins backpack of never-ending things. Nathalie wiped the saliva from her face, grimacing when she had to pull the skin near her eye to get it all.

She took her time cleaning herself, then unceremoniously dropped the tissue in front of Carissa.

Her steps were like the ticking of a clock, a timer counting down till the monster inside me was going to spring free.

"You asked me what curse would be worth breaking the laws of hospitality. I wanted you to *hurt*," Carissa said suddenly, her hoarse voice cracking unevenly. "To know what it felt like to lose your mind. Even if he killed me, it would have been worth it."

Just before she entered the Le Fay mansion, Nathalie paused.

"Don't kill her, August. I don't want that on my conscience. Get the information and go back to the car. I'll join you after I find what I need."

My fists clenched, but I accepted I couldn't kill Carissa. That was okay.

I'd already decided on a worse punishment. One that she wouldn't be able to escape.

NATHALIE

I walked out of the Le Fay mansion with empty hands and an emptier heart. Like I suspected, Mother had kept records of Marcel's condition. Thorough, detailed, excruciatingly clear records. I was doubtful Carissa knew about them given the multitude of cloaking spells they were hidden under. Our mother was a paranoid woman. She didn't want anyone accessing her secret logs when she died, not even her daughters. The lack of intention for us to ever see them made them even more cut-and-dry. The things she'd done to him . . .

I shook my head, fighting the bile that wanted to climb my throat.

He was being given a potion with oleander and a combination of hard-to-find herbal supplements. It was also poisoning him. What she'd known about his disorder? Next to nothing. Except that no matter what they gave him it always came back with a vengeance. His tolerance to their potions and poisons built up rapidly. By the time Dolores Le Fay passed, nearly eleven months ago now, Marcel had been taking five times the lethal amount of oleander.

By all measures, he should be dead already.

Yet he wasn't. Somehow his magic was sustaining and killing him at once. It was like he was born with the power of an immortal, but not the body of one. Which explained why she and The Morrigan had wanted him to impregnate me or my sister.

There were mentions of the Le Fay matriarch that died that night as well. While she wasn't there most of the time, she requested to be present for any particularly radical experiments . . .

My stomach turned again, and I forced that thought back as I tried to focus on the facts.

Mother had given him a year at most in her last entry. It was dated two days before she died. I could say a lot of things about her, most of them awful, but she was meticulous in her research. If how he'd looked last was anything to go by, I'd be lucky if we made it to the one-year mark.

These thoughts consumed me as I pushed through the main doors. The fresh air outside was welcome but still tasted stale somehow. Dead. Like this land had managed to taint it too.

I was going to burn the whole fucking place to the ground one day.

My steps fell short.

At the bottom of the stairs, Carissa was curled forward into a ball, the top of her head pressing into the wood. One arm bent awkwardly as she rubbed at herself furiously through her dirty dress. It disgusted me on every level.

August leaned over her, whispering so low I couldn't hear.

An irrational sort of jealousy hit me. I'd asked him to do this. I wasn't jealous, truly. He wasn't touching her. He didn't look at her like he did me. But old insecurities were sometimes hard to fight when I saw them so close together.

I watched for another moment. Whatever he said made her collapse the rest of the way to the ground and weep. A loud, keening cry made the crows scatter.

August lifted his eyes to me as he stood up.

Some of his earlier fury had settled in light of whatever he'd done.

I both wanted to know and didn't.

"I'm ready."

He nodded. "Let's go." He stepped around Carissa like she was an obstacle in his path and not a sobbing woman.

August extended his hand as I met him halfway down the stairs. We linked fingers and walked the rest of the way to the car in silence. It was only when we were seated, buckled, and pulling onto the highway that either of us spoke.

"Your sister . . ." he started. I shook my head.

"I don't want to know."

"Are you sure?"

"Quite." Unlike some people, if I wasn't up for the truth, be it good or bad, I didn't ask. In this case, the only thing that mattered was he kept her alive. Beyond that, my conscience was better off not knowing.

"I would never touch. You know that, right?" he asked in a voice that was nearly vulnerable. I laughed softly.

"Thank you, but I'm not worried about that. Not with you. I just don't want to know. Not unless she somehow figured out something my mother hadn't that could save Marcel."

He sighed. I knew the answer before he said it. My heart withered more, impossible as that was. I didn't really have hope that she had, but I also did. It was hard to explain. "I'm afraid not. I think she was actually telling the truth about that bit. Shocking as it seems, she had nothing to do with trying to heal him—or at least she doesn't remember it if she did."

I nodded solemnly and didn't respond.

We drove the rest of the way back to my place in a comfortable but anxious silence. I knew August had questions. I could see them in the corner of my periphery even when he didn't think I was watching, but I wasn't in any place to talk about Lucifer right now. Marcel's past, present, and future all but swirled together in a hazy montage of flashbacks and imaginings brought on by grief I shouldn't even feel.

He was still here, damnit.

But his clock was ticking toward an unknown countdown.

Lucifer had been equally quiet, and the silence was shocking in some ways. When I had a ghost around twenty-four seven coupled with August demanding my attention, and now answers about my ghostly company, I didn't often get to be physically alone these days, so a quiet environment was hard to come by. Either way, I was grateful for the peace and the opportunity to ruminate.

I'd found the answers I was searching for, only to have twice as many questions come to mind in light of them. My only hope at this point was that Marcel could shed some clarity on his situation and by some act of divine intervention knew something I might be able to use to save his life.

"You ready?"

My eyes refocused, and I realized I'd just been sort of walking blindly, lost in space, not paying attention to my surroundings at all. I didn't even remember most of the drive back. Or parking. Which was both a miracle and scary as fuck for me.

Good way to get yourself killed, Bad Nat scolded in a far-off recess of my mind.

Oh hush, you. No one is sneaking up on her if August is by her side. He's her protector. Caretaker wasn't wrong, but I didn't want to listen to them argue.

I shook both of them off and pressed my lips together in a forced smile.

"Yep." One word was all I could even manage. Great. This was going to go well. I had a lot to say, but my vocabulary was already lacking.

The look on August's face turned skeptical. "Nathalie," he started, but I held a hand up and interrupted him.

"I really don't want to talk about the ghost right now. I know you have questions. Just . . . not now."

"I was going to ask if you were okay."

"Sorry." My cheeks flushed. *Way to be an asshole, Nat.* "I'm okay, August. Really. It's just a lot to process. My brain is tired, but I don't have much time for rest, do I?"

"Is there anything I can do to help?"

The sincerity in his voice kindled a warm feeling in my chest. Now wasn't the time to tell him that him going with me was enough. Accepting me when he thought I was my sister was enough. I needed someone by my side more than I wanted to admit, and just . . . He was enough. More than.

Reaching out, I took his hand in mine, lacing my fingers through his while I shook my head gently. "I have to do this next part on my own."

August nodded in understanding, but his eyes darkened slightly, the glamour around them shifting. One day I'd ask him about it. Today wasn't that day.

Twisting our entwined hands, he lifted them as he

KEL CARPENTER & AURELIA JANE

turned mine toward him and pressed a firm but gentle kiss. Tingles spread up my arm.

As he let go, his fingers trailed my skin slowly, and I exhaled.

He turned around and opened his apartment door.

Anders sat on the couch, shuffling a deck of cards. Without looking up, he simply said, "You owe me."

Perusing the two empty bottles of liquor sitting on the counter, August raised an eyebrow. "Do I?"

Anders glanced at the hallway that led down to Marcel's guest room, then shifted his gaze back to us. "Fuck you. And yes."

"I sincerely doubt that."

"You said you'd be a 'few hours.'" Anders chuckled, glancing at me. "I should have known better."

Warmth spread across my cheeks from . . . what? Embarrassment? I didn't feel shame about spending my time with August. Maybe I just didn't like someone calling me out for fucking almost nonstop since last night. I left them to bicker, shaking my head as I walked down to his room and tapped my knuckles on the door lightly.

Marcel opened it, wearing his glamour once again. It was so easy to believe he was okay. Even if my eyes recognized it as a glamour, I couldn't see what was beneath it. The fragile part of my psyche that wanted to protect me was telling me this was the real thing. He wasn't sick. None of this was real.

In an opposite corner of my mind, Ann was there to remind me of the truth. They all were. Along with the polaroid photos my mother had kept of him during her "experiments."

"Hey, sunbeam." He greeted me with a lazy smile.

"I went to see Carissa this morning," I said, stepping in the room.

"Guess we're skipping the formalities," he muttered, shutting the door behind me. "C'mon in."

Sighing, I began pacing the room. "I didn't mean to be rude. My mind is just preoccupied with everything I learned."

"And what is that?" Marcel's interest was piqued, and he sat down on the edge of the bed, leaning forward and resting his elbows on his thighs.

"Well, first, something weird is going on with Carissa," I started, gesturing as I spoke.

"Something weird is always going on with her. She's a horrid cow."

"This was different, Marcel. She's not the same witch we saw the day you left."

"How so?"

"She looks young again, but disgusting. She hasn't showered since we left her, but she has magic again. And her memory is . . . Well, she's pretending like she doesn't remember anything about that day or the last few months entirely."

Marcel shook his head. "I don't believe that for a second. She was always a master manipulator."

I ran my hands through my hair. "Yeah, she is. Always has been. But as venomous and hateful as she was earlier—and I can't believe I am about to use these words in the same sentence as her name—her confusion seemed sincere."

He sat up straight and scrunched his face like he'd bitten into a lemon. "Nope. Can't say I like that word associated with her at all."

I huffed a small laugh and slowed my stride. "No joke."

"Nothing about her seemed different. Nothing changed when I was there. She was just as shitty as she's always been. Her not remembering any of it? I don't know what that all means, or what could even cause that. Maybe she fucked with the wrong person? That or some kind of spell she tried could have backfired. I don't know, but I'm not buying it."

"Me either. Not yet, anyway. My entire life I've been able to see who she really is, but this confused the hell out of me." I dropped onto the reading chair, leaning back.

Marcel watched me closely, tilting his head to the side. "So where does that leave us?"

Chewing on my lip, I knew what I had to do. I had been considering the options since I'd found my mother's journals. "I need to take some of your blood."

A frown cut between Marcel's brows, and his voice dropped when he spoke. "What for?"

I clasped my hands and pressed them between my thighs to stop from fidgeting. "I know, I know. Don't give away your blood—supernatural rules 101. But I need you to trust me—"

"I'd give you anything, Nat. Trust isn't the issue. I just don't understand what it's for."

My stomach twisted when he said the words that echoed of our past. He'd always told me how much he trusted me, and I'd always believed him . . . until the day my mother told me he was going to marry Kat. Hearing it all over again stung. The context was different now. There was no reason for him to lie to me, but it was just another reminder that the trust that was once between us had been so brutally severed. So many lies had been told over the past three years . . .

I cleared my throat before speaking again. "I need to do more research. If I look closely at your blood, maybe I can figure out the illness."

His face fell a little, like our efforts to take a deeper look would be fruitless. "You know they've already done that. Your family, I mean. No one knows what I have."

"I know they looked. I found my mother's journals . . ." I struggled with what to say, and he grabbed my hand, interlocking our fingers together and squeezing. It was the touch I needed to ground me and remember to breathe. "She was good, but I'm better. I need to look at it for myself to find a cure." I sighed, dreading the next part. "But I also need to make a new potion for you. Until I know what I'm looking at, I won't know how to formulate one."

"So she didn't write down the recipe? Figures. That's such a Dolores thing to do. Finding a way to fuck me over even from beyond the grave." He ran a hand through his hair, glancing up at the ceiling in disappointment.

"She did, actually . . ." As my voice trailed off, I took a deep breath.

Marcel's eyes met mine, an eager shine brightening at the prospect. "Then what's the problem?"

"The problem is that it was also killing you slowly . . ." I said, searching his face for a reaction. I did my best to not wince as I said it, but delivering news like that was painful on an emotional level.

"That can't be . . . They've been giving it to me for years. It's what's kept me alive."

"As best as I could tell, they weren't trying to kill you slowly. If they'd wanted to do that, they would have. You and I both know my mother was more than happy to drop anyone she or The Morrigan consider deadweight—myself included. What this is, is an unfortunate, if ironic, side effect of keeping you alive."

"But you have the formula. We can make it again to buy us some time."

"I can't do that," I said softly and gave a small shake of my head. I knew he was a fighter; that he wouldn't give in easily. That he was still alive was all the testament needed to prove that.

Marcel stood up, talking with his hands as he spoke. "Nat, I've been taking it for how long? Over seven years? Eight? Okay, so it was killing me over time. Not really the greatest news, but most medications have negative side effects. If we know what it is, I can take it and go through the normal cycle of feeling like shit then getting better. I'm dying as we speak. There's no 'slow' to it. I'd rather take it and buy time than let this thing kill me right here and now."

I shook my head again and struggled to maintain an even voice. "You've been without it for too long. Your body is . . . weak. Far weaker than it already was, I mean. The potion would kill you now. Not slowly. Just flat-out kill you."

"How can you know that?"

I grit my teeth in frustration. It wasn't wrong that he wanted to fight back, but pretending he was stronger than he was wouldn't do us any favors. "Because I'm a genius, Marcel. Because I know the plants used and their properties. Because I can smell the faintest hint of it on you and I have for years, I just never thought about why. Because I saw the state your body was in when you took off the glamour. Because the potion is also poison, and the amount you were taking when my mother was still alive was five times a lethal dose. Any immunity you built up to withstand it is gone. You're in no condition to fight off a poison of that magnitude now."

A long silence spread between us. Marcel held my gaze, searching for a counterpoint. He could fight me on it, but I wasn't going to give in. Not on this. There was no way I would hand him a poison I knew for certain would kill him. I wouldn't be his executioner. So I waited. No matter what he threw at me, I had my rebuttal ready. When he closed his eyes, the crease between his brows loosened as resignation took over. "Okay."

"Okay?" I didn't expect compliance. Like most of our encounters of late, I expected pure conflict.

"Yeah. I don't know what else to say. Just . . . okay."

"You aren't going to argue with me?"

"I said I trust you, Nat. I do. I'm not going to underestimate you anymore. Do I want to fight back and say my body can handle it? Yes. Every part of me wants to tell you that you're wrong." He ended with a pause, leaving something hanging, like maybe he didn't want to finish.

"But?" I prompted.

"I don't think you are." He plopped down on the bed again, and rolled up his sleeve as he held his arm out to me. "So how are we going to do this?"

I blinked a few times, finally believing he wasn't going to push back. Slapping my palms on my thighs and rubbing the sweat off of them, I stood up. "The good old-fashioned way." Reaching into my bag, I pulled out a phlebotomy kit. "We'll need a clean draw to get a good look at this. I don't want anything tainting it."

"All yours, Doc." He grabbed a pillow and tucked it under his arm as I grabbed the desk chair and brought it over to the bed. Setting it down in front of him, I took my seat and opened my kit. The gloves were a tad tighter than necessary, but I'd make do. I attached the needle to the hub and laid out the collection tubes. Grabbing the tourniquet, I tied it on his upper arm, and he automatically squeezed his fist. "You'll need to bear with me. It's been a while."

"I'm sure it'll be fine." His calm response was soothing, but it really had been a long time.

I'd learned how to do such things when I'd volunteered in the clinics I funded. It was important to be cross-trained and able to help wherever someone was needed. Sometimes that was in the donor banks. Sometimes it was with doctors and healers. Knowing how to find a vein and take blood was a useful trait. Still, it would've been better if I'd been more in-practice than I was now.

I swabbed his arm with an alcohol pad and felt around with my middle finger until I found the spot I needed.

Grabbing the needle, I angled it properly and as I pressed it into his vein, I whispered, "Sorry."

Marcel exhaled sharply through his nose, but said, "Nah, you're good."

"You're such a liar," I said softly while pressing a collection tube into the hub. The blood started filling it, but it was moving slowly. Removing the tourniquet and his hand releasing the tension didn't do anything for it. I knew there were many reasons this could happen. Maybe he wasn't hydrated well. Maybe—quite likely—I hadn't picked the best vein. But logic didn't stand at the forefront of potential explanations. What teased at the corner of my mind was the level of his illness. The magic trying to escape, draining him of his life force.

Blood continued to dribble into the tube at a glacial

pace. It was going to take longer than I thought, and I still needed two more vials.

Twisting my lips, I looked around the room awkwardly. My eyes landed on a stack of books next to the bed, and another stack on the desk. "So . . . read any good books lately?"

Marcel chuckled lightly, staying careful to not jostle his arm. "My prison guard has a decent collection in the room across from mine. Some scholarly, some classics. Different languages. It's intriguing. Not much to do except read, so I'm going through them pretty quickly."

I nodded noncommittally when a thought popped into my head. I had the Eye, but I knew fuck all about what to do with it. Marcel was probably the most educated and well-read person I knew, except maybe August. It was possible somewhere in his studies, he'd learned about it. "Were there any scholarly texts that you've never read before?" I asked in a casual tone. "I assume you started with those."

"There were, actually." Collection tube number one was full, so I pulled it out and swapped it for the second. "He's got books dating back further than Morgan Le Fay was even alive. Some ancient scrolls. He had a few spelled against people outside himself reading them, but that wasn't exactly difficult for me to get around."

"Find anything useful?"

"Nothing about an illness close to mine, if that's what you're asking."

I hummed in response. "What about artifacts?"

He angled his head, narrowing his gaze a fraction. "What are you getting at?"

"Just musing, really. Thinking about different books at the Le Fay mansion and if artifacts could play a part in finding a cure." I focused on his arm, waiting for the blood to reach a certain level.

"Such as?"

"Do you remember reading the collection *Relics of the Old World*?"

"Somewhat. It wasn't my focus, so I didn't prioritize reading those. There's like, what, eight volumes now?"

"Nine." I shrugged. "At any rate, it had magically imbued artifacts that had been found or lost over time. Things like the Tarnhelm, Ariadne's diadem . . . the Eye of Parcae. Just thinking through things that could help strengthen a potion or help us find a cure." Of course, I knew what had happened to the first two.

"The Tarnhelm was destroyed in Pompeii and Ariadne's diadem wouldn't help us. It was supposedly used to create rifts between realms. The prevailing suspicion was that Lucifer had it. He's dead, so if he did, we'll never know."

Movement in the corner of the room caught my attention. I acted as though my muscles were strained and stretched my neck, allowing myself a clean line of sight to see Lucifer leaning against the wall with his arms crossed. He shook his head at the accusation. Not that I needed the diadem, but I'd question him about it later.

"What about the Eye of Parcae?" I eased the second collection tube out and replaced it with the final one.

"Not much has been written on it. Supposed to help you find what you need, whatever that means. The texts weren't always clear about what exactly it was the Eye was rumored to do. Even if it could help us, there's been no trace of it for centuries."

"I've always wondered how it works, though. Anytime I found a mention of it, none of those texts described how to actually use it."

"I don't know that anyone knows. Everything I ever read on it was incredibly vague. Almost like it was a myth rather than a true artifact. We'd have better luck finding the Lost City of Atlantis."

I gave a small laugh, and a tiny smile found its way to the surface. "That was Kat's favorite story when we were little. She wanted us to find it. Run away there, just the two of us, and live like queens. She said if the Atlanteans didn't accept us, she'd spell them."

What a different time that had been. It felt like a million years ago. Another lifetime, with another person. My twin. Not the spiteful witch she'd turned into.

"How is Kat doing in hiding, by the way?" Marcel's question was so casual, but it caught me off guard completely.

"Wh-what?"

Marcel's eyes softened, and he gave me a lopsided smile. "Carissa and Kat were the only ones alive that knew I was sick, sunbeam. Carissa didn't tell you so you could help me. Give me a little bit of credit. I know Kat came to you. It's not hard to put two and two together."

I sighed. "She's . . . surviving, I guess. She didn't say much. Stuck around long enough to throw some shade, as usual, and to tell me you were sick. She wasn't willing to share why she's run off into hiding."

"Didn't imagine she would tell any of us. Could be an olive branch, trusting you with this." He sounded hopeful. It was sweet, but naïve on his part. Kat would never forgive me for killing Prudence. There wasn't an olive branch strong enough to bear the weight of my actions, nor hers.

"Ha! No, I can assure you it's not. Too much has happened between us. Too much that can never be undone."

225

KEL CARPENTER & AURELIA JANE

Memories of splattered blood and shattered glass flashed through my mind. My sister's lifeless body, and her friend's life hanging in the balance. The screams echoed in my ears, and I clenched my teeth.

In the dark attic of the loci, a door rattled, and my chest seized.

"Nat?" Marcel calling my name jolted me back to the present.

"Sorry, got lost for a minute," I admitted, taking out the last tube and pulling out the needle. I pressed a cotton ball to the puncture and stuck a bandage on top.

"Where'd you go?" he asked, taking my chin between his thumb and forefinger. "When you disappear like that, where do you go?"

"Memories," I answered. It was the most I was willing to admit.

He'd asked that once before, but I'd avoided the question then as well. No one knew, and I wanted to keep it that way.

When my silence had spoken for me, he sighed. "What happened between you and Kat wasn't your fault. Your mother played us. I wasn't willing to let her hurt you—"

"We were all pawns in my mother's schemes." I couldn't hear it again—the reasoning behind his marriage to my sister. I knew he wanted my forgiveness, but I couldn't focus on that *and* saving him. One thing at a time. "She was going to sacrifice me one way or another. It was only a matter of time, apparently."

"She sacrificed both of you. You were both means to an end."

"Kat told me, by the way."

"You'll have to be more specific." He spoke slowly and remained guarded, but the tiniest inflection in his voice sounded hopeful once again. I realized at that moment he wanted me to know their real relationship, but he hadn't been willing to share her secrets. If one of them had told me the damn truth, it would have saved me so much pain. At least his keeping this to himself was honorable—or that's what I was going to tell myself. It stung too, since it felt like him still choosing her over me in some way.

"That she's gay." Silence. "But you knew that already."

"Of course I knew. Kat became my best friend. We were never anything more to each other than that. Dolores could force us to marry, but she couldn't force your sister to be someone she wasn't, and she couldn't force me to not love you. She just never knew the truth about what the relationship was for me and Kat."

"Kat told me that you guys didn't . . ."

"Consummate our marriage? Yeah," he said with a snort. "I told you that too."

I cringed. "You did. I suppose I owe you an apology for not believing you."

"No. No, you don't. You don't owe anyone shit, Nat. Least of all me," he said softly. The pain in his voice resonated, mingling with my own.

Pain that he was on the cusp of life and death.

Pain that we might not find a potion or cure before it was too late.

Pain from our past.

Pain from the years of lies.

Pain that our lives had been ripped off course and out of our control for so long.

I felt it all too—in the deepest part of me—but I didn't want to anymore.

Enough was enough.

"I understand why you did what you did, Marcel," I

started, using a gentle tone so the meaning behind my words was understood as sincere and true. "I don't expect you to regret that decision either. You'd do it again to save me from my family. I recognize that. I really do. But the explanation doesn't negate the impact it had on me. I need . . ." I trailed off, wanting to say time, but I knew we didn't have it. "I need to process it all a bit longer."

He gave me a sad smile.

"I know. You may never forgive me, but at least you know the truth. More than anything, that was what I wanted you to understand."

"I have to go," I whispered. "I need to run these as soon as possible."

Packing up the collection kit and blood samples, I stood up quietly.

Marcel caught my hand, lacing his fingers through mine, and I let him, feeling his warm palm against mine. He twisted my hand the same way August had, placing a gentle kiss on top, and my skin heated at the contact. Conflicting emotions lanced through as I thought of both of them, then glanced up at Lucifer.

"You know where to find me." He started to release his hold, but he squeezed it tightly as if to enunciate his words. "If anyone can find out how to save me, it's you."

"No pressure," I teased, trying to ease the tension. "I'll call you tomorrow, okay? Hopefully I'll know something."

Turning around, I headed for the door.

"Nathalie?"

"Hmm?" I turned back to face him.

"Just in case I—"

"Don't say the rest of that sentence, Marcel." A knot formed in my stomach, twisting violently.

"Let me finish. Please. You know it's possible . . ." When

I didn't speak again, he took that as permission to continue. "Just in case something happens before we find a way to stop this, I need you to know something." He paused and I waited, counting the hammering within my chest that beat in time with the silent seconds. "No matter what happens, I've always loved you, sunbeam. It was always you."

This was the most vulnerable he'd ever been. My breath caught, and I nodded, not willing to trust my voice enough to attempt a response. I knew he loved me. What tore at me was that deep down, I never stopped loving him but didn't have the guts to say it.

I was completely and utterly confused.

Lucifer's ghostly form stood in the room—my accidental familiar—tied to me in a way that surpassed that bond. And I didn't hate it, or him.

In the other room was an immortal incubus I'd fallen for despite my better judgment.

And here I stood, in front of my ex . . . who, despite his choices, was earning my forgiveness and had never truly lost my love.

So I needed to figure out how to handle the three of them, save the life of one of them, bond or not with another, and deal with my growing feelings for what amounted to a poltergeist with a sex-on-a-stick voice.

Plus solve a few murders, run a city, figure out the Eye of Parcae, and find Sasha in the veil.

It was just another Tuesday in the shitshow known as my life.

I could really use some sort of miracle right about now. Time slowing down or pausing would be a great start, but I'd take anything. Just something to show me that we were all going to be okay.

Instead, I barely held back tears saying goodbye to

Marcel, terrified that he could die while I was gone. Instead, I barely managed to talk to August on my way out, trying not to think that it could be the last time I saw him before Sasha woke up and they completed the bond, even if he insisted it wouldn't happen. Instead, a bird shit on my shoulder on the way back to my car.

Message received, universe.

Message received.

nineteen

NATHALIE

I needed a few supplies before I could cast the spells I needed on Marcel's blood samples. After visiting one of the clinics I funded, there was just one more stop to make.

"What's the purpose of the machine you borrowed?" Lucifer angled his head toward the box in the back seat.

"It's a centrifuge," I answered, turning on my blinker and heading toward my apartment building. "It separates the blood and plasma."

"But you know whatever has caused his illness is magical in nature. Human medicine isn't going to help him."

"First of all, supernaturals devalue human history, technology, and ideas. My family included. My mother was brilliant and kept meticulous records, but she never would have lowered herself to use science to look at his blood in its most simplistic form. Second, whether or not they want to admit it, what they used was a base that humans have used for centuries. All medicine started off as herbology. My mother just mixed nature with magic."

"Baggage doesn't think you'll find a cure."

I shot him a glare from the corner of my eye and ground my teeth together. "Stop calling him that."

"Well, well. Starting to feel a little defensive over your ex?"

"He's not my baggage," I started, then sighed. "We have our shit to work out, but knowing how much my mother screwed with us changes a lot of what I have to process. You and August calling him that doesn't help. It just makes you both assholes."

"I never claimed I wasn't one," he countered.

"Where's salt when you need it?" I muttered my useless threat, and he chuckled darkly, tracing a phantom finger up my arm. Goosebumps pebbled on my skin, and I shivered.

"I don't think salt will work anymore, little witch."

I scoffed, but I knew he was right. His form had changed too much, but I still didn't know what that meant. There was just too much going on for me to explore it.

Lucifer made a show of breathing in as though he were exasperated beyond measure. "But if it matters to you, I'll stop calling him that."

"Really?" My eyebrows rose in surprise, but I wondered silently what he wanted in return. When he said nothing, I turned to him slightly. "That's it?"

"If it makes you happy."

"Why are you giving in so easily?"

"Should I make it harder?" he asked with a playful smile tugging at the corners of his mouth.

You make everything harder, I thought, but rather than voicing that, I just shook my head. "Nope."

I wasn't going to play with fire. Every time I played with Lucifer I got burned, so right now it was just better to take the win—if it really was one—and keep my mouth shut.

Pulling in front of my building, I came to a stop and got

out of the car. The door to Señora Rosara's shop creaked when I opened it, and several pairs of eyes drifted in my direction. A cat walked up to me, rubbing itself against my leg with a soft meow.

The moment Lucifer showed himself behind me, it hissed, narrowing its eyes in his direction. No surprise there. Animals had a sixth sense about the veil, especially cats. I wondered if that's why the señora kept so many of them.

"Señora?" I called out just as she came out of the back. Her long skirt swished as she sauntered to behind the counter.

"Nathalie," she greeted, briefly flicking her gaze to the ghost at my side. "I've been expecting you." Bending down, she picked up a medium-sized box before setting it on the counter.

I perused the contents, not too surprised that the seer knew I'd come to her for supplies to test Marcel's blood.

"Thanks," I said quietly, wondering if I should ask her the thoughts weighing on my mind. Before I could even form the words, she spoke.

"I know what you want to ask. No. I haven't had a vision of you finding a cure." I pressed my lips together and exhaled through my nose. "But I haven't seen you failing either," she added.

"I don't suppose you can tell me more about the 'not failing' option? Namely how I get there?"

Her smile was tight, but it was genuine. "Abernathys are notoriously stubborn, and even harder to kill. He's doing everything he can to survive because he wants to be with you."

I swallowed, trying to make the lump in my throat go

away. "I don't know if that's going to be enough to keep him alive while I try to work through all this."

"Time will tell, won't it?" She nudged the box that sat between us. "I don't have all the answers, but you're on the right path to find them . . . just take care not to run yourself into the ground while searching. You have a lot on your plate, and the consequences will soon exact a toll."

"I'm trying, but right now my best doesn't feel like it's cutting it." Chewing on my bottom lip, I shifted my weight and glanced at the door that led to the secure room where I knew my friend's body was being safely guarded. "I've not had any luck finding Sasha either. The stupid planchette moved once, and it hasn't done a damn thing since."

"Have you called for her today?"

I shook my head, guilt making my stomach roil. No, I hadn't. I'd spent the previous night in August's arms, then gone over to Carissa, then went to see Marcel. And we were running out of time.

Some friend you are, Bad Nat said in a mocking tone.

Ann and The Warden immediately shot her a glare.

Everything she does is for her friends, Caretaker countered.

Right. Getting dicked all night by a hot incubus was for "her friends." I bet Sasha will totally agree—if Prime ever makes time to find her, that is. Or maybe, plot twist, she doesn't want to find her.

My breath caught at the accusation, and I shuttered my mind, drowning out their bickering.

I wanted nothing more than to shove Bad Nat in a closet. I'm pretty sure everyone else did too, except Caretaker. She cared about everyone, even those who probably didn't deserve it.

"I'm, um . . . I'm heading up to start some spells on

Marcel's blood, then I plan on using the board to call to her again."

"Nathalie," the señora used my name to scold me. "You can't look for her every waking hour. Staying up all night out of stubbornness and guilt won't make her appear."

"I haven't—"

"Don't lie to me."

I bit my lip and sighed. "There's only so much time. I can't search all day and night, so I'm splitting the hours between priorities as best I can."

"Without taking care of yourself."

"I—" The words stuck in my throat. I lowered my face into one hand. "I know," I settled on eventually. "But Sasha and Marcel are running out of time. I'll sleep . . . later." The end of that saying made my eyes water because I couldn't accept that possibility for either of them.

"You need to prepare to lose this battle," she said gently, but firmly. My jaw clenched. "If Sasha doesn't find her way out of the veil tonight, she's lost. I can't keep her body alive beyond Samhain. It's cruel to tie her to this plane for an outcome that won't come to pass. She doesn't deserve that." My gaze unconsciously flicked to one of her cats. The moment I met her eyes again, I winced. I kept my mouth shut, having promised I wouldn't ask questions about her collection of enslaved felines. "*They* deserved it," she added after seeing the gesture, her tone far harsher. It made me wonder what they did to deserve it.

"What are my odds?" I asked, dodging the mention of her pets.

She shrugged. "They were never very good, but with the spell mingled with her mate's essence and tonight being Samhain, it's the best chance she has. Even with that, the odds aren't in your favor. As it stands, if she does come

235

back, she's not going to be right in the head. Surviving in the veil for that long . . ."

"Alters your reality," I said, finishing her sentence. She dipped her chin, acknowledging my assessment.

A thought occurred to me while I hovered, not making a move to leave. I'd already asked Marcel, and he didn't know. If I brought it up to Señora Rosara, it meant revealing more than I wanted to. Truth be told, there was a good chance she knew it already, since she seemed to have future sight of me most of the time, anyway. She was always ready for whatever shitshow I brought in.

"There's one more thing," I began, and she raised an eyebrow in response. "What do you know about the Eye of Parcae?"

Her lips pursed in assessment. "Everything, or close to it." Her gaze sharpened. "Why?"

My heart leaped with hope. "You know how it works?"

"Why are you asking about it?" The señora's voice lowered as she spoke, caution and curiosity filling each word.

A knot twisted in my stomach. She didn't know, for once. I could see it on her face. "I, uh . . ."

Her lips parted a bit. "You have it, don't you?" She inhaled sharply when I nodded in confirmation. "I can't see the Eye. No seer can, no matter what kind of sight they have. The magic that created it is not of this world, so our own can't follow it. It's why no one has been able to find it for centuries." She flicked her gaze over my form. "Except you, it would seem."

I wasn't going to correct her by admitting I'd only been tracking it, and my sister killed the man who'd found it. Those were insignificant details. At least I thought they were. Were they? I didn't know anymore.

The truth was I'd wanted it to find the Illuminati. Piper had dealt with them before the twins were born, and they'd caused a lot of damage. Lives were lost. They were a cult, and while Piper had made an impact, I'd wanted to find them and learn whether or not they remained a threat to my city and world.

Now I needed the Eye to find a way to save Marcel's life. "How do I use it?"

"Why haven't you asked him?" she asked tersely, nodding in the direction where Lucifer stood. "Your ghostly companion could have answered that for you."

My jaw dropped, and I squeezed my fist as I turned my head in his direction. Dropping all pretenses about his existence, and not caring that I looked crazy yelling at a ghost, I went after him. "The fuck! Seriously, asshole? You *knew*? Why didn't you say something?"

Lucifer remained silent, his hands tucked away in his pockets. Finally, he shrugged. "You didn't ask."

"Dickhead," I muttered so quietly it was surprising he heard. "You knew I had it. You were there when I got it for fuck's sake. You've had plenty of time to tell me. You heard me ask Marcel just a couple of hours ago, and you *still* didn't say anything. You're supposed to be honest." I shook my head, pinching the bridge of my nose.

"You didn't directly ask me, little witch," he said, enunciating every word slowly. "I'm not obligated to give you answers to unasked questions."

Indignation consumed me. For a brief moment in the car, I thought he'd been doing something nice for me by conceding to stop using the nickname Baggage when talking about my ex.

Now, I felt like I should have known better.

"I could have perhaps already found a cure for Marcel if

you hadn't kept this from me." My voice was tight, and the anger I felt was making it hard to speak. I walked toward him. "That's what you wanted, wasn't it? You wanted him to die, so you were going to keep this a secret and then he'd be out of the picture?"

"It won't help you find a cure, Nathalie," Señora Rosara said, interrupting me.

"Why the hell not?" I asked, turning back to her.

"The Eye doesn't help you find the unknown or what is lost. It allows you to wield the items of fate." The answer didn't come from Señora Rosara, but from Lucifer.

Time felt like it stopped. Blood rushed to my head, roaring in my ears.

The spindle, the loom, and the shears.

The items of fate. I knew of them, but I didn't have them. I didn't even know where to start looking. They were likely just as hard to find as the Eye had been. My heart sank.

Sucking in a ragged breath, I cracked my neck from side to side. "Okay . . . I have contacts all over the world. I can still use this to my advantage," I said, desperately thinking through the ways I could manipulate this to work in my favor. "If I have them, it will help me find—"

"Nathalie," Señora said, her voice as gentle as I'd ever heard it. "It's never that simple. The Eye requires a sacrifice most are not willing or able to give."

"Which is?"

"An eye for an eye," she said solemnly. "To use the Eye of Parcae, a supernatural with chaos magic must give up their own and replace it with the item in question. Only then can you wield the items of fate. But there is no guarantee it will help you, either, and the process is not reversible. Only when the wearer is dead can the Eye be removed."

I stared blankly, trying to let that sink in. "I'm sorry, what? I would have to *take out my own eyeball*, and put the Eye of Parcae . . ."

"In your eye socket, yes," she finished, nodding.

Fuck me sideways, this had to be a joke. Goosebumps rose on my arms as I thought about what I'd have to do. *Cut out my eye?*

I took a deep breath, centering myself. One thing at a time. Right now, I just needed information. What I chose to do with it . . .

"But it will help me find what I'm looking for, though, right?"

Señora pressed her lips together before speaking. That simple action told me I wasn't going to like what she had to say. "That's not how it works. The spindle, the loom, and the shears control the threads of fate. No one can see these threads, not even you." She gave me a hard glare. "The only way to see those threads is with the Eye of Parcae. That's its purpose."

"But will it help me find what I'm looking for, Señora?"

She sighed. "Not without a thread to follow first."

Closing my eyes, I exhaled loudly and tilted my face to the ceiling. Tears stung as they threatened to fall but I refused to let that happen. Rarely did I hit brick walls this big. I was Nathalie Le Fay. I could find anything.

At least I used to.

Now I couldn't find a group of shitheads that had once kidnapped Piper.

I couldn't find Sasha in the veil.

I couldn't find a cure for Marcel.

I couldn't even find my own fucking sister.

The overwhelming feeling of failure threatened to consume me.

"This is why I didn't tell you," Lucifer whispered. I shot him a glare, but he didn't back down. "Using it won't necessarily get you what you want, but what you give up never comes back. The process can't be undone."

"How do you know all this?" I asked him quietly. In truth, I was thankful he'd spoken up so he could distract my thoughts and keep them from spiraling.

"It's a family heirloom," he muttered, turning away from me. Señora Rosara's lips twitched at his admission. A twinkle shone in her eye.

"And you, Señora?" I began, facing her again. "How do you know? I've scoured texts my entire life, whole libraries of information, and never found this much on it."

"I've been around a long time, Nathalie. Some questions are better left unanswered." She pushed the box a few inches, reminding me I still had work to do. "Begin your spells. Call for Sasha. That is all you can do right now. Once the witching hour passes, you're out of time."

"Put this on my tab," I said, grabbing the box. "And let me know if anything changes down here."

Señora had already turned and was heading into the back room again, her skirt swishing in her wake. She waved over her shoulder, not turning around.

Lucifer's hand grazed the small of my back.

"I'm still mad at you," I said, heading to the elevators carrying the cumbersome box, thinking of what I needed to start first as we rode to my floor.

"You can stay mad at me. I didn't tell you because it won't do you any good. You gouging out your eye helps no one. It accomplishes nothing because it finds nothing for certain." He fell in step beside me as we walked into the hallway and headed toward my apartment.

"You could have told me so I at least knew what it did."

"To what purpose? So in your desperation in Marcel's final hour you could try to prove me wrong?" He scoffed, crossing his arms. "I think not."

Slamming the box on the kitchen counter, I spun to him, annoyance filling every word. "I wouldn't make a rash decision like that, and certainly not just to prove you wrong. You keeping secrets is—"

"Necessary sometimes, and should be unsurprising, considering you know who I am," he said, cutting me off. "The phrase 'desperate times call for desperate measures' exists for a reason. Would you have made a deal with me in exchange for that knowledge if you knew I had it?"

"No," I said, my tone firm and curt. I'd learned my lesson on that front.

"Exactly." He grinned. "Which is why I didn't offer to tell you."

"What would you have asked for, hypothetically speaking?"

"I'd have made you promise not to use it."

"Because you want to see Marcel die?" I couldn't believe him. What a selfish, arrogant, egotistical—

"So I don't have to watch you suffer for nothing, little witch," he answered, running his thumb down my cheek.

The genuine nature of his tone shocked me almost as much as the admission itself.

Standing in place, I leaned into his touch, and it grounded me. He had a habit of doing that. His reasoning wasn't all that different from something I would do for someone I loved. The thought of the *L* word made a shiver run up my spine. That was my justification and emotion, not his, but the logic was in the same vein.

Whatever version of love he could feel was unknown to me, but I knew he cared about Sasha. I knew, beyond whatever undefined thing we were, he cared about me—as weird as that sounded.

"It's hard to argue with you when I would probably do something similar, if I were in your place."

Something wicked crossed his features, but that was nothing new. He loved it when I had to agree with him. I was still kind of mad he'd kept it from me, but I also knew I was essentially blaming him for something he couldn't control. Marcel's illness wasn't his fault. If he had been the one to tell me about the Eye of Parcae, I'd have been mad at him for that too, and wondered if he were lying about how to use it.

Why? Because I didn't want it to be the truth.

There were a lot of truths I didn't want to face. Like what it meant if I didn't find Sasha. Today was my last chance. That sad, desperate voice inside of me said I had to find her. That finding her would absolve me of my unbidden thoughts.

We spent the next ten minutes preparing the room for what I knew to be a long night.

While I worked, I thought about how Lucifer had kept an eye on the board for me, watching for any sign of movement—no questions asked and not in return for a favor. He'd simply done it for me, and for Sasha, I presumed.

Regardless, it was an act of generosity; a kindness I didn't think he wanted me to realize he was capable of.

Or maybe he did? He wasn't much for words when he wasn't needling me or attempting to turn me on, so maybe this was his way of showing me.

With candles lit and the lights turned off, I sat down on the floor in front of the Ouija board. Lucifer settled in next to me, and his presence was more comforting than I wanted to admit.

But if he could show me those small gestures, I could return them in my own way.

A give-and-take, but this time without the prearranged agreement.

"Thank you," I whispered, scooting into a position that didn't hurt my lower back. He raised his eyebrows in question. "For staying with me while I do this."

"Anything for you, little witch." Lucifer leaned in to brush a gentle kiss over my lips. Tingles spread through my body. His touch was stronger on Samhain. While he was always with me—even when I didn't want him to be—for the first time, it felt like he was truly there.

And I liked it.

twenty

NATHALIE

We'd only been sitting for an hour when my body decided being on the floor sucked. I'd twist and turn, trying to stay comfortable. Moving between the couch and seated on the floor, it really didn't matter. I was pretty sure my bones were just tired and, no matter what I did, everything felt achy.

After my umpteenth complaint, Lucifer shifted himself to sitting on the couch behind me.

"May I?" He pressed his fingertips into the muscles in my lower back, massaging at the knots that had formed.

I couldn't answer him. Instead, it felt so good I just managed an incoherent "yep" mingled with moans while I slumped over. His thumbs glided up and down the sides of my spine, while his hands raked over the rest of my back, loosening the tension.

"Thanks." I gave him a small smile as I sat up.

After three hours of calling for Sasha with the Ouija board, I considered the possibility that I was going crazy. Sitting and talking to cardboard in a candlelit room with a ghost for company could do that to a person.

Thoughts of doubt raced through my mind, and I questioned everything.

Maybe she'd never moved the planchette that first day. Maybe I had imagined her presence. Maybe my desperation to find her was what made me think it had moved. Maybe she was just . . . gone.

While those fears swirled in my head, it happened.

The tiniest jerk of the planchette, moving of its own accord.

My eyes widened, and without looking away from the board, I whispered to Lucifer. "Do you see what I'm seeing? It's moving, right?"

"It's moving." I almost smiled when he answered me in a quiet voice, as though someone else could hear him.

Overwhelming hope, excitement, and happiness surged inside me while my heart leaped into my throat.

"Sasha, is that you?" I said into the empty room.

The planchette moved, but it was painstakingly slow.

Gliding to the corner of the board, it landed on the word I needed to see.

Yes.

Relief flooded me.

"Are you okay?" The words came fumbling out as I choked back a sob.

What I wanted to see was a shake or a wiggle over the word Yes, but instead it moved to the opposite corner of the board.

No.

Anxiety pulsed in my chest. I needed to ask her so many questions, but it would take so long for her to spell it out. I tried to think of how to guide her to her body. She was here and I couldn't afford to waste time.

KEL CARPENTER & AURELIA JANE

"Sasha, your body is in this building. It's with Señora Rosara—"

A slow glide across the board . . .

Yes.

"You know where your body is?" I asked, surprise filling my tone.

A shake and a wiggle . . .

Yes.

"Sasha, she's left a small rift in the protective spell. Follow—" A tight lump formed in my throat, causing the words to come out hoarse, but I didn't care. "Follow August's scent. The spell, Sasha. Follow his magic. It's calling to you. It'll guide you to the opening. Follow his essence."

Another glide across the board moved the planchette to hover over . . .

No.

Glancing at Lucifer, we made eye contact, and a crease formed between his brows. I imagined we had the same look on our faces.

"Why not?" My voice wavered as I asked. It seemed like the kind of question you need an answer to, but you didn't want it.

N . . . O . . .

And then it stopped between *T* and *S*.

"Sasha?" I asked in barely a whisper, reaching over to Lucifer to thread my fingers through his. Holding his hand for support, I repeated her name, letting moments pass by.

After an hour of waiting to see if she'd come back, I looked at Lucifer.

"Any idea for what *N-O-T* or *N-O-S* could mean?" I asked, finally addressing him instead of calling her name.

He shrugged. "Maybe writing No Spell? Like she can't find the spell to follow?"

"No Scent?" I suggested, thinking out loud. "No Samhain? Not . . . something?"

We were grasping at straws. Neither of us knew, and it didn't matter how many ideas we came up with, we wouldn't know unless she came back. It wasn't enough to go on. My eyelids felt heavy, and a big yawn forced its way out.

"You need a break. You've been doing this all afternoon."

I shook my head in response. "What if she comes back?"

"You've told her to follow August's magic. There's nothing more you can do. She either comes back or she doesn't."

Something about his words resonated. He was right. I had done everything I could. There was literally nothing left I could do. I had made contact. I told her about the spell. The location of her body. If I could have, I would have led her to her body, but that's not how the veil worked. Still, I had trouble moving. If I walked away . . .

"Scoot forward," he said with a sigh. As I did, he moved to settle in behind me, sliding a leg on either side of me.

"What are you doing?"

"If you don't sleep, you're going to pass out. You spent the night trying to fuck your problems away and then faced those problems all day," he said, dropping his voice lower when I tried to interject. "I'm going to watch the board. If anything changes, I'll wake you. You're right here. All you'll have to do is open your eyes."

Every cell in my body screamed for sleep. It was hard to argue when I was running on fumes. It was also hard to ignore the desire to argue with him on principle. Glancing over my shoulder, I caved. "Just a nap, okay?"

"Of course."

I shuffled back, fitting myself into the curve of his body. The illusion of warmth comforted me, and I wondered how tired I really was to feel something so intense when it wasn't there.

Still, I couldn't fall asleep.

Tracing my index finger over my thumb, I tried to quell my anxiety. Lucifer noticed, then grazed his hands over my arms gently, rhythmically caressing my skin. The methodical movement may as well have been a lullaby. Dropping my head back onto his broad shoulder, I let sleep consume me.

TEETERING on the edge of a dream and consciousness, I could hear myself let out a breathy moan as strong arms enveloped me, holding me tight against a hardened body. Flashes of golden eyes watching me as I orgasmed raced through my mind. His breath tickled my skin when he whispered in my ear as I came undone around August.

A hum vibrating against my cheek took me from that half-dream state and my eyelids fluttered open, finding that I had tucked myself into the crook of a warm neck. Inhaling sharply, it took a moment to figure out my surroundings.

As I tensed, Lucifer loosened his hold around my waist. "It's just me." His deep voice washed over me, and I shuddered, responding with a throaty purr. "Unless, of course, you want me to pretend to be someone else?" he asked. The flirtatious tone in his voice made me want to smile and smack him simultaneously.

Glancing at the board, I knew I didn't need to ask. If anything had happened, he would have woken me up. I knew that. Instead, I stared at the planchette in disappointment, replaying the truth in my head. There was nothing more that I could do. The clock on the shelf read after seven-thirty at night.

"Who is it you think I'd want you to pretend to be?" Rocking forward, I stumbled onto my feet. My body was stiff, and I stretched and twisted to work out the kinks.

"The incubus, for one."

Glancing at him over my shoulder, his eyes heated the way they had when August and I had fucked in the restaurant. It was what I was dreaming about. I wondered if that was replaying in his head as well. "I don't need you to pretend to be him."

"Yes, you've had him quite a bit by now, haven't you?" he taunted wickedly.

"Does it matter?"

"Oh no, I rather enjoyed watching you get ravaged by him while your eyes were on me. Though, I think you like it when I'm around too, don't you?"

Heat pooled in my belly, but I tried to push it down. "Do you talk this much because you like hearing your own voice, or is it for some other reason?"

"Oh, it's very much to get a reaction out of you." I scoffed, turning away and walking toward the kitchen. "It's working, by the way."

Whipping around, I realized he was up as well. And now he was walking toward me with a feline grace. I edged backward, stopping near the door.

I opened my mouth to respond, but Lucifer shook his

head and leaned in until he was an inch away from me. "Were you about to lie to me?"

"Probably." Because I hadn't thought better of it until he pointed it out.

He grinned. "What were you dreaming about just now?"

"Why?" I said, my voice hoarse.

"Because you were digging your nails into my thighs and moaning. I want to know if you were dreaming about me. Were you, little witch?"

The rules of the game whispered a reminder in my thoughts . . . *I swear to tell you the truth in return for your own truth, but for every lie or non-answer, I will claim a kiss.*

My mouth dropped open slightly, and I stood there with my cheeks flushed. I had a choice. I could tell the truth, with no idea what would come from it. Or I could lie, and he would kiss me. Where that would go, I didn't know.

Everything about him was fire. The sexual tension in the air was thick and heady. It was like he was there, and I was lying if I said I didn't want to feel something with him. After Samhain, I didn't know how much of him would fade until the next year. Tethered to me always, yes. But how strong would he be? I didn't want to think about the possibility things would be different. He was safe. And so many things in my life were about to change.

Some distant part of my mind saw this for what it was. A cliff. A precipice. Dark, churning waters awaited me if I jumped.

I'd either swim or drown.

Only one way to find out.

So I lied.

And he knew it.

Lucifer broke into a wicked smile as he quietly

answered, "You lied on purpose."

"Maybe I did." I pushed against him, closing the minimal space left between us. My lips covered his as he growled into my mouth, wrapping his arms around me as he moved our bodies.

My back hit the paneled wood door. The curved edge pressed uncomfortably into my shoulder blade, putting just enough pressure against the bone that I gasped, breaking the kiss. My back arched as Lucifer's lips wreaked havoc on me. He peppered my skin with tiny bites and when his canines came close to breaking the surface, my core tightened.

"Do you want to . . . taste me?" I asked softly. I almost didn't voice it. Another day, another night, I might have pretended I didn't notice the way his jaw strained at the word "taste." The white brands that marked him as a demon peeked out from beneath the unbuttoned collar of his shirt, glowing faintly from his desire. Or mine.

Maybe they were one and the same.

"More than you know," Lucifer answered after a suspended moment. I shuddered in his arms. My fingers loosened in his hair as my breathing went from shallow to labored.

"Then tell me."

He scraped the pointed edge of one fang over my carotid artery. My pulse stuttered like the needle on a record when they first touched. He made my blood sing.

"I died with the taste of you on my lips. Your blood. Its essence." He spoke quietly, but there was no softness to his tone. His words had bite to them. A hiss that was distinctly primal. "For three hundred days and nights, I've thought of tasting little else."

I gasped when he sucked at the point where my neck

met my shoulder until it was tender.

"You're a self-proclaimed hedonist and demon of desire," I breathed. "That hardly means a thing. A drunk would crave the last drink he had before sobriety, just like a burning man would crave a drop of water." I was grasping at straws and flimsy dismissals. It was a half-assed attempt at stepping back into the light and out of the devil's embrace. I wasn't even sure why I tried.

"I'm not craving blood, Nathalie." He drew back to stare down at me with a gaze of pure liquid gold only broken in half by black slitted pupils. He'd never looked more beautiful or more monstrous than he did at that moment. "I'm craving *you*. Your blood. Your sweat. Your arousal."

His hard length pressed against my belly, tempting me to sin like nothing else.

"If I asked you to stop, would you?"

Lucifer stilled. His chest stopped, mimicking breathing.

"Stop craving you, or . . ." His silence finished the question for him.

I swallowed hard. Every Nat in the loci was paying very careful attention to what came next. Bad Nat most of all.

"If I let you taste me. Would you stop if I told you to?"

"Yes."

He answered without hesitation.

"Why?"

His eyes narrowed. "Because you told me to."

I shook my head faintly. "Yes, but *why*? Is it because you're my familiar? You've told me hundreds of times how you'd take what you want if given the chance. Well, here it is." My eyes flicked down to our bodies that were pressed together. It shouldn't have been possible.

None of this should have.

Día de los Muertos.

The day of the dead.

Samhain.

"You're practically flesh and blood. We're alone in my apartment. There's no one here to stop you—"

"I may be a monster." He slowly closed the gap between us, lips skimming across my cheek as he breathed me in before whispering in my ear. "But I want you to see me as a man."

His hands on my hips turned brutal. "A man," I sighed. Then laughed once softly. "Men can be monsters too."

"You know what I mean," Lucifer growled in frustration.

The emotion in his voice didn't match the burning intensity of his eyes. He sounded vulnerable, and yet looked like the ultimate apex predator.

It was a juxtaposition that I was confounded by.

"Why does it matter how I see you? It's not like I can get rid of you."

His nails turned sharp and pointed as they pressed into my hip bones. I'd have fingerprint bruises in the morning.

"I want you."

"We've established that—"

"No. I don't think you're getting it. I want *you*."

My pulse picked up, like the beginning of a song that hadn't even really started yet. We were racing toward a crescendo with consequences I couldn't anticipate.

"Not just your body. Not just your soul." He kissed my neck softly, somehow making the action more intimate than sexual. "I want to be more to you. More than a regret. So if you say no, then the answer is no. Whether that's to your blood or your body. You are the only thing I want, which means your opinion of me is the only thing that matters."

My stomach twisted, but not with dread. With . . . feelings.

Butterflies.

His fingers slid under the hem of my shirt. The place where his skin touched mine was straight ecstasy. Where his nails threatened to break the skin turned to fire.

There was hooking up with an incubus, and then there was hooking up with the devil.

A lot didn't even begin to describe it.

"Why me?" I asked. "And don't bullshit me about how 'special' I am. If it's because I'm your only real option right now, I'd rather you say that instead of pretend."

"I've had many lovers, and I hurt them all, in one way or another," he said with a sigh. "Some of them went insane. Not all creatures can withstand being near my magic, even passively. Some died in wars *because* of me, some died *for* me. I never cared. I don't feel remorse. By all accounts, I *am* a monster and I'm okay with that." His hands skimmed up my sides, dragging my shirt up with them. It was wrong on so many levels that he was admitting this, and yet it did nothing to tamp down my libido. I was embarrassingly wet and practically quaking with the need for release. "But I care what you think. I don't like it when you're in pain. I feel compelled to watch you and try to understand every little thing that makes you tick. On paper, you're just a weak witch, even with your chaos magic. You're beautiful, but not exceptionally so. Your grades were good, but not great. You didn't excel in any form of magic like—"

"Did you have a point you were getting to, or do you just enjoy insulting me?"

Lucifer chuckled, leaning his forehead against mine. "I swore an oath of honesty. If you prefer shallow compliments, you'll need to strike a new bargain."

"What would you even bargain for?" I asked, finding myself perversely curious about what he would want. I twisted my lips, unnerved by how close his were—and yet we were talking. He hadn't simply gone for the kill and fucked me, even though he must certainly know that I was weak right now. I licked my bottom lip, unable to help it. "You got the truth or a kiss. You know I won't resurrect you."

Lucifer didn't answer right away.

His thumbs skimmed beneath my bra line and my nipples pebbled. I sucked in a sharp noise.

"Nothing. I have everything I desire."

I squinted at him. "You don't have my soul."

"You're trying to provoke me," he said suddenly, muscles taut but still touching me. "Do you want me to take from you? To pull the truth from your lips like you do to me? To claim my kiss by wringing orgasms from your tight cunt every time you lie?"

My lips parted. "Why would you think—"

"Because you want me and you're afraid to admit it. I think you'd rather I take everything—your blood, your body—so then you can still believe that I'm just another monster. After all, it's so much easier to not have to deal with feelings if I remain the devil you know and hate."

He struck me speechless.

Bad Nat whistled under her breath. "He called you *out.*"

In the greenhouse, Peace paced. She was torn between the feelings he elicited and the low-conflict life we wanted to lead. Caring for him in any way was dangerous because we were in an impossible situation.

He wanted to come back permanently and uproot our entire lives.

I wanted . . . I wasn't entirely sure anymore.

August came to mind, but that was also a complicated relationship. Then there was Marcel, who'd finally given me the truth and made me reevaluate my entire past—including the admission to myself that I still loved him.

I shook my head. Tumbling into bed with him was me trying to clear it, not add to the many things I needed to work through.

"You're right," I said after a suspended beat. "Everything you said. I would rather you take and make it easy on me. I've had my magic and will stolen before. I survived that and I would survive this . . . but I don't know how I'm going to survive you. I mean, you said it: you're the devil. You're nine thousand years old and I'm . . ."

"Twenty-three."

I swallowed. "Yeah. That's probably not even a blink of an eye to you after how long you've existed. I'm just a witch with a mortal lifespan. In another fifty years, I'll be dead—the final kind. For you, feelings may be a novelty, but I've had them before and they *hurt*. I can break up with a boyfriend. I can dissolve an aurae bond. I can't get rid of you. Anything between us would be . . ."

I pushed against his chest, suddenly finding it hard to inhale. He remained where he was though, not shifting a hair.

"If fifty years is all we have, then it will be the best fifty years of my life."

"I'm not ready for a lifelong commitment," I said.

"Bit too late for that, little witch. I hate to break it to you, but in your own words—twenty-three isn't a blink to me. Fifty? I want you and that won't change, neither will me being your familiar." His thumbnail scraped over the thin material of my bra cup, making my nipple harden further. I groaned, biting my lip in an attempt to hide it. "I told you, Nat, till death do we part. I'm here now and for the rest of your life—however long or short it may be."

I shuddered as an embarrassing amount of wetness dampened my underwear. My jeans were sticking to me uncomfortably.

"That may be true right now, but your mind changes like the wind. I can't trust this version of you will be the same one I have in five years or ten."

"Yes, you can. I can only ever be honest with you—"

"Because you let me off easy," I said, scrambling for some kind of leverage to convince myself this was wrong. That me wanting him was wrong, because it was beginning to feel right. "It's not like you claimed my soul. You asked for less than you offered. Why is that? You had to know I would've accepted less than complete honesty forever from you in return for what I wanted to know. We both heard Sienna. She said you want nothing short of someone's soul. So why did you let me off easy?"

He let out a deep sigh, eyes dropping to my pulse at my neck. That wicked thumb continued to trace circles around my nipple, making it hard to think.

"That you still believe all I traded was the truth speaks to both how little you realize and how much I actually stole."

His cryptic answer had the opposite effect of what I intended. Instead of triumphant, I felt desperate. Weak. Like the one person—technically not a person—who was supposed to theoretically be mine, had found a way to screw me.

I waited, expecting him to talk when the silence felt uncomfortable, but he didn't. Instead, his tongue swept across his bottom lip as he looked me up and down like a starved man eyeing a feast.

Flustered, I tightened my hands on his shoulders, unsure if I wanted to push him away or bring him closer.

"Oh, come on, do you honestly think I'm going to drop it there? What is it exactly that you think you stole?"

Hope.

It flared in my chest like a seed planted.

Except this seed wasn't planted in Peace's greenhouse of the memory loci. This one grew through the cracks in my foundation, despite the odds. With no sunlight, no water, it defied all probabilities as it sprouted in the center of the living room.

For a plant that represented hope, it looked the opposite.

A black, vine-like thing whose leaves carried a golden sheen.

I wanted to curse myself because hope was the last thing I should be feeling. Hope that he didn't screw me. That he was being as overly dramatic as always.

Lucifer sighed. He dropped his hands from my body and came up to tap my chin, lifting my face closer to his. "If you make me spell this out for you, I don't think tonight will end the way that we both want it to." While searing, his expression wasn't simply heated. It was also serious.

"First, that's presumptuous to think tonight will end in that way—"

"I can smell your arousal, little witch, and it has nothing to do with the fuckboy or incubus."

"Again, presumptuous."

He lurched forward despite the little bit of space I'd put between us, showing that it was very much a choice on his part. Even dead, he could overpower me. Fucking Samhain.

"Is it presumptuous when you whisper my name while you sleep?"

Heat crept up my cheeks. I knew he watched me sometimes, but I rarely remembered my dreams, let alone what I might say during them.

"Maybe I'm telling you to fuck off and the rest just doesn't make it out."

He snorted, then moved his face to the side to whisper in my ear. "If the way your fingers slip into your panties is anything to go by, I'd say there is fucking involved."

I gasped. "You're lying."

He chuckled, but it was underlaid with hardness. "I can't. Not to you. I didn't then and I'm not now. Almost every night in the last week, you've rubbed that tight little cunt like you can't get enough. You've moaned my name and *begged* me. I'm only putting two and two together here, Nathalie. I did not lie to you. I have not betrayed your trust. Isn't that enough for tonight? If I promise to explain in the morning, can you let it go until tomorrow?" I hesitated, torn between my piqued curiosity and heated body that wanted to throw caution to the wind. "I suppose the real question is not can you, but will you? We both know how marvelous you are at compartmentalizing things you don't really want to face. It's been a long day. A long month. Let me have you; I promise to take care."

My choices ricocheted around in my mind.

He couldn't lie to me. I knew this.

"Will it change things between us?" I asked quietly. Call me ignorant, but it was a luxury I was rarely afforded.

And sometimes, bliss was what was needed.

"No," he answered, the picture of utter surety.

I arched up on my tiptoes, my lips brushing his.

"All right. I'll play this game. One night. I'll give you one night, and tomorrow morning you will tell me all of it."

twenty-one

LUCIFER

Victory had never tasted so sweet.

Nathalie softened in my arms, going from all coiled muscles to lush feminine curves. Her tan skin flushed when I grabbed her sides, pressing my fingers firmly into her waist. Her chest rose and fell as she panted lightly, releasing wafts of lilac and juniper from her parted lips.

I kissed up her neck, scraping the side of her jaw with the blunt edge of my teeth. She shivered, the scent of arousal thickening the air. I dropped my hands lower, cupping her ass.

"Wrap your legs around me."

She obeyed without hesitation, letting me take her weight as she wound her legs around my waist, ankles hooking at the small of my back. This position put her flush with my painfully hard cock.

The air hissed between her lips as she ground into me, all heat and sensation. Nathalie moaned low and loud, her head tipping back when I took her lips again. She kissed like she fucked, with everything she had.

Our tongues dueled for dominance. It was cute that she thought she'd ever win with me unless I let her.

"I'm close," she groaned. One hand gripped my shoulder while the other wrapped around my neck. She fisted my shirt with both hands, nails biting into muscle that shouldn't be there. "How is that possible? It's like I'm sixteen again—"

I sucked the bottom lip that she seemed to be perpetually gnawing on as I reached for the door.

"I'm the embodiment of desire, little witch. I could make you come with my voice alone if I wanted to." The handle turned easily, and I stepped inside, not needing to look to know where to go. I'd walked this room hundreds of times. If not for my lack of a physical body I would have worn a path through her rugs and into the floor after the number of times I'd paced this room at night.

It smelled like her shampoo and sweet musk. She'd left the bedside lamp on earlier, providing dim but not overly bright light.

"I don't think I believe you," Nathalie mumbled, desperately rocking her hips against mine in search of relief. I chuckled, knowing exactly what she was doing.

"Is that so?"

"Mmhmm," she hummed in impatience.

"And if I don't want you to come yet?" I mused, stopping before her bed. Nathalie's eyes opened in thin slits, glaring at me.

"I might actually salt you," she deadpanned.

I lifted both eyebrows, trying and failing to hide my mirth. As much as she threatened it, Nathalie would never actually get rid of me—even if she could. "That would be a terrible idea. I might decide to play a different game in the bedroom and be the boogeyman you'd rather believe I am." Her pulse sped up, cheeks turning a deep auburn color. "Would you like that, little witch? If I climbed into your bed one of those nights you were dreaming and couldn't be sated? I'd peel the clothes from your body and pound into the slick cunt you've been teasing me with for weeks." At my filthy words Nathalie let out a strangled sound and the scent of her arousal flooded the room, enough that I could almost believe it was one of those nights. One of those dreams. "I'd fuck you in that fevered state until you came, milking my cock with this pretty pussy." She clawed at my shirt, clinging to me with all her strength. "You'd wake up full of me and satisfied for once. Free of guilt because I took what I wanted. For a woman so strong and independent, you like the idea of me having my wicked way with you, don't you?"

"Yes," Nathalie whispered against my lips. "Yes," she repeated, nearing her precipice. I could feel her legs tightening with excitement. She was roiling with it.

I slid her down my body, letting her feel every inch of my hardness for her.

"Who do you want tonight?"

She paused, half-lidded eyes clouding in confusion. "What do you mean?"

"Do you want me or the devil?" I rephrased slowly.

Most people believed they were one and the same. That me, the man, was the same as me, the nightmare. What they didn't know was that, like my witch, I compartmentalized pieces of myself. The man I needed to be to rule the Underworld was powerful and charismatic, but he was a monster by all measures. A true boogeyman. If she wanted the vision I painted for her, it was him she'd be playing with. I would enjoy it either way, but there was a connection that it lacked. That I wanted with her.

The *me* that I was with Nathalie was a newer me. A vulnerable version that I wanted to show her but wasn't sure she was ready to see.

"If I choose the devil . . ." Her question trailed into silence.

"Then I'll ravage you till dawn and bring every filthy fantasy you won't even voice to life." She swallowed. Her tiny hands rubbed over my chest absentmindedly.

"And you?"

One corner of my mouth hiked up at the side. I grabbed her hips and pushed her back. "I'll worship you like the queen you are—but there won't be any games. No false pretenses. No pretending." Her back touched the down-filled comforter, hair sprawling in every direction. It was longer than she usually kept it, the length dragging her brown waves out so that it was nearly straight. She had no idea how many nights I sat next to her while she slept, playing with her hair—relishing that it was the closest thing to feeling I had.

Not tonight.

I'd feel it all. The anticipation left me both calm and impatient. I'd lived a long time and yet the wait for this, for her, felt longer than any before it.

Nathalie wet her parted lips with her tongue subconsciously. "What if I want both?"

My cock twitched. I lifted an eyebrow, sliding one knee onto her bed. The mattress dipped. She didn't notice or react, her eyes trained wholly on me.

"The monster and the man?" I checked.

Her chin dipped as she nodded silently. I leaned forward, resting a hand on each side of her waist to support my weight.

"That's a fine line to walk." I lowered my face between

her thighs, running the tip of my nose over her pants-clad apex. Her legs shivered as I inhaled deeply. "What if it's too much for you?"

I didn't like to ask it, but her human sensibilities had to be acknowledged and appeased. While I was confident I could push her past what she believed to be her limits and make her love it—crave it—she'd also hate me for it.

Permission and consent were important to her.

"I'll tell you," she whispered. "Red means stop. Mercy means—"

"I know your rules, little witch."

"Then what are you waiting for?" she sassed back, lifting a brow back like she was mocking me. I stifled my amusement as I looked up her body, between the valley of her breasts, to her swirling whiskey gaze.

I snapped my fingers and the front clasp on her bra opened. The cups flew to each side, spilling her perfect, unmarred breasts. Dusky pink nipples pointed to attention.

Unable to deny myself after so long, I crawled up her body. My hard shaft pressed against her heated center. Nathalie writhed beneath me.

"Please," she begged, a whine entering her voice. I tsked, and telekinetic fingers gripped her hips to press her into the bed. She groaned when I denied her that friction, instead choosing to send her into a state of insatiable lust. I wanted her as desperate for me as I was her.

She tried to reach between us and rub herself. I growled under my breath, pushing her hands aside before pinning those too.

"You asked for both," I reminded her. My breath touched her heated skin in the cool air. Goosebumps started up her chest.

"I wanted to be ravished and worship—"

"I'll do both, in good time."

She groaned with pent-up frustration; her body strung as tightly as the strings on an instrument that I was a master at playing.

I lowered myself so that our bodies touched but none of my weight was on her. "You prance around in your little tank tops every night, torturing me with these." My hand cupped her right breast, thumb brushing over her nipple. It tightened to a stiff peak. "I think it's my turn to do a little torturing, don't you think?"

"That's not—ahh!"

There it was. Music to my ears.

I sucked that tight bud between my lips, tasting the essence of her. Desire bloomed inside her. I groaned at the feel of it and pinched her other nipple. Nathalie gasped, her body jerking beneath me.

"Lying is futile."

"I'm not!" She wasn't, but it was all part of the game. The monster in me sought control. Power. It understood punishments and rewards, especially where my little witch was concerned.

I wouldn't let myself near her in an actual situation where my control had flayed, and my anger made me cruel. In a controlled environment, under different circumstances, I could loosen those reins. Not let my baser desires run free, so to speak, but I gave them room to stretch and breathe.

"You mean to tell me, you didn't know what they did to me?" I ran the flat of my tongue over her nipple, waiting for a reply.

"I. . . ."

My assault paused.

"So you *did* know?"

"They're my pajamas. What do you want me to do? Buy

new ones—" She inhaled sharply, the breath hissing between her teeth when I bit the side of her breast. Not hard enough to break skin. Barely. It would bruise all the same.

That thought left me with supreme satisfaction.

"That's what you wore, walking around the apartment when Piper lived here?" I asked, already knowing the answer. "When my brother was here all the time? You let Ronan see you in that?"

A thread of actual jealousy snaked through me. I couldn't help it.

She could wear what she wanted. Fuck where she wanted. I would never stop *her,* but unless I was with her, inside her, wrapped around her—the irrational urge to kill everyone else became overwhelming.

"Well, no, but even if he did, it wouldn't have mattered. He's only ever had eyes for Piper."

I lifted an eyebrow, not agreeing with her argument one bit.

"And Anders? Did you dress this way when he was over all the time?"

"No, but—"

"But?" I cocked a brow, letting a dangerous edge enter my tone. I was very quickly approaching the line that I couldn't cross, talking about other men and her while we were in bed. "He's never been into Piper, and only sees Sasha and Sienna as very close friends."

"He's obsessed with Bree."

"Bree hasn't always been here. Before her, you would have been just his type. Petite. Curvy. Intelligent. Long hair a man can fist while pounding into your tight cunt—"

"No," she rasped, voice husky as if her throat were dry.

"I've never worn those pajamas around him." I curved a smile against her breast that she couldn't see.

"But you wear them for me?"

She opened and closed her mouth, a hot blush creeping up her chest. "I wore them because I like them. Not every-thing revolves around you, asshole."

I bit the other side of her breast, this time, breaking the skin.

Two tiny drops of blood welled where my fangs were. I locked eyes with Nathalie as I swept my tongue over them.

The first taste hit me like a dose of ecstasy.

My body came alive at the taste of her. The white brands that covered the upper half of me vibrated with energy. With *desire*.

Nathalie let out a keeled wailing and arched her back so hard I thought she might snap her spine. "Oh my god," she breathed.

When a demon gave blood, the receiver gained a single drop of their magic. To most supernaturals, a single drop was the most they could take. Too much and most people die. Their bodies weren't like ours.

On that same note, the vampire's curse for blood came from us. We craved it with those that created powerful emotion in us. Hate could lead to bloodlust, just as love could lead to binding.

Nathalie had taken blood from three demons to date, including me.

I could taste it inside her. The subtle notes of both Piper and Ronan. Mine was the strongest, but there were still traces of them.

The devil inside me wanted to eliminate it.

It wanted to drain her dry, to the edge of death, just so I

could fill her up again with *my blood*. It was the only blood that should be running through her veins.

The desire to take her in every way imaginable intensified with those two little drops, and I wasn't the only one feeling it.

"Please, Lucifer," she groaned. "Please. I need you."

My cock twitched, hardening further to the edge of pain.

"Then tell the truth." My voice came out deeper, more a rumble in my chest than anything.

"I wasn't trying to torture you," she moaned. "I was just . . . teasing."

"Teasing," I repeated.

She nodded her head yes, and it tasted of truth. The slight distinction made little difference to me.

Keeping my psychic hold on her, I crawled backwards off the bed. She whimpered at my distance.

"I'm sorry," she whined, lost to the haze that drinking her blood had caused.

"No, you're not," I said while unbuckling her jeans. "But you will be."

She squirmed, trying to break free, but it was useless. I tugged her jeans over her hips and down her legs. Her lacy black panties contrasted against her skin.

"Spread your legs." Nathalie quivered slightly but obeyed. My mouth watered at the sight.

"Do you know what it feels like when desire turns so sharp it hurts?" I asked her softly. Her lips parted.

"Yes."

Interesting. I wanted to ask but knew the answer would tip me over that boundary. I pushed my own curiosity aside.

"You've probably felt it for minutes. Maybe hours." She

averted her gaze, swallowing hard. "Imagine it happening for days. Weeks. Except there's no relief."

Her warm eyes snapped back to mine. A sheen of gold was already covering them and becoming brighter by the minute. They'd be twin suns by the time I gave her relief.

"But you're dead."

I knelt on the edge of the bed. "I never fully died, Nathalie. The only way to kill a demon on this plane is to drain them of every single drop of blood. You took mine when you tried to save me. That's why I can feel, and that's why I've felt so real to you. My soul is quite literally desire. If there's anything I can feel, it's my need for you."

She opened then closed her mouth, licking her bottom lip to wet it.

"I didn't realize."

"You tortured me all the same." My stomach pressed against the bed as I reached under her and grabbed a handful of her ass. I lowered my face to the wet patch of arousal I could smell, running the tip of my nose along that slit.

Her thighs quivered. She threw her legs over my shoulders, planting her heels in my back in a poor attempt at pulling me in. I chuckled.

"Please, Luci," she whined again. Her voice hitting a breathy high note of desperation. "We only have one night. I thought you wanted to spend it inside me?"

I'd spend every moment of the day inside her if that were an option, but it wasn't. Instead of answering, I licked the sensitive skin where her thigh met her pussy. My tongue dipped underneath the edge of the lace underwear. Traces of her arousal exploded on my tongue. Nathalie's body stiffened, muscles tightening with every fiber of her strength. She moaned so loud the people on the street might have heard it, if not for the silencing charms. I sucked her skin between my lips. Her voice cracked.

"It hurts," she groaned. "I need to come. Please—"

"You'll come on my cock and not a second sooner," I said in an unhurried tone. I'd barely gotten started, and she was caving. Sex really was her weakness.

"Fuck me," she commanded, switching tactics. I pushed the slit of fabric aside with my nose to lick her weeping center.

"Please!"

"I love hearing you beg."

I did. The sick, perverted part of me reveled in this.

"Not enough to do anything about it—"

I turned my face into her thigh like I was going to nuzzle it. Instead, I bit down without preamble, drawing a lot more than two drops of blood. Nathalie screamed as desire burned through her veins.

I lapped up every drop then sucked at the twin bite marks.

"How are you feeling now?" My voice was gruff and not nearly as even as it had been.

"I will give you anything if you put your cock in me right now."

I tilted my head. My fingers toyed with the fabric.

"Anything?"

She started to nod fervently, before pausing. It clicked in her brain and Nat's bottom lip trembled. "Maybe."

Her admission shocked me speechless for a moment. "You would bring me back? For sex?"

Nathalie let out something between a sigh and a groan. "Maybe. I don't know. I'd need to see if the sex is worth it first."

She wasn't quite lying, but that wasn't everything. "And?"

"Need to find someone really awful so that I don't feel guilty killing them." Something like disappointment touched me. I tried to push it down. "And there would need to be boundaries. You can't fuck up the lives of everyone I love. If I brought you back, you'd need to find a purpose."

My disappointment evaporated, something else taking form.

"Purpose? Outside of fucking you every chance I get?" That was a pretty grand purpose from my perspective.

"Outside of that," she parroted, utterly breathless. Sweat dampened her forehead. Her cheeks were rosy and eyes bright. She was at the end of her line, but I wasn't sure if she'd stay there.

"That's oddly selfish of you to be willing to gamble that all so I can make you come. I'm proud of you, little witch. Why don't we try that apology again instead? If you can show me you really mean it, I might take pity on you." My words were punctuated with the sound of her underwear ripping. Tossing them aside, I ran the flat of my tongue over her clit and she yelped.

"*Please.*"

"That's not an apology."

"I'm sorry for teasing you," she blurted out. Tears ran from her eyes as I put a single finger inside her. They weren't tears of pain, but desperation. "I just thought we were flirting harmlessly. You kept whispering things to me when you thought I was sleeping and then started reading my smutty books. I—"

I climbed up her body and kissed her senseless.

There was no hesitation when she kissed me back. No

271

reserve. Nathalie parted her lips and sucked on my tongue with a fierce need.

I rolled my hips, rocking into her. She clutched at me like I was her lifeline and she'd never let me go.

"I need you to take my blood."

She stared up at me, so much gold filling her gaze the pupil was gone. "Why?"

I sat back on my haunches to undo my shirt. As the material fell away, her eyes devoured my bare chest.

"I can taste Piper and Ronan in your blood still," I said, unbuttoning my slacks. "I need my own signature to drown them out. I . . . I will have a very hard time controlling my aggression while tasting my brother in you."

"Oh." She blinked then licked her bottom lip. "Will it force me to do your bidding or something?"

"No."

"Okay."

"You'll do it?"

"It changes nothing," she breathed. I'd let up on the psychic holds enough she could sit up and start inching toward me. "As you love telling me, we're together till the end. If it won't control me, I'm done fighting this."

My heart seemed to beat louder as I crawled over her body.

Of all the things she'd said and done tonight, it was those words that wrapped around me. Those words that made my brands change, because the entire fiber of my being had changed.

I thrust into her, unable to hold back any longer.

The haze over my mind cleared.

The insanity quieted.

"Oh my—"

I bit my tongue and then pressed my lips to hers. My

hips rocked back before punching forward, making her mouth open as she stretched around me. I sealed my lips over hers, forcing a mouthful down her throat. She choked for a second and her pussy constricted.

I grabbed her ass with one hand and planted my forearm on one side of her face with the other. She was shaking from how tightly she'd been drawn. All she needed was to fall over the edge.

I angled her pelvis toward mine so I could go deeper, and I pounded harder and harder, pushing further inside her. She exhaled and grunted with each thrust.

Nathalie sucked on my bottom lip before throwing her head back. Red stained her teeth. Gold filled her room. With my cock dragging over the most sensitive part inside her, her legs began to tremble. I licked up the column of her throat. My breath fanned her ear, making her shiver when I skimmed the shell with my nose.

"Come on my cock, little witch. You've been a very bad girl and owe me my pound of flesh."

I nipped at her pulse point and Nathalie shattered.

A vicelike grip clamped down on my shaft. Her mouth opened in a silent scream as gold magic literally flooded the room.

I pumped into her tight channel until my release tore me to shreds as my cock pulsed inside her.

My skin cracked, pieces flaking away in the violent storm of magic. Her own brand of chaos filled me in return, sealing the pieces of my soul that threatened to break away. The veil pulled, but its call was little more than a whisper with every second that went on.

When her body stopped twitching and her insides were bathed in my release, I pulled out. My dick wasn't soft in the slightest, but that had more to do with the serious release of magic that happened between the two of us. It demanded that we consummate it. That I take her in every way, fill her with more.

"Holy shit," she murmured. "I've never had an orgasm like that. I feel like I need a power nap before round two." Some of it was the orgasm. Some was the magic she didn't realize she'd released. A yawn escaped her as her eyes closed. She wasn't kidding. Ready as I was for round two, Nathalie needed a power nap.

I rolled over and pulled her into me. Her face settled against my chest, jaw slack from sleep, as I pulled her leg over my waist.

"Sleep well. You'll need that energy because I promised to bring every fantasy to life tonight." My lips pressed against her forehead.

She mumbled in her sleep.

"Don't want you to go."

My chest tightened, and I held her flush against me.

Little did my witch know, I wouldn't be going anywhere.

Not without her.

twenty-two

NATHALIE

Fingers traced my skin.

I leaned into the touch, groaning but still half asleep. My limbs hurt in the best kind of way. Flashes of the night before made me squirm, thighs rubbing together subconsciously. A warm body pressed against my front.

"*Lucifer,*" Bad Nat offered casually.

"*Luci,*" Peace corrected.

Ann rolled her eyes at them both.

"You slept like the dead."

I squinted up at the inhumanly beautiful face before me. Tousled white hair and half-lidded eyes weren't what I expected. Neither was the strange sensation of warmth that filled me at seeing him this way. The fingers running along my side stopped as he smoothed his hand over my skin.

My breath hitched.

"I can still feel you." My voice was thick from sleep and raspy from overuse last night.

"I'd hope so," he said, lifting one corner of his mouth in a lazy smirk. "I fucked you half a dozen times last night and only stopped because your body gave out. You needed your rest. What kind of familiar would I be to deny you?" He lifted an eyebrow. I swatted at his chest, unable to ignore how hard and masculine it was. White brands wound around it and down his arms. They climbed up his neck, stopping at the edge of his jaw.

"That's not what I meant," I started.

"You expected to wake up alone because we fucked?" he guessed, hand trailing down my side, past my hip and around the curve of my ass.

"Yes. Wait, I mean no—" The words got jumbled when he stopped partway down my thigh and pulled it across his lap so that I was straddling him. I pressed my hands against his chest and leaned back, pushing up.

"Cat got your tongue?" Lucifer said, leaning forward to catch me in a searing kiss. "And by that, I mean this pu—"

I put my hand over his mouth.

Very adult-like. I know.

"I thought I'd be alone because Samhain passed. The veil isn't thin anymore. I thought . . ." My voice trailed as my thoughts turned to Sasha and I knew the truth. If she'd returned, they would have come to get me. "I need to go check in with Señora. Arrangements will need to be made. Sienna and Hallie will need grief counseling. I may need to take Hallie for a while so Sienna can work through it. Anders will want to be closer. Shit, maybe I should contact the builders and see how long it will be until my house is finished. They can all stay with me then and be close to Piper. Hallie is going to need Orson. Hell, maybe I should just get a therapist on retainer for all of us. We can do weekly group sessions." Another thought occurred to me that made my eyes water. "I'll need to plan the funeral. I don't even know what she would want—"

He grabbed my wrist and pulled my hand away so that he could curl my fingers over his and kiss each knuckle. "Breathe, Nathalie." The command made me pause, chest already heaving from my racing thoughts alone. "First things first. Unless you want to give everyone a show, you need clothes. Get dressed. Brush your teeth. Wash your face. Your ten-minute morning routine isn't going to change anything, little witch. Start there."

I let out a breath I didn't know I was holding. "Thank you," I said quietly.

He smiled, but it didn't quite reach his eyes.

I hopped out of bed and went about picking my clothes for the day. I could almost believe it was just another day, and that I hadn't boned the devil. He sat in the bed like always and complimented my style as he often did. Lucifer shared my love of luxury clothing and knew most of the brands I wore. He remarked on the weather, letting me know what to expect since the Weather Channel wasn't exactly a thing anymore. Neither were apps. I had a color-changing wind chime outside my window to tell me what temperature it was, but I didn't stop him because I liked that he cared enough about me to say.

I could almost pretend he was dressed in a suit and not naked. Pretend I hadn't licked every inch of his body last night. Pretend that I hadn't noticed his brands changed overnight.

It would be easy to pretend.

But I didn't want to.

"Piper said a demon's brands are their true name," I began, brushing my hair. "But unlike chosen names, it changes with you."

"Mmhmm," Lucifer hummed, watching me. Our eyes locked in the mirror.

"Yours changed last night."

"I'd say I'm surprised you noticed, but I'm not. You notice far more than you let people believe, don't you?"

My mouth went dry. I looked away but the faint pull of our bargain yanked me back, demanding I answer or give a kiss. "Yes, I do."

"Do you have a question about them, little witch?" Them, being his brands. I was unsurprised he talked about them like a living, breathing entity. To some extent, they were. As best as I understood it, demon brands were *alive*. Their magic was in their blood and the brands signified it.

"Not so much a question, really," I murmured, then sighed. I was beating around the bush—and why? To act like I didn't recognize one of the symbols that appeared? To feign ignorance, like I wasn't aware of what exactly it meant?

I spun around to find him standing in front of me. My eyes were level with his sternum and the brand in question sat right there in front of me, just a little to the left.

"That's my name."

"It is." His astute agreement was so Lucifer, it was infuriating. I started to turn away, but he held me fast by my chin, drawing my face back to his. It didn't even take him a second to read me. "Setting aside my burning curiosity about how you know what your name is written as in a language man can't understand, you're surprised to find it there. On me."

I swallowed. "It's not the brand itself—"

"Don't lie," he said distastefully. "It's insulting at this point."

I huffed a rueful laugh. "I'm sorry. I wasn't meaning to lie. It's second nature to me to smooth things over. Yes, I'm surprised by the brand for a few reasons. From what Piper has told me, they're intrinsic to who you are as a person. Hers have only changed a few times since she got them." I lifted a hand to count on my fingers. "When she decided to put my safety before her secret, my name appeared. When she bonded with Ronan, his did. When you died and she lost control, it changed again. Then when she consumed the Source, her brands spread. Those were all big things and last night . . . I don't want to dismiss it, but it's not like we're a mated pair."

He nodded slowly. "No, we're not, but I am your familiar. It's not uncommon for familiars to bear their bonded witch's mark."

"Yes." I hesitated but forced the rest out. "But the placement is . . . telling."

Understanding lit his expression. He inhaled sharply.

Lucifer took my hand in his and then purposely pressed it against the brand.

Over his heart.

"I suppose it is."

While dramatic in many, many ways, his quiet admission hit me so much harder. It burrowed deeper, sinking its toxic love spikes into me. Because there was little doubt in my mind now what this was. For better or worse, despite any good or bad that may come of it—Lucifer loved me.

He could be charming and devilish and downright flirtatious.

But brands didn't lie. He *couldn't* lie.

My brain stopped, focusing on that last thought.

He couldn't lie.

He couldn't lie.

He couldn't—

"We get the fucking point, Prime," Bad Nat hollered from her room.

In a much gentler but still exasperated voice, The Warden looked up from her book to remind me, "Last night he never said what he bargained for."

I wanted to slap myself in the head. I was so busy being dickstruck, my priorities were out of whack.

"I need to put a kettle on before I go downstairs. You told me you'd explain what you meant last night about how little I realize and how much you stole when we made a bargain. Time to pay the piper." He released me and my hand dropped away from his chest as I stepped back. I could have sworn a shadow passed over his eyes.

"Very well, you walk and I'll talk." He motioned to the door behind me. I turned on my heel and started down the hallway.

"Sienna warned you that I wouldn't bargain for anything less than your soul."

She had, but she was wrong. *Right?* A small voice in the back of my head was starting to wonder.

"I may be a man, but I've never claimed to be a very good one. I knew your soul wasn't one I could take, so I made a bargain not for your soul or your truths, but for mine." I rounded the counter and filled the kettle, trying to process and figure out where this was going at once. "You've been lied to so many times," he said. "You hate liars, even though you are one."

"Lying for survival is different."

"Is that what you call denying your feelings?"

"I'm not—"

He moved so fast, he was around the corner before I could blink. Strong arms caged me against the edge of the sink. Water ran over the lip of the kettle, down my hands, as his front pressed against my back. "Do you love Marcel?"

I frowned, but answered all the same. "Yes. Not that it's relevant."

"And August? Do you love him?"

Ah, hell. He was forcing me to say this out loud . . . I knew where this was going. "Yes, but—"

"What about me?"

Yep. There it was. Should have known he'd never settle for confessing his feelings and leaving mine to me. His stupid ego would never go for that.

"I don't know," I replied hotly.

He pulled my hair to one side and licked up the length of my neck. "Your lies may taste sweet, but you're going to regret this one. You don't have to like it, Nathalie, though frankly, it pisses me off that you'll admit your feelings finally for the other two after what they've done but it's me that you're still in denial about."

My indignation left me in a whoosh, draining out and taking my frustration with it. Maybe it wasn't his ego so much as the fear of rejection. It was easy to forget how old he was sometimes and in all those lifetimes, he'd been loved and worshiped as a god but never returned it.

Now he did, but it was me holding out on him.

"Luci," I whispered. "I—"

"Don't finish that sentence. If you say it out of pity, even if it's true, you'll see a side of me I have been working very hard to contain." The timbre of his voice made me shiver. He rarely used that tone with me. The one of a god. A demon. The devil.

"You're right," I said. "I'm sorry. That was . . . shitty of me."

He nuzzled my neck affectionately, letting me know he

accepted my apology. "For the record, I wasn't saying it to get after you. I don't think lying is inherently 'bad.' You use it to further your business, to get yourself out of trouble, and to establish dominance in a room when other immortals might otherwise think to belittle you. I don't judge you for that, but I knew you would never open up to me unless I could only speak honestly. Without that, you wouldn't believe a word I said and by extension, never trust or care for me. You needed safety, just as I needed you."

One by one his words clicked into place.

"I don't understand. You tricked me?" I whispered.

"No. I was honest with you." He reached around me to shut off the faucet. "I've been honest with you since the very beginning. You simply didn't want to believe it, so I found a way to make you see. It was your own desire to prove your sister's innocence that forced your hand. You're a logical creature by nature. It infuriated me at first, but I have grown to appreciate that quality about you. I knew all I needed to do was bait you with the information I had on Katherine and you would take the deal." He kissed my neck softly. "To be fair, anyone would have. From your perspective, it was a fabulous deal. You shouldn't regret it just because I meant for all this to happen."

I pulled away from him and his wicked lips. He sighed and let me, but didn't move.

"So you what? Manipulated me so that I would *like you*? So I was sorry for you?" I shook my head, struggling to understand him more than ever. Crossing my arms, I turned and faced him. My back pressed into the edge of the granite while my arms fit snug between his chest and mine. "Fat lotta good it will do you now that I know this was all one big manipulation tactic. I can go back to ignoring you and living my life."

I didn't have time for this.

He was right before, but I was kicking myself for that apology now. He didn't deserve it. He wasn't some stupidly in love guy that was earning my heart. He was the devil and decided that instead of working for it, he'd maneuver pieces on a board to attain his desired outcome.

It occurred to me that we were not so different in that.

I didn't do it to partners, and he did, but I had no problem playing chess with the lives of so many other people.

I shook my head, not wanting to think about this right now.

"Hypocrite," Bad Nat said, throwing her bowl of popcorn at the TV as if my thoughts and feelings were little more than a reality show for her entertainment.

Fed up with both of them, I uncrossed my arms and reached behind me for the saltshaker. As many times as I'd threatened it, I never actually thought I'd salt him.

Guess I was wrong there too.

My fingers wrapped around the glass. I hooked my thumbnail under the metal cap, prying it open. The seal released with a pop.

I tossed the entire thing at him.

The shaker bounced off his chest and fell to the ground between us. White crystals littered my kitchen. They clung to my sweater and dusted his bare chest.

My mouth dropped.

Lucifer cocked a brow.

"That's not going to work anymore, I'm afraid." He smiled, some of that monster from only minutes before now lurking in his eyes. "Sienna warned you, Nathalie. She told you the rules. You knew exactly how the game would end. But you still chose to play and did exactly what I knew you would do."

"And what is that?" I sneered.

"You fell for me. Not just the ghost but the man." He said it with complete and utter surety. Except how could he? Unless it was true. My stomach turned. "You give and give and give to everyone else, only to receive scraps in return. All you really wanted was for someone to *see you*. To want you just as you are. I do. I told you I want all of you. The good. The bad. The ugly. You know that *and you love it* even though you won't admit it." If I could have backed up, I would have. As it was, I could only stand there and listen. "You want the bad boy who won't be intimidated by you or cowed by your success, but you don't want the baggage that comes with it. You want bad, but only if it's safe for you. I'm yours in every way. I am tethered to you tighter than any marriage can ever be, and because of our bargain, I am honest. You trust me, despite every preconceived notion that tells you not to. Enough to let this conversation go last night because you want me, and instead of letting your mind get ahead of you, you took what you wanted. And what is *want* but another word for desire?"

One by one. *Click. Click. Click.*

The picture started to form.

"Rage feeds Piper," he continued, golden eyes glowing —no, *brimming* with power. "Death feeds Marcel and Katherine. Spirit feeds Anders. Chaos feeds *you*, which is why you're always doing a hundred things at once. You live and thrive in it. So tell me, who does desire feed, Nathalie?"

It was right there. All of it. I felt so stupid when it was this obvious.

"You."

"That's right," Lucifer purred. "Desire feeds the devil.

Your desire, to be specific. Our magic is our souls, little witch. So you see, Sienna was right. I did steal your soul. But if it's any consolation, you stole mine first."

To say I was angry was an understatement. I couldn't afford to be this enraged. I didn't have time for that. So when Rage started to beat at the door, all it took was a glance from me for her to quiet because this was *not* the time. "Why? Why did you do all of this? What's the point?"

Footsteps sounded down the hall. I recognized Mist's gait.

Shit. Why was she sleeping here and not at Sienna's? Shit shit shit.

I was the worst friend and guardian right now.

"Hey, Nat—" Her voice cut off and her footsteps paused at the end of the hallway.

"Everything okay?" I asked without turning. I didn't want to give Lucifer my back. Two knocks came at the door. Lucifer gave me a cool look and telekinetically unlocked my door. I glared at him, and he lifted his hands in surrender, then stepped back to give me room to slip by.

I reached for the door and had my hand on the knob when Mist spoke again.

"Why is there a man here?"

Everything in me froze. I spun around.

"You can *see him*?" I rasped, voice still scratchy.

"Uh-huh," Mist answered, clearly uncomfortable. She pulled at her long shirt sleeves and her wings folded forward, partially hiding her body.

"Hello, Mist, I am Lucifer. Do not compel me." His brands flared and power pulsed from his words. Her jaw audibly snapped shut.

"Nathalie?" She was beginning to panic.

So tell me, who does desire feed, Nathalie?

Who does desire feed?

Desire.

Desire . . . feeds—fuck me.

Lucifer smiled, and I finally understood.

The door shook as someone else knocked, but I couldn't be arsed to answer it. I hadn't been imagining it every time his presence felt more solid . . . more real. *Who does desire feed?* I hadn't been reading into it when I thought it was strange his brands changed suddenly.

Lucifer was back.

My desire *fed* him. It gave him the strength. The medium he needed.

Fucking me on Samhain had given him exactly what he wanted.

Another chance at life.

"Fine, I'll do it." Lucifer moved toward me, putting a hand on my waist as he leaned past me to open it.

It was probably Señora Rosara bringing the horrible news I already expected, and I was just not ready to hear it.

"Lucifer?" The melodic yet husky voice that spoke his name was not the señora's.

It belonged to Sasha.

To be continued...

Please consider leaving a review on Amazon or Goodreads if you enjoyed this story. TikTok reviews/recs are also greatly appreciated!

Nat's story will continue in Premonition of Peace. This will be the third and final book in her story.

Join our SMS text list to be notified when Premonition of Peace releases:
Text "Books" to (844) 506-1510

Join our Facebook Readers Group, The Crow's Nest, for the latest updates on our stories and to commiserate with other readers.

acknowledgments

Writing this book was a bit tumultuous. The urge to get the words down during the first half was overwhelming, but it came to a crawl by the end. Typically it's the opposite for us, so we thought we knew how to get around that. You make plans and the universe laughs at you, right? So we hit a few speed bumps along the way. Dodged a few grenades. The usual.

It's life.

Anyway, we both have a lot of people to thank: our partners, kiddos, publishing team, and family. We love you all, but straight truth, we're too tired to write the mushy stuff so we're going to trust that you know it.

Our biggest thank you is to our readers for continuing Nat's story. We appreciate all of you so much for following us where all our crazy ideas go, even when they completely diverge from the plan. (Looking at you, *August*.)

Until next time in New Chicago,

Kel and Aurelia

Printed in the USA
CPSIA information can be obtained
at www.ICGtesting.com
LVHW091817221223
767208LV00031B/62